CRY ME A RIVER

Robert Michael

CRY ME A RIVER
Robert Michael

INFINITE WORD PRESS
Broken Arrow, Oklahoma

Printed in the United States of America
ISBN: 0615728626
ISBN13: 978-0615728629

Families are what make our lives special. My life is extra special. I want to thank my family—Tracey, Nate, Eden, Seth & Isaac—for giving me the encouragement and support to follow my dreams.

CHAPTER ONE

Claire Eppington held the black steel box in her lap. It was strange to her that she was around thirty thousand feet from earth with the remains of a deceased person in her lap. She never missed the irony of this situation.

Claire's job involved taking the remains of someone's family member to a remote location to deposit them. The job offered many benefits: exotic travel, little to no supervision, and plenty of time alone. Although it was not her career of choice, it certainly fit the bill for the moment.

Her only reservation about her occupation was that she never really felt comfortable during the ceremonies that she had to have recorded for the families. Her company usually made arrangements for a religious official to preside over the ceremony and either Claire or a media professional would document the proceedings for the family.

When a priest, minister, or rabbi would say words that were meant to be comforting, Claire was unimpressed. The words always seemed hollow. They felt insufficient and disingenuous. The loss of life was final. No one living wanted to come to grips with that reality.

Despite the burden on her lap, it was her current environment that was causing her discomfort. The air in the plane was stale. Airplanes are notorious for this phenomenon, especially overseas flights. Basements, mausoleums, and old warehouses all have that cloying no-scent of staleness. Delta Airlines Flight 311 to Bogotá, Colombia was a classic example of the oxymoron of purified stale air. Air breathed by those in the cabin for the past two hours was being filtered and re-circulated. The air played with the fringes of Claire's minor case of claustrophobia.

Claire opened her datebook. Fiddled with the apps on her smart phone. Picked up and discarded the airline magazine. Finally, to pass the time and take her mind off of her distress, she made faces at the four-year old girl across the aisle and two seats up from her. Blonde, replete with pony tail and Dora the Explorer crocs, she would sneak a peek every minute or so to check on Claire. Energy seemed to crackle in her eyes. All hail youth.

"Valerie, turn around. Color a picture. Or draw Mommy a dog."

The mother, as fidgety as Claire, seemed occupied with her iPhone most of the time. A paperback Grisham novel thrust itself out of her bag along with a stuffed animal, a Nintendo DS and an Oregon University cap. The novel had a bookmark protruding about at the half way point. Claire speculated she had been reading the novel for a long time and intended to read it on the trip. Claire's money would be on the novel remaining unfinished. She knew about these things.

With a sigh, Claire waited for Valerie to turn around again. She rested her hands loosely over the steel box in her lap. *Unfinished business.*

She glanced around at the other passengers, all fiercely engaged in frittering away the four hour flight. Each passenger anxiously awaiting the infamous crumbs left by the stewardesses and dreaming of the day that first class was achievable.

Oh, caviar and London broil. Mussels and linguini in white wine sauce. Surely, a half-pound cheeseburger with a side of onion rings or a cheese-dripping Philly, heavy on the peppers with a side of Hellman's would be more appropriate. Five hours. Sheesh. Pretzels and Seltzer water. Stale crackers and cheese; she noted wryly the expiration date was two months ago.

Figures.

Claire had been to Dublin twice, Amsterdam regularly, Switzerland sporadically over the span of two years--once with a client, morbidly romantic mere days after the death of his mother. Ireland was Claire's favorite. Florence was dirtier and more boring than she anticipated. Thankfully, she had never been cleared for the Mount Everest assignment, a special package that required a team of "remains location specialists" and included the placement of a unique urn rather than the customary spreading of the ashes.

These longer flights often meant longer layovers and better service than domestic flights. They also were characterized by decidedly better-looking passengers; all olive-skinned, Latino-styled slick hair, or wavy no-fuss-just-got-off-the-polo-horse quaffs. These passengers were punctuated by perfectly styled shoes, arched eyebrows and hard cheekbones, their bags genuine leather, their accents vividly sexy.

Oh, Claire! Stop it, you're bored.

Five hours seemed a lifetime when you wanted feet firmly on the ground. Take no chances; put your life securely in your own hands where gravity has less leverage: that was her motto. No one forcing you to eat out of date food, breathe stale, purified air, and numbly watch other folk suffer along with you.

Now, nature was inevitably calling. Silently cursing the three cups of coffee in the terminal at Atlanta, Claire sat the black box on the window seat and got up. Claire imagined as she walked the unlit walkway of the airplane aisle a fashion runway where she tripped headlong into the Rastafarian in 12F.

First she was uncomfortable with the stuffy cabin and now she could not control her bladder function. Crazily, she thought of all those long road trips her father forced on her.

"Daddy, please stop. I gotta peeeee!"

She would squeeze her legs together and lean forward between the seats, pleading for Frank to stop.

"Honey, just hold on unless you are prepared to go on the road. Daddy can't stop yet, Tucson's just a few more miles. Can you hang on?"

Oh yeah. Few more miles. Classic. Like this stroll from 10B to the back wing, the whine of the engines intensifying, the rocking of the plane more evident the farther back she got. Not to mention the pleasant experience she was dreading the most: the bathroom.

It is gonna be a mess, I just know.

It had not escaped Claire's attention that the elderly gentleman and the Rastafarian had recently made their obligatory trips. If twelve years living alone with her father had taught her anything, she knew she would have to clean up before sitting down. *Great!*

On her way back to her seat, Claire noticed Valerie nodding off. Claire retrieved the steel black box, feeling its comforting coldness calm her. Something about holding the cold steel in her lap seemed to anesthetize her. She thought of it as a tranquilizer or music to tame the savage beast. Always in a hurry, impatient, easily distracted, Claire needed a center.

Her occupation seemed odd to her family and friends. They failed to see how carrying the ashes of the deceased to exotic global locales could be exciting or rewarding. Her father had not figured it out yet. He consistently and doggedly hounded her.

"Find your path, Claire. Blaze your destiny. A globe-trotting mortician cannot be your permanent career," he would tell her.

Boyfriends thought of her as a stewardess and the length of her relationships were subject to this attitude.

Love me and leave me.

Unfinished. Not that this pattern disturbed her. It sometimes suited her restless spirit. Sometimes, though, it saddened her. Like now. She glanced down at the box in her lap. She realized she had been tracing the gilded letters absently with the tips of her fingers.

"Katherine Borche" spelled out in embossed silver to match the silver roses and artistic swirls etched into the surface of the glossy black box. She noticed her nails were ragged.

She was distracted by a low sob beside her. Across the aisle, a brunette lady dabbed her nose with a tissue. Her eyes, reddened and leaking steady tears, stared at a cross she held in her other hand. Claire realized she was oblivious to anyone else, and was experiencing personal pain. However, Claire could not help herself. Probably out of boredom. Probably.

"Excuse me, ma'am. Are you alright?" Claire asked.

Dumb question. Sounded like some guy question. Are you alright?! Dumb!

The lady turned to her and Claire noted she was heavier than she first appeared. Sadness seemed to drag her face, pulling at the folds and drawing down her mouth. Her neck jiggled as she turned and Claire forced herself to stare into her eyes. Green eyes, and worried. Claire realized that one could only read so much into the facial features of the distressed. She was quite sure, though, she had opened Pandora's Box.

"I'm sorry. Am I disturbing you?" She was genuine. Not a tinge of sarcasm or malice.

"Oh no. Not at all. I am sorry for bothering you. I am sure you don't need a complete stranger bugging you right now. Please forgive me." The lady paused. She daubed at her makeup with the tissue which did not help at all but streaked and smeared her mascara.

"Don't be sorry. You are probably concerned or curious." She turned back and bowed her head to look at the wooden cross. It was attached to a silver string which the lady wrapped around her hand, the cross resting in her palm.

"That's hardly an excuse." The lady sniffled and turned back to Claire, apparently trying to compose herself enough to seem brave or normal.

"My name is Nancy. My husband passed away."

Knowing it was the wrong thing to say, but like so many others, going right on ahead and saying it because the right thing to say was nothing at all…

"I'm sorry."

"Yeah…Me too." She half-smiled, showing crooked but healthy teeth. With the smeared makeup and the grief chiseled on her face, she probably would pass for sixty. Claire decided she was at least forty.

"My mom passed when I was nine. I don't think my dad forgives God to this day." *Don't know why I just said that!*

"I don't blame God. I blame James. James knew that bike would be the death of him. Our son George bought it for him as a mid-life crisis thing." She looked disgusted for a moment. "I suppose I could blame George. But, George, James, God, what does it matter? He's gone."

She was shocked into a moment of silence. Claire had the realization that she was on the precipice of enormous emotional upheaval. She was confused as to whether it was hers or Nancy's, though. She felt an irresistible urge to shout, to cry and flail violently. She could feel the heat of tears forcing themselves to her eyes. She could feel the warmth of others witnessing her folly of breaching the sanctity of grief. But she was here already, no going back now. No do-overs.

A question that had chased her for years reared its ugly head. It was a question that had nagged her from the time she was a little girl, sitting on her mother's lap at church services.

Again, after her mother had passed, the source of the question came from her father's unmitigated hatred for Christianity, for the God of his Hebrew ancestry, for anything religious. In her college and early adult years, the question persisted during long discussions with professors, lovers, and of course her almost combative anti-god role model, her father, Frank.

Nancy paused in squeezing the cross, dabbed at another tear and turned to Claire.

"Do you believe in God?"

"Of course." This seemed the safest course, always. For where else did one go from there? Downhill. All speculation and conjecture, faith and legend, tradition and idealism, presupposition and logic. Not a topic for even a full five-hour flight.

Surely, they would be descending any moment now. Claire could hear the intensification of foreign dialect, a sort of Spanish, spoken swiftly with deft accent upon the more guttural consonants and lazier around the vowels and verb endings. A directness of syntax more closely related to Portuguese or the Caribbean.

"Not everyone believes. James didn't. He thought he would live forever. I guess that is what makes me so sad. He only existed to experience life. I suppose that was ok. He died happy. Good family, faithful wife, got to re-live his childhood. I suppose I should be glad he lived a life he enjoyed."

"That's all anyone can ask," Claire agreed meekly.

"Yes. I suppose… except I know that this world is not all there is to live for. Knowing that there is something else…you know?" She looked at Claire, imploring understanding.

"I understand," She nodded, but of course, she did not. But it was easier this way. Quicker.

"I knew you would. Thank you. Again, I am sorry for bothering you with my blubbering." Nancy stowed her tissue and returned a warm smile. She looked up ahead of her at several conversations going on in Spanish. "Looks like we sparked a lively conversation."

Claire looked around. Absently, she wondered if anyone recognized that she was carrying the dust of the deceased. Maybe it attracted these occurrences. They seemed to happen more frequently of late.

"Yeah. I guess this sort of discussion often does. Seems no one wants to be left out."

"It's very comforting, isn't it?" Inexplicably, this did not inspire comfort for Claire. Only trepidation that she was more alone on the flight than she imagined.

"I suppose so." Claire picked up the flight magazine again, hoping to find a distraction worthy of breaking the conversation.

She could not shake the feeling that she had avoided something big. She could not ignore the gnawing at her stomach that she had lied. Not for the last time on this trip, Claire felt that she had narrowly missed something, had left something unfinished.

CHAPTER TWO

Paul tapped his fingers nervously. He was hoping that he had not missed her. Her description was abrupt and her flight was packed. But when he saw the steel black box and the inevitable American personification of her dress, her walk, her air, Paul knew he had found Claire Eppington. She appeared comfortable but curious. In charge, but out of place. Paul smiled.

She looked like so many of the mission workers that came annually for their week's worth of penance and "help." Honestly, they all turned out to be more trouble than they were worth; except, Paul needed the financial support. He did not require much for Nina and himself, but the orphanage and the widows needed continual assistance to keep them from the civil rights atrocities that constantly rocked Colombia.

American money was the only cushion he could provide in the face of the cartels, the militants and the corrupt and subversive elements of Colombia's government. By God's mercy he hammered out agreements, bought food and shelter, provided protection, pardon and patronage from civil rights activists for the less fortunate. In Colombia, the less fortunate were numerous.

He stood up, seeing that Claire was searching for him. Paul put on his warmest missionary smile and adjusted his collar. The leather bag at his seat was quickly in hand and he walked purposefully toward her. She was not the least suspicious. This could be dangerous, he thought.

Finally, she smiled and set down her carry-on bag. She extended her hand to shake.

"Brother Paul, I presume?"

"Yes. Glad to meet you Miss Eppington." He took her hand in his and then gently pulled her to him. He lightly kissed her cheek: jasmine and vanilla, light but sweet. He was not sure if it was soap or the same body spray his wife, Nina, used.

"Don't let this scare you, but Miss Eppington—"

"Please, call me Claire."

Still smiling, Paul replied, "Claire, I don't mean to alarm, but it would be best during your visit here to not appear so trusting. Don't assume anything. Although I am Paul Rodriquez, born in Miami, parents of Colombian and Cuban descent, I could just as easily be Luis Esponel, noted henchman for the FARC rebels in Medellin's criminal district. *Comprende?*"

"*Comprende, hermano.*" Suddenly serious, Claire seemed more at ease.

"*Bueno.* Now, if you want, we can grab some grub, as my young interns term it."

"I am famished. What do you suggest?"

"How about McDonald's?"

"You're a man after my own heart."

"I think you put it aptly, Miss—I mean, Claire. And call me Paul, will you?"

"Boy, you can drop that accent quick when you need to sound American, huh?"

"They both serve me well. When in Rome…" He grabbed her carry-on luggage and turned to go to the baggage claim.

"Oh, we don't need to go to baggage. I pack light. Just gonna be here a few nights. Company pays for new duds if I stay longer or if weather is inclement."

Paul changed directions and led her down the stairs to Customs.

After a brief meeting with the Immigration and Customs agents, they stopped at the Duty Free. Paul recognized that the worker there

10

was particularly surly so he kept their visit short and to the point. He then escorted Claire to the public transportation.

Many of the modern amenities of the terminal--varnished wood, gleaming chrome and glass--clashed with the colors and styles of the original airport construction and its 1980's remodel. The ceiling was dingy, the staff was too small for the renewed tourism and the city was looking forward to the new construction next door.

The never-ending bustle of a crowded international airport lent to the mass confusion and sensory overload Paul wanted to avoid. The sooner they exited the terminal, the better, he thought.

"Hey, what's that contraption?" Claire inquired.

"Oh, that's the public transportation. It's new. We'll take it into the capitol district. Your company is putting you up at the Platinum Suite Hotel?"

"Yes. It seems it is the closest to the American Embassy in case I have trouble."

"Very wise. I have your transportation to Yondo finalized and confirmed. Do you have any other needs?"

"Uh, yes. I had trouble getting the right specs for the digital photos and I would rather have the expertise of a professional. Our client is not a demanding person, but it seems John Olshan, Cremation International's president, is a good friend of Dr. Borche, the deceased's husband. He wants the best and is throwing in extras without charge."

"Yes. That is how I am involved. I know Dr. Borche. His wife," Paul pointed at the black box still nestled between Claire's arm and bosom, "was a dear friend. I actually introduced them."

"You amaze me, Mr. Rodriquez. I had no idea the ceremony would be so intimate. It explains why Dr. Borche did not come personally, he trusts you with his wife's last rites?"

"Well, Clay would have loved to come. I suppose it is not appropriate, however. He is not well-loved among the family and

Katherine's mother requested that her remains be scattered along the river where she grew up. Dr. Borche has great respect for her family's wishes and does not want to interfere. We discussed this while Katherine was sick. He refused to bring her to Colombia then, knowing that the volatility here would only worry her more and affect her level of comfort."

"I wish now I had met Dr. Borche personally. I only received the assignment last week and the remains were shipped to me for transport. It sounds as though Dr. Borche is an extraordinary man."

"Very much so. I meet many great men such as Clay. Some are even Americans." Paul turned to smile back at Claire.

"Well, it is kind of you to say so, Mr. Rodriguez."

Paul laughed. "If you have time, I would like to have you over for lunch. I believe my wife Nina would love you—you remind me of our daughter, Emily."

"You have many children?"

"I am afraid not. Emily was murdered by a paramilitary seven years ago."

"I am sorry."

Paul stopped and glanced back. His smile dropped. He detected sadness and his compassion for Claire spiked. He could tell she was hurting, but he felt that she was not even aware she was feeling it. Something had numbed her. He had seen it many times on the faces of the little children. Their parents were slaves, raped, murdered, or subjected to incredible atrocities. They had witnessed so much grief, human suffering and emotional and physical neglect; they no longer recognized the sadness that was evident enough to those that cared to notice.

Accustomed to the signs, he was nonetheless surprised by this young woman and her obvious baggage. He determined silently to drag it out of her during the long trip up the Rio de Magdalena.

To break the spell, he put his finger to his chin. "Hey, I think I can help."

"Huh?"

"Your photographer. I have just the person that will fit the bill. I will arrange a meeting in the morning at breakfast. If you like, he can accompany us on our journey. I warn you though, he eats like a mule. You might offer food as part of your bargain. Although money buys food, he never seems to want to pass up a free lunch."

"Sounds like a plan. Thank you very much. I was worried I would have to figure out how to make contact at the last minute. I will agree to meet with him in the morning. Be sure to tell him to bring along his digital equipment. And if he has filming capabilities that would be great."

"Oh, trust me. Manuel will come prepared. Better than you."

"Oh, is that a challenge?"

"No, merely an observation. You will want to be wearing pants on our trip to the village. So if you packed only Columbia shorts and LL Bean men's shirts, you will want to check out the local outfitter tonight."

"Duly noted. Thank you. When in Rome, right?"

"You catch on quick." Paul loaded the bag onto the bus and paid the fare. Claire sat down, careful of her cargo. Soon, they were shuttling along the busy thoroughfares of Bogotá.

What Claire noticed most about Paul was that his hands never seemed to rest. One minute his right hand was at his clean-shaven chin. Then, he would scratch his forehead consecutively three times and then drop his left hand to his side.

If either hand stopped for more than one minute, it began to twitch and then to bounce and then it was back in motion or touching something—his collar, his luggage, his cell phone would flip open and closed, open and closed. Claire was not sure what to make of this unusual habit, but marked it up to a smoking habit barely controlled or a nervous habit around strangers.

She tried not to notice. Paul, although pleasant, had evidently exhausted his repertoire of small talk and was probably mulling over how to ask her some important, pending question.

She could see it etched there on his tongue. She could feel it oozing from his pores. Maybe that was the reason for the twitch.

During the break in the conversation, she turned her attention to the outside. The bus ran along quietly, but the world outside the bus was louder than the terminal at La Guardia. People yelled, horns screeched, semis roared, and cars zoomed by.

She could not help but be surprised by the architecture. Although she expected some plantation-like Spanish buildings with clay tiles and stucco, she was not prepared for the gleaming glass, the multitude of colors, the striking modern shapes that lined the streets of downtown Bogotá.

Finally, she could stand the twitch no more. Even the distraction outside could not contain her. She turned to Paul.

"Ok. I know we just met but I can tell there is something you want to say to me or ask me."

Paul looked amused but did not take the bait.

He raised his eyebrows, "And?"

"And, well, I am sure you want to know if I believe in God, or have I been saved or where would I go if I died today?"

"Why would I ask you any of those questions?"

"You are a minister, a missionary, a man of the cloth. Isn't it your duty to ask me questions like that?"

Paul looked at Claire earnestly, "My duty, Claire, is to share. I do not need to know answers to very personal questions about you. Unless you wish to share them with me.

I don't expect that your life is a short chapter book I am going to read from here to your hotel. And in the same turn, what I have to share with you, when you are ready, will require more experience with who I am before you are prepared to receive it. Understand?"

"I don't suppose I do. I mean, aren't you going to whip out the Bible, quote me some scripture that pertains to some sin you notice or some mention of Jesus as my Savior?"

"Again, dear Claire, you misinterpret me. Of course I know the Word of God very well and what it contains is very important to me. I do have the compulsion and the duty to share it with others, but I do not force it on anyone. As you get to know me, you will ask better questions. I only hope we will be together long enough for you to trust my judgment and seek my advice as you feel fit."

Claire was silent for a second, contemplating. She looked down at the black box, ashamed she had so brazenly opened up this same line of questioning that had gotten her in a tight spot on the plane.

What are you thinking, Claire? I honestly think you are coming unhinged.

"Well, I suppose I can't argue with your humility, Mr. Rodriguez."

Paul's right hand drifted between his nose and upper lip. "I thought we were on a first name basis?"

"You are right. I guess I'm defensive. It's just that with my job, I work alongside many priests, ministers, pastors—whatever—and they either creep me out right away or treat me like a lesser individual. Like I need to be taught something. Plus, I grew up around a dad that is devoutly atheist."

"All that would make anyone defensive, I suppose. I am not offended, Claire." Claire glanced over at him, his eyes gleaming with pent-up moisture.

Great! Now you're gonna make a grown man cry, Claire!

She considered hugging him. He looked like a man who needed a hug. Not in a pathetic way, just in a demonstration of humanity.

"It's just that Dr. Borche and Katherine were such close friends of mine, I wanted this trip to be special. Sort of like a home-coming. I am still not done grieving for our loss."

"I understand, Paul. Together, we'll make sure it is like a homecoming." She smiled broadly, attempting to reassure him and set the conversation back on solid ground. "And you know something; I think we are going to be friends before this is all through."

Paul laughed—a sort of a surprised cough--and dabbed at his eyes as he turned back. "Well, I certainly hope so, Claire."

CHAPTER THREE

Manuel removed the lens from his Nikon digital camera and carefully stored it in a large case. He glanced over the tools of his trade: camera, back-up camera, video camera, several lenses, extra batteries, hoods, lighting meters, special filters and a modified Kel-Tec P11 with laser sights and four magazines of 9mm ammo. Old habits never seemed to die. Especially habits designed to keep you alive.

The permanently dusty flat he shared with his mother and brother was sticky with humidity. Wiping his brow, Manuel closed up the case and moved to the kitchen.

The street noises here were hard to get used to at first, but after nine months, he had adjusted to the chaos that was common with Bogotá. Manuel checked his cell phone, turned off his laptop and packed it away, threw his extra jacket and a small flashlight into the backpack with his laptop and exited the kitchen.

Manuel was intercepted in the foyer by Lucia, his mother.

"Where are you going, now?"

"Mom, I'm thirty five years old. Do I really need to check out every time?"

Lucia looked hurt. Her graying hair and loss of weight over the last few years had been the most alarming changes to Manuel. She looked like a ghost of the mother he remembered playing stickball growing up.

"But, Manny, I still worry about you." Her face softened and that quick smile sped to his rescue. He needed that smile even as a grown adult. "You will always be my baby. You know that. Besides, I need you to pick up some chicken for dinner."

"Hmm. I am amused, Mom. But if you're serious about the chicken, I can't help. Paul found me a job for the next two days."

"That is excellent. And was that so hard, really? Now get going, you don't want to be late."

"Sure, Mom." Feeling like a kid again and strangely in an excellent mood, Manuel leapt down the wooden stairs and jogged to the street corner. A job, a change in his life, pride in himself. All the pain, the sacrifice, the heartache that he still experienced seemed distant the closer he got to living the life of his dreams. He could not believe his luck.

∞

Closing the door, Lucia's smile faded. Somehow, even the obvious relief of her son was not enough to erase the frown from her features.

She watched him cross the corner and blend into the crowd moving north toward the plaza downtown. His bags and bright red shirt were the only way she could track him as he moved quickly and eventually disappeared into the mass of people.

It was too bad he could not sense something was wrong. Some part of her wanted him to find out. Lucia had many secrets. Deep in her heart, she was tired of carrying their burden.

She let the curtain go and moved to the kitchen. She almost did not notice the man sitting in the darkened nook that was the dining room.

"How long will he be gone?" The dry tone and the thick accent were so familiar, but the man so foreign to her.

She stared at him and did not answer. She reached for the coffee and turned her back to him.

She knew this was dangerous. She was fed up with being conservative and not defending her family in a more tangible way.

"You know, you cannot protect him forever. We have allowed him to have this opportunity to realize his mistake naturally and return to us. Our next move will be to gently remind him of his destiny. Once. After that, we will not be so gentle, so generous as we have been."

His dark suit blended with her antique chair, his thin tie a silhouette on his gray shirt. His arrogance, his assurance was all wrapped up in the gold watch at his wrist, his diamond rings along his thin hands, and the pearl handle of the .45 caliber pistol under his suit jacket. She no longer felt intimidated by his presence. She feared only for her sons.

"Why are you threatening me? What does this have to do with me?" She dropped the cubes of sugar into the coffee as she asked this, splashing herself with hot coffee. She winced.

"Lucia. You are his mother. You have influence no one else has. I do not threaten you, but only remind you what to expect. A timeline has been established to bring Manny back to our fold. We wish only for him to realize his error, turn back to his duty and leave these spiritual platitudes that cloud his judgment. The sooner he realizes this, the less tenuous his situation. The sooner you can feel secure about his safety. Understand?"

"It strikes me as strange that I have never heard you so talkative. Are you losing faith that he will come back? Feeling desperate?" Years working with her husband had honed her sense of finding the soft spot.

"Mocking me gets you no closer to saving Manny." He picked up the Bible lying on the table, its gold gilded edges reflecting the light from the kitchen. He smirked, turned it over and set it near him, his hands neatly folded. He arched his eyebrows, his smile sardonic.

She set the coffee down on the counter. Her hands were shaking. Lucia could not tell if she was more scared or angry. How dare he threaten her with Manny's life! Lucia understood this to be more threat than actuality. Alfonso had always demonstrated an aptitude for cruelty and bullying.

"Ahem. Well, I don't know why you continue to torment me. Why can't you go directly to Manny yourself?"

"I have explained this to you before, Lucia. I do not have the time now to continue this discussion. I must report back and set up our tracking network. The good news for you is that Manny is never out of our sight. He is safe for now."

"I suppose I need to thank you?"

He stood, his dark hair falling across his forehead. His dark brown eyes flashed amusement for a second. He reached out and grabbed her arm gently. She recoiled.

"No, Aunt Lucia. You need not thank me. I enjoy keeping a watchful eye upon my cousin." He moved past her, smelling of strong cologne and cigarettes. She did not watch as he walked briskly out of the house. She stood rooted to the spot. Sobbing, she poured her coffee down the sink, moved to the cabinet and took down a bottle of Scotch and a glass.

∞

The thing that bothered Manuel the most over the past two weeks was he was getting soft. He had lost the edge. This was all according to plan. *Lose yourself in the new you. Create a new life. Start over.* His past would haunt him forever, but he knew he would never be the man he once was.

He could not keep going back to the old Manuel, feeling the same way, acting the same way, and thinking the same way. He had to push forward and blaze a new trail for his life, no matter the struggle and sacrifice, the baggage, and the memories. He must replace his nightmare of his past with the dreams of his future.

But, he still had the nagging feeling that he needed to cling to some of the more essential features of the old Manny. He needed to keep his survival instincts, distrust of everyone, analysis of every detail, awareness of his surroundings at all times, decisiveness and his uncanny sense of danger. Lately, he felt he had lost touch with all these features.

No better example of this was his present situation. He was caught up in the euphoria of a new job, being re-united with his mentor, Paul, and getting to be outside. He looked forward to being away from the confines of the city and his brother Oscar's flat. He was now practically skipping down the crowded street.

He was only dimly aware of his surroundings. He knew of his destination and could think nothing of his journey there. The din of the crowd numbed his senses. The wash of people, the conversations, the pungent odors of the marketplace, the feel of the gradually warming day already bringing beads of sweat to his back, the weight and tug of his equipment were surface concerns Manny processed automatically. In the life he abandoned, he would have processed all this input and analyzed every face, every wary glance, considered every smell, and been in tune with his own body more.

He thought of the Kel-Tec in his bag. He knew he could justify it, but it was the one habit, the last vestige of his old self. Not that the nine millimeter was his sidearm of choice. However, it represented the same thing that he had come to feel a level of comfort about: intimidation, power, death-bringing. Guns were an aphrodisiac of immense power, a primordial draw. A killer with the will to use it could strike fear, could melt hearts, and could ruin lives. That kind of power was addictive.

Thinking himself beyond those base feelings now, Manuel clung to the belief that the new and improved Manny would only use a gun if forced to defend his family. If death came to his own door, he was determined to answer it with a smile. He was ready to move on because he knew what awaited him.

He stopped for a moment in the middle of the bustle.

"Stop and smell the roses, even if they stink," his father had said many times.

He wondered at that moment whether maybe over the past few months, as he immersed himself in the new Manny, perhaps he had missed something. There was always the nagging feeling that getting out was too easy. Too clean. At least as far as his brother Domingo was concerned. The rest of the business of leaving had been messy. Manny tried to put the memories of that week out of his mind.

He always expected some sort of repercussions. To date, he had experienced nothing more than a cold shoulder from some of the soldiers. His brother had even sent him a Christmas card. No present, but what did he expect? They were not teenagers anymore, competing for their father's attention and against each other in a thousand ways.

He loved Domingo. If only he could be sure his brother still trusted him. He picked up his pace; the station was just ahead and he was fairly certain he had seen Paul, standing a head taller than everyone else. Paul had not noticed him yet, though. Manny chuckled.

He remembered joking with Paul once, teasing. "Your head is always in the clouds, Paul."

Manny tried to blend in with the crowd.

CHAPTER FOUR

Carlos stared intently out the window of the three story brick building overlooking the plaza. Among the throng of people below, he managed to pick out several Americans. He could spot a foreigner within seconds. He had a knack, especially, for seeing through the cultural and racial subtleties of North, Central and South Americans. His job entailed tracking and sometimes eliminating targets who often wished to maintain a low profile.

He put out his cigarette in the tray by his bed. A knock at the door and he was up, pistol ready.

"It's me, Carlos. Time to open up."

Carlos did not want a visit from Alfonso today. Not after botching the last assignment. He let him in anyway.

"Nice to see you in one piece after last month, *mi amigo*."

"Yeah. Close one."

Alfonso had a way of moving through a room while making small talk. He seemed to be gathering information, storing away details for later use. He turned back to Carlos as he made his trip around the little room that Carlos had called home the last three weeks.

"We have another assignment for you. Observation and report only. We wouldn't want you getting trigger happy." Alfonso glanced down at the pistol at Carlos' side.

"Don't worry, I can handle myself."

"So I hear."

"Careful what you say—"

Before he could finish the sentence, Alfonso had him against the wall, his knuckles bearing into Carlos' throat. Carlos could feel the sharp point of a knife at his gut.

"Threaten me again and I'll gut you. Now, give me the pistol."

Carlos handed it over. Numb and beginning to see stars from lack of oxygen, Carlos choked. Alfonso let him down and turned his back.

Carlos watched him as he held the barrel of the .22 and pocketed it. Then, from an inside pocket of his jacket Alfonso extracted his pearl handled .45. He turned back to Carlos and ran the barrel of the pistol down his cheek to his chin. The light through the window framed him and darkened his features. He squinted through the haze of light and gloom.

"Are you interested in the assignment, or should I just put you out of your misery now? You are of little use to me. Don't forget that."

Carlos, still choking, managed: "Yes. Tell me what you want."

"Good." He straightened his tie, "I need you to watch after Manny again"

Alfonso backed away slowly. Alfonso's smoldering eyes never left his.

"This time, though, get some information about this new employer. She is American. See what her value is and let me know. I see some opportunity here. If you help me capitalize upon it, maybe we can graduate you back to your old status."

"Manny, huh? Can't believe you'd chance that."

Alfonso closed the gap and raised Carlos back to his feet. "Carlos. . .Carlos, we should not be having this conversation, you know. Just do what I tell you and then see how you are rewarded. I can tell you now; you will like it much more than if you fail me."

He walked back to the door, leaving Carlos to lean against the flimsy card table, knocking over a beer and spilling its stale contents on the magazines there.

"Yes, Alfonso."

"Simple enough." Alfonso turned to Carlos and with a grin asked, "Does your sister still live in that flat above the bakery? I should go and see her again soon. I hear she misses me."

"She has moved. I have not heard from her in weeks."

"That is too bad. She was delicious. Let her know I asked about her next time you see her. Give her my number. And Carlos…"

"Yes?"

"Do not engage Manny at all, you understand?"

"Yes." *Thank God for small favors*, he thought.

Alfonso stared at him a moment longer and then left. Carlos could hear his footsteps echo down the corridor and then descend the stairs.

He could feel the hatred and fury welling up inside him. It was fruitless. He had no choice. His family had no choice. His gift had doomed him to be of service to the cartels, the paramilitary, the FARC. Now, he had to track his old boss. *This could be the death of me*, he thought. Needless to say, regardless of his course, his death was near. As close as he had been to death over the past decade, they should be good friends by now. Somehow, familiarity had bred contempt.

As Alfonso descended the stairs, he pulled from his pocket the .22. He had made sure to use his sleeve as he extracted it from his pocket. It was all coming together now. Only Manny could upset the balance. He put the gun into a baggie and back into his jacket pocket.

His cell phone rang.

"Alfonso here…Yes, *Capo* Domingo. We are still monitoring him. I spoke to your mother this morning. She mentioned he has a job now. I have my best man . . . Yes, Domingo. Have faith in me, my cousin."

Domingo shifted uncomfortably. He hated bowing to Domingo. He was anxious for the ruse to be over.

"Manny will be back in the fold soon. For the moment, though, am I not fulfilling his work admirably? Oh, come on, Domingo. That was only one instance. How was I to know that she was connected? Huh?"

Alfonso lit a cigarette and sat down on the bench just outside of Carlos' apartment building. The crowd bustling by did not faze him. He was focused. This was important.

"Yes, I know, *Capo*. I will. Yes. This is all in good hands here. We have good men working, doing what Domingo Villarreal does best. Make money, right cousin? Anything else you need from me, boss? Good. I will get in contact with you as soon as I hear anything new. Great. Bye."

As he hung up the phone, he crossed the street, dodging the traffic, stopping some cars, sliding around a bus and then entered a building just across the street from Carlos' apartment. It was an old furniture factory, abandoned several years ago. Alfonso had purchased it with money from a blackmail ring he ran independently right under Domingo's nose. The door slammed shut and he walked through the empty lobby into the old manager's office and then into what appeared to be a closet. He entered a combination into the keypad on the wall, pressed his finger to an identity port and waited for the "beep" that signaled that the security system was disarmed.

The room he entered next was large and full of men. Mostly, they had been slouching and playing cards, cleaning weapons, stacking money and fighting over the soccer match between Venezuela and Ireland on a television sitting on a coffin by the microwave stand. Two men near monitors had already fallen into the routine of appearing "busy." They knew Alfonso had dropped in. The others were caught off guard.

"Listen up! Get your gear and take the van over to Val de Sol y Rue Dies. Time for some surveillance, boys! Stay out of sight and report back to Jessica by email every fifteen minutes. Be there by 10 am sharp or you will miss them. Don't be late or it's your hide. I will call you with the target in an hour on the secure line. Go!"

"The rest of you, get that shipment loaded on the flat bed and delivered. Make sure you collect from Minister Aroucheville before you leave this time. Don't let any of Domingo's boys see."

Without words, the men broke up and began to pack, to move, to obey, but none looked Alfonso in the eye. Out of fear, resentment, loyalty or apathy, each man in the room did not want the attention of Alfonso Marianas.

CHAPTER FIVE

He could not help missing his younger brother. His pride reminded him that he was better off without the guilt associated with having Manny exposed and in harm's way. Domingo owed Manny his life. He was tired of feeling dependent upon Manny's abilities and loyalty. Domingo thought maybe this move would be good for him. It was not good for everyone to think of you as weak because your younger brother was around to watch out for you. It was not good for his image.

Alfonso could not be trusted. He understood that. But Al's way with people, his absolute control at all times was daunting. Domingo respected that. Alfonso was a born leader. Domingo predicted that soon Al would spread his wings and move on to bigger and better things. The trade-off for Al's positive traits was greatly dwarfed by his severe liability to the organization. Domingo decided he would not worry about Al or Manny for now. He had business to conduct and his guests should arrive soon.

The frozen cocktail stung Domingo's hand as he held it, watching the valley from his third story balcony. Condensation dripped onto the glass table at his side and ran along his cell phone, forgotten. He could hear the stirring of the two guards behind him and he wondered how long they could stand there in this heat before they asked for something to drink.

"Don Villarreal, your guests have arrived." A tall, slim Mexican woman dressed in a bright orange and yellow pant suit smiled briefly at the patio door, a clipboard propped against her waist. She ignored the looks from his bodyguards. She was cool and professional. A real find.

Domingo stared into her deep chocolate eyes and followed the shape of her luxurious dark silken hair as it spilled over her shoulders and framed her almond-shaped face. The horn rimmed glasses were fake, he knew, but they did not detract from the image.

"Maria, thank you. Please escort them in and have Christiana bring up the refreshments we have planned, please."

"As you wish, Don." She did not bow, or cow-tow. She briskly turned and marched away. Domingo watched his men follow her exit from the room and smiled. The benefit to allowing such beautiful women access among so many men with crude appetites was that she was unattainable, unassailable. They had no chance and they knew it.

Although Maria did not carry a gun, run a platoon of men, or perform the dangerous task of escorting coca, her station was above almost everyone in his organization. Manny had seen to that. He had hired her, fought off her most fervent advances, trained her and now, after five years serving directly for Domingo, she was Domingo's most valued assistant.

Some people assumed Domingo had slept with her, but nothing could be farther from the truth. Domingo was a faithful husband, and more importantly, he knew to mix business with pleasure—no matter how exquisite—would be a disaster.

Henry Frônçeau and his escort entered the terrace, a smile playing coyly upon his features, his hand extended. Domingo rose and crossed in front of the table to shake Henry's large black hand. He was at least four inches taller than Domingo and outweighed him by almost a hundred pounds.

"Nice to see you again, *mon ami*," Henry hooked a finger over his back.

"You allow us to be checked twice for weapons, now? What, do you trust no one since Manny is not around to watch your back?" Henry teased.

Domingo dropped his smile. "It seems it is a more dangerous world today, Henry. Please, do not let it offend you. It is merely their job. I am glad they perform it seriously."

Henry, continuing to smile, gestured to the empty seat. "Is it alright if I sit while we talk or am I constrained to be baking my bald head in this sun?"

"Please. Let us sit." The shade of the canopy was only slightly more comfortable.

Seated, Domingo glanced into the doorway and noted that Henry's bodyguards were chatting politely with Rodrigo and Martin, his own personal escort. He could not hear them, but by their facial expressions and sneers, he imagined that the topic was Maria.

"So, you are expanding into Africa. That is it?"

"You're information is perfect. I think it will be the best route into Europe. Europe is naturally less dangerous than the US though better guarded than here. There is no security. Only fifteen percent of my product reaches its destination."

"Surprising." Henry motioned grandly, his arms encompassing the terrace, his eyes taking in the beautiful mountaintop grandeur that was the Villarreal headquarters.

"Don't let appearances blind you to the truth, Henry. Fifteen percent of our production at today's street values is still more than the gross national product of some Third World countries. I am more concerned about our efficiency and our dwindling availability of qualified personnel."

"I supply you with the best trained men, and the best armaments, do I not?"

"Yes, yes. That is true. Except, I suspect that allegiances are growing weary. Our political differences notwithstanding, the two guerilla groups and the paramilitaries dancing around each other because of some sort of agreement is about as absurd as me inviting President Uribe to dinner. Besides, your connections and the sheer numbers are greater in Western Africa, are they not? Or is my information incorrect?"

Henry smiled, reached into his cargo shirt pocket and extracted a cigar. He clipped the end off and stared at it before rolling it in his fingers.

"In Africa, we have many thousands of armed men, hundreds of informants, dozens of qualified agents and tons of equipment at my disposal. This is true. Even better, the environment is ripe for strife and conflict. Money flowing to this area would spark much trouble, I am sure."

"Seems there is trouble no matter where we go. Is it trouble we can control and manipulate? Like our government here perhaps?"

"We probably do not have to be that sophisticated, Domingo. Political upheaval is a draw for organizations such as ours because there is little threat from a decentralized government. But yes, we can certainly pull strings here and tuck things under the carpet there. In the end, I think you may be right about the risk." His lips smacked audibly and he considered the cigar. Its smoke rose lazily in the humid air.

"I am sure of it. The only problem is we will be stepping on many people's toes."

"Again, you are talking security, Don Domingo."

"Yes. At home, it will be fierce. The other cartels will appreciate less competition, but be jealous of any success we have. Our contacts will feel they are being abandoned. The *cocaleros* will be offended we are no longer paying top peso for their coca paste. Others will see our venture as foolish and short-lived; maybe a sign of weakness or distraction."

"All of these things sound like opportunities for breaches of security and added risk. Seems you cannot escape it altogether."

"Henry. What do we do for a living? We are not producing American movies or selling cigars! God forbid that we sell cars or make farm implements! We sell cocaine—one of the world's most sought after agricultural commodities! Danger and risk come with the territory."

"So where do we start?"

"Get an organization on the ground there off the western coast of Africa. Just make sure it is the right fit. Your connections in the French government should come in handy in keeping an eye out for Interpol and EU. I trust you, Henry. My father trusted your father so, why not? We shall keep this in the families, am I right?"

"Yes." Domingo raised his cocktail, dripping with condensation and Henry met it with his cigar, "To our families. May they live long, strong and prosper."

"You said it all right there." Domingo laughed quietly.

CHAPTER SIX

So, this is what a Colombian photographer looks like.

Claire knew that Manuel Villarreal was more than he appeared. She had met men like him all over the world. They all seemed simple and unfettered, laid back, but intense. Their exterior roughness usually belied a shrewd and dangerous mind. They were capable guides, invaluable diplomats, and trustworthy security blankets in dicey situations.

Manuel had approached Paul from his blind side and practically tackled him. After so many warnings from Paul recently to be alert, she was startled at first.

Despite this, her first impressions of Manny were influenced as much by his gregarious attitude as his dark olive skin, his chiseled chin and his well-maintained body.

"You must meet my friend here, your potential employer, Ms. Claire Eppington," Paul said as way of introduction.

Manuel, suddenly serious, brushed his long dark hair from his fascinating chestnut brown eyes and thrust out his hand in a traditional North American greeting.

"A pleasure to meet you Ms. Eppington. If you would allow me, I have brought along my professional profile so you can browse my work…"

"No need. Paul vouches for your work and I am in a hurry," Claire smiled and returned the handshake and let go. She looked at him with mock appraisal and shrugged. "You will do in a pinch."

"Paul, she is about as ornery as you, it seems."

"Impossible," Paul deadpanned.

Manuel slung his bag onto his shoulder and bent over to pick up Claire's shopping bag.

"She is not hiring you to be her Sherpa, Manny."

"No. Let him. I haven't had the pleasure of having someone wait on me hand and foot before. I think I might like being spoiled."

"She sounds American, that's for sure." Manny smirked.

"Do I pay extra for the compliments?"

He turned to Paul, and grabbed his elbow.

"They are free, aren't they Paul?"

"I have got to say, Manny, you really shine in a job interview," Paul said sarcastically.

"Hey, I'm nervous around you, Paul. What can I say?"

"Just tell me you aren't going to eat so much that you embarrass me like last time."

"So where are we eating?" Claire asked.

"Someplace special. I think you will enjoy it. Manny here won't tell his mom he secretly craves the food here more than at home, will you Manny?"

"I don't know about you, Paul, but I am a firm believer in keeping my hide. You know momma doesn't like me eating away from home."

"So, how do you hide it from her?" Claire asked, enjoying the banter and beginning to feel comfortable.

"He eats double portions, *a su casa y a* "Basket of Plenty.""

Laughing, Manny said, "Don't let Paul fool you, we are taking you to a lunch line run by one of the members of his church. We are going to serve lunch as well as eat. Paul's idea of a good time."

Although Claire did not have this on her itinerary, she did not mind short excursions. This was especially true when the company was worth it.

"I know I said I was in a hurry, but it sounds great. When do we start?"

"Lunch isn't until twelve, but we must help them prepare the meal. Then we will serve. Once we have eaten and helped John clean, his son will take us down the Rio De Magdalena."

"Did I mention I can't cook?"

"Don't worry, mostly you will be cleaning vegetables and cutting up chickens," added Manny. "That's all he'll let me do, anyway. But it's a small price to pay for the wonderful food."

Manny was right about the food. Once they had arrived at the northern end of the block where they had met, Claire could see several outdoor kitchens being constructed. Iron pots on gas burning stoves surrounded by makeshift tables spread with all sorts of produce and meats. The smells of the city somehow did not encroach here. Excited women bustled around, some yelling, some laughing.

Everyone seemed occupied, but as soon as a lady dressed in a loose white blouse, burgundy flowing skirt and thin leather sandals noticed Paul, she screamed, "Brother Rodriguez! Man of God is here to bless us! Quick, get him a chair and some water."

She motioned to a young girl, already carrying a metal pitcher in one hand and several plastic bags with what appeared to be corn tortillas in the other. "Go, girl, can you not see? Look there! It is Brother Paul. He is gracious to help today, you must wait on him!"

"Ai! Mama! Brother Paul is here every day and my waiting on him only embarrasses him. He makes fun of me! Now go and cook, mama, before we make the people starve."

The girl sat the pitcher down on a table so hard, the water spilled out. She rolled her eyes at Paul, mockingly, and set off at a jog for a long metal grill set over a wood fire.

"Lord, have mercy, Paul! Did you hear that? On the mouth of a girl from my womb! Can you believe?"

"Angelina, I can only believe that the girl is now thirteen and she is becoming a woman of her own mind. Sort of like her mother was at that age, if I remember."

"Remind me to rub some dirt on your empanada, Mr. Rodriguez."

Soon, Claire was up to her elbows in corn shucks. They roasted the buttered cobs over the embers of a fire. Dozens of yucca lay in bowls atop multicolored resin stools. On one table, Claire noticed what she was afraid were several iguanas. She hoped that she could avoid whatever dish they were going into.

Manny sauntered up, his shirt sleeves rolled up, sweat beading his forehead.

"Can you believe in this heat, we are having *ajiaco*?" he asked.

"Ajiaco? What is that? Does it have iguana in it?"

Laughing, he replied, "No, the iguana and what little chicken we could find is for the *carimanolas*. *Ajiaco* is the soup of Bogotá. We have it almost all the time. Potatoes, heavy cream, avocados, some capers. Very rich if you want it that way. I dip the corn in it or *pain de maize* for a change."

"You mean corn bread?"

"Yeah, you think Americans thought of those themselves? Hmm. You should get around more."

"I am not much of a food critic. But I am certain I will not like iguana."

"Don't knock it until you try it. Besides, if there is any left by the time we eat, I doubt you will know what you are eating."

"That's what I am scared of."

All the ladies doted over Paul, but Claire noticed they almost avoided Manny. Manuel went back to peeling potatoes and joked around with some of the older men and the boys who were setting up low tables and mismatched chairs at the fringes of the street.

All the workers seemed excited and happy. No one argued, it seemed, and most were focused on their task. Even the children bustled around, apparently aware of their roles. Utensils were laid and plates stacked at one end of the square. As the preparations for the lunch neared completion, Claire noticed the first customers begin to arrive.

The whole square was filled with people within minutes. The air was charged with voices, the aroma of cooking food, and warm Colombian sun. Angelina and her husband, Christian, doted over every person in line. Their generosity and dedication to the orphans and the homeless was touching.

Claire had known many charitable people growing up—her father's best friend was the curator at the University museum in Chicago. But, Paul and the members of his congregation were genuinely concerned about the well-being of everyone there and she listened as Paul asked about loved ones, family members, friends at work. He seemed to know everyone and recall intimate details about their lives. Claire realized Paul was a remarkable man. She was anxious to meet Nina and she was sure she would like her.

Claire raised her eyebrows as a girl with light brown hair and big cheeks smiled at her and spoke something she could not understand. Claire nodded and offered a corn cob. The girl shook her head and pointed above Claire's head. She turned in time to catch Manny putting bunny ears behind her head. Manuel shrugged and ran off to his station. The girl giggled and moved on down the line. She glanced over at him; Manny was teasing a young boy. It seemed his popularity here was concentrated mostly among the younger generations. They treated him like a famous athlete or a cherished uncle. She could not quite figure that one out. She made a note to ask Paul about that later.

CHAPTER SEVEN

Oscar hated it when she chewed her nails. His mother had maintained this habit since he was a child. He understood that something was gnawing at her, so she in turn, gnawed at her nails. It was a disgusting habit, but it was a dead give-away that he needed to pry from Lucia what was bothering her.

With all she had experienced in her lifetime, it could be anything. For a moment, Oscar considered the wisdom in exposing his mother's concerns. What if she told him some dark secret about Domingo, or told him of some illegal act she was involved in with his father?

He did not want to know such things.

He had worked diligently since before his father was murdered to distance himself from his family's self-centered, opportunistic and illegal tendencies.

He stopped himself from thinking "evil."

After his father died, Oscar had invited Lucia to join him in Bogotá. His father's murder had set off a chain reaction of betrayal and competition over the Villarreal estate. Lucia would not have survived in the Valle de Cauca. Lucia had not been involved with the day to day business of the Villarreal organization. Initially, Oscar knew, the draw for Lucia to join him was to help take care of Carmen, his ill wife. He welcomed her, thankful for her presence and grateful that his mother was safe.

He thought he had saved her.

It was sad he could not save his wife.

Just a year after his mother moved in, Carmen passed one night in her sleep. The cancer had taken over too quickly. Oscar was never the same.

Nine years later, Oscar had found a new purpose in his life.

It had begun with a call from Manny. He had met someone who had changed his life, he said. Oscar was surprised to hear from his youngest brother. He had never gotten over the transformation of Manny from young soccer star and heart throb of the girls in the villages to Manuel, the cold-hearted killer and security chief for the Villarreal organization. He had heard of Manny's ruthlessness, his focus and his wits.

The Manny he knew did not call his estranged older brother at eleven in the evening, sounding confused and sad.

Manny did not want to go into details, but wondered if he could stay with Oscar and their mother for a while.

"But what about the estate? What about Domingo?"

"I can't go back there now. I have decided to turn another page in my life. Can I come? It would mean a lot to me. I can help with the rent."

"You don't need to worry about that, Manny…It's just that, it has been a long time. I've gotten away from the Villarreal curse. I will always love you Manny, but I don't want to be exposed to the dangers of the illicit and notorious things our family practices."

"I understand, Oscar. Maybe that is why I am calling you. I respect what you have done. I want to join you. Please, brother. It will mean the world to me. It will make the difference."

Oscar had not realized that he would be instrumental in saving Manny from the life he and Domingo had created from the ashes of their father's legacy.

After meeting Paul, Oscar more fully understood and accepted Manny's change.

Despite this, in his heart, Oscar always knew that there was still some dark pall that hung across the shoulders of his youngest brother. He did not pry, though.

Glad that he had rescued both his mother and youngest brother, Oscar had sought to lure Domingo from the corruption. He would have to battle furiously to save Domingo. He was in deep.

For all his intelligence, his schooling and world travelling, Domingo had a deep-rooted desire to rise above, to fulfill their father's destiny, and make the Villarreal name famous throughout the world. Riches, power and self-love appealed most to Domingo Villarreal.

Now, Oscar could not decide whether his mother was upset over a decision to go shopping with her gossipy friend, Justina, or some memory he did not want her to dredge up for his sake.

Finally, he decided valor was in order. He stepped in feet first.

"Mom, what is wrong? You seem nervous."

She glanced at him and put her right hand on the table folded neatly over her left. She arched her eyebrows. He watched as she glanced to her right. He sensed a lie or a diversion coming. He could read her like a book, now.

"Um. What do you mean, nervous?"

"Mom, don't play games with me. I'm your son and I can tell perfectly well when something is bothering you. Now, come out with it or I'll tell Justina you didn't have that doctor's appointment last week."

"Oscar! You wouldn't. I just couldn't go to that wedding with her. I barely know the Marcen's. And, besides, she was just trying to set me up with some guy from her support group."

"Is that it?"

"What?" She looked genuinely confused.

"The guy. You aren't going to remain single the rest of your life, are you?"

"Are you?" He should have expected that. But it hurt anyway.

"Mom, I'm talking about you. You're chewing away at your nails like a dog after the ham hock. I know something's up. Just tell me. Maybe I can help."

His mother sighed, looked at her nails and said with a frown, "Oscar. You don't want to get involved. I can handle it. I'm just a little worried, that's all."

"Then why can't you tell me? And besides the family business and crocheting, what don't I want to get involved in?"

"Exactly."

"You're worried about crocheting?" He tried to be funny whenever he could. It seemed to calm him.

"Oscar. Don't be silly. It is family business and it does not involve me directly. I'm just worried, like I said."

"Well, if you say so. Actually, I am glad you have been thinking about the business. I have been considering calling Domingo again to arrange a time for us all to have dinner together. Big happy family. We haven't had many meals together, or holidays since Dad died."

"I know. But I don't think the time is right. See, with Manny gone, Domingo is probably under a lot of pressure and feels insecure. Give him a few months, eh? You all are big boys now; it is not so unusual to be separated and live your own lives. I am just glad you, Manny, and I have been so close these past few months. It is good to have my boys back together."

"Which is exactly why I thought of inviting Domingo over. I really want to see him dissolve the family business, Mom. We have enough money to live comfortably. And maybe it is time for Domingo and Manny to have a family before it is too late."

"Like it is for you?"

He stared at his mother. He couldn't tell if she had blurted that out, or if it was an intentional barb meant to change the subject and distract him. His mother was a clever manipulator. His father had discovered this and had used her skills to further his empire. Lucia had an uncanny grace and beauty. Even now, nearing sixty, her olive skin was unblemished, her hair trimmed neatly, her dress modest but fashionable.

She took a deep breath and he could see she was displeased with herself. Which meant the comment was deliberate and he should let it roll off his back and dig deeper into what was bugging her. But not now. Her guard was up and he would not be able to crack her resolve.

"Ok Mom. I'll drop it. But I'm still calling Domingo. I think it is important to keep in touch. You never know."

He could tell she was relieved. But she had not offered an apology.

"Yeah, you never know, Oscar. But thanks for the concern, honey." Lucia jerked her head in mock alarm and said, "Oh, I forgot! I left a note from Manny for you on the kitchen sink. You should read it. I didn't, but he wanted me to make sure it got to you."

"Manny left me a note?"

"Yes. Haven't you heard?" She beamed with pride, but he could detect a suspicious note. "Manny got a job this weekend."

"A job? Well that is great! I'll get the note and read it when I get back. I'm going out to get some tools to fix that deadbolt for the door out back. It seems to have gotten some metal shavings in it and it won't stay locked."

"Uh. Sure, hon. Could you get me some bananas and walnuts? I'll make some bread for the ladies from church."

"Yes, mom. I'll be back soon." He picked up his wallet from the mantel, smiled over his shoulder and left.

She still hasn't apologized, he thought. *Of course, I wasn't exactly sensitive to her feelings, either. I guess that road goes both ways. Welcome to the Villarreal family.*

As he tucked the note into his pocket and made his way down the dirty street, he failed to notice the black Dodge van parked across the street from their flat.

CHAPTER EIGHT

Alfonso waited impatiently by the curb. He checked his watch again. The noon sun was beginning to make him perspire. He did not want the American to see him sweat. He glanced around, took out his handkerchief and reached inside each sleeve of his jacket to wipe away the moisture there. He briefly sniffed the handkerchief and decided to put it back in his pocket. Rotten idea to wear a suit, but he had an image to uphold.

Alfonso had grown up watching American gangster movies. He had idolized the Mafia and tried to emulate their attitudes. He loved the way they seemed invincible, arrogant and proud. He felt that way himself. This American agent did not intimidate Alfonso, but he was an important tool. Almost too valuable. He did not like feeling that without Agent Alvarez, his operations would be seriously hampered and his hopes of inheriting the Villarreal cartel would be dashed.

He was an integral part of Alfonso's plan. The problem was deeper, though. As Alfonso knew all too well, Alvarez had his own agenda and was using Alfonso as much as he was using the American DEA agent. Plus, Alfonso also understood from his own personal actions and intentions that a man that would betray one ally would betray another without a second thought. "No honor among thieves," he had overheard once.

He leaned against his Lincoln again, feeling the sun baking the glossy black fender and the heat it radiated. He could hear the metal *plomp-plomp* as he applied more of his weight to the car. He took out a cigarette and thought twice about lighting it.

The American was peculiar. He would drift away and stand back speaking softly if Alfonso smoked or had been drinking. It was almost as if he could not stand someone else's vices. Alfonso did not mind the judgment. It was just that he was unnerved by the guy's hypocrisy.

Just as Alfonso tucked the cigarette back into his inner pocket of his jacket, a car rolled gently around the corner and approached the other side of the street. Its brakes squealed and it came to an abrupt stop. Its engine sputtered quietly. It was Alvarez's red Toyota Corolla. He looked completely out of place in it.

Agent Alvarez unfolded his six foot four inch frame from the small vehicle. He appeared dazed, shielding his eyes with his hand. He looked up and down the street. His jacket was not pressed. His shoes were embarrassingly untidy. His black glasses seemed cliché and his mustache marked him as a man beyond vanity. One side was trimmed much shorter than the other and his stubble was thick, at least two days' growth.

He did not smile, but had an air of mirth. He nodded almost imperceptibly and then checked the street again. He did not look at Alfonso again until he was standing near him. Alfonso found it uncanny that Agent Alvarez would never stand straight in front of him. He would always approach at an angle. If Alfonso moved, the agent would move, almost like a distant dance or a cameraman following a movie star.

Alfonso felt a compulsion to light the cigarette for spite. He was unsure about this man. He was an enigma. He was off-putting but commanding, gangly in his physical attributes, but compact in his manner of speaking and engaging.

"Well." Not a question, but posed as one. A usual greeting.

"I told you we can control this thing," Alfonso replied. It was best to take a confident stance with Alvarez. The man could smell weakness as well as he could cigarette smoke and alcohol. The only difference was his reaction.

"We?"

"Yes. You have the inside here and I have the key to Domingo's African expansion." He saw a gleam of understanding, but a flash of danger. Confused, he continued, "If you cover me for one more week, I can get Domingo reined in."

"Really? And how is this supposed to interest me? I am aground here. You put me in a difficult position." He looked down the street to the bustling traffic on *Av Dos*. He shuffled his feet and put his hands in his pockets. These were sure signs that he would leave soon.

"Wait. Let me explain." Alfonso stood up straighter and shifted forward. He noticed that Alvarez shifted away immediately and took his left hand from his pocket.

"You see, Domingo is not as vulnerable as you need him to be. He has too many competing interests. His father built a strong organization but it relies too heavily on others to keep it afloat. Paras to protect the routes, the government insiders to blind the crop sprayers, the corrupt middle men in Mexico, and the labs in America that degrade the purity of our product to multiply their profits and cut us out. His losses are covered, sure, but the losses are tremendous. You understand?"

"Completely." His hand went back to the pocket. He looked down at Alfonso and gave that crooked smile. He removed his glasses and wiped his brow with a wrinkled sleeve of his two-button suit.

"Of course. But do you see? Domingo feels that the risks of the loss are acceptable because the dividends are so great. Like a great stock market of coca, he plays with the fortune of his father. Soon, the rising prices from the cocaleros will cost him even more. It will only be a matter of time before it will crumble around his ears," Alfonso continued, gaining steam. He ignored the bored look in Alvarez's eyes.

"Africa is his ticket to all of Europe. He thinks that if he rides the initial wave, he will make as much profit on the first shipment to cover the costs to start up the venture and enough revenue in two more shipments to pay for the losses of his North American routes altogether."

Alfonso paused to let this sink in.

Alvarez sucked his teeth and looked down the street again. And then he put the glasses on his face. It was a deliberate gesture, an attempt at intimidation.

"Listen here, Mr. Marianas. Listen close." Alfonso could see the little blue eyes boring through the dark lenses of the glasses. "I am not interested in Africa. I care only to keep the status quo. Africa and Europe and Canada and everywhere but the good ole' U-S of A is of no interest whatsoever to me."

"I see, but—"

"No buts. Just listen." He pursed his lips, licked them and said, "I will only say this once and then our business is finished. I don't want anything to do with Africa. If you can keep Domingo's operations focused on staying consistent, staying put, I will support your attempts. I will cover your proverbial backside. But don't expect me to lift a finger if your intent is to trash the North American branches of the Villarreal cartel to carve out some temporary turf in Europe."

"Why?" He knew it was dangerous, but he was not scared of Alvarez. He was only intimidated by losing his alliance because Alfonso's only real concern was going it alone. Without Alvarez, he had no protection from the American patrols, the Colombian police or the prying eyes of the Colombian government. The government was so desperate for a martyr to prove their intent to gain American financial support, they would literally invent rebels and drug lords to put a feather in their cap.

"I need not expose my intents. But surely, you can see my energies have been focused on building a working relationship that supports routes north to the US. An interruption of those routes would be an affront to my hard work and my sacrifice."

"Would a new venue like Europe not deflect attention from your activities and provide you more protection?"

"You do not understand the risks I take. Or perhaps you do. You too play a dangerous game. Two dangerous games can get you hurt, Alfonso. Remember that. You want my support? Keep Villarreal in line. Discourage his expansion. Or take the blasted thing over yourself and honor our agreement." He glanced up the street again and then looked over to his Corolla. He smirked and then looked up into the sun.

"Take care, Alfonso. I have to fill up and get back to the office. Don't call me again if you don't have anything important. I have other contacts and a day job to maintain."

"Sure."

Alfonso was nervous. He could not remember when he had lost control. Somewhere in the conversation, he began working for what passed for the American government here in Colombia. He watched with a sick feeling in the pit of his stomach as Agent Alvarez folded himself comically back into his compact vehicle and pulled out into traffic.

Alfonso sighed. It was going to be a long day.

CHAPTER NINE

The Rio De Magdalena was not sexy. Although the river was surrounded by lush vegetation, the sounds and images of bright birds and the colors of spectacularly beautiful flowers and shrubs, Claire could not see past the murky brown stain of the river.

Its latte coloration was distracting and purposeful. The river was swollen to the banks. She understood that just weeks prior, before the rains, the banks were full of alligators and other predators. Now, they lurked just beneath the surface or in temporary lairs hidden in the nearby forest.

When Claire had begun her journey, she had been afraid that it might storm. Now, drenched in perspiration from the humidity and heat, she felt as though she had experienced the storm after all. She pulled out the handkerchief she had purchased this morning in the market. It was as wet as her clothing. She tucked it back in her backpack and frowned. The riverboat they had rented was large and with the hold below, she had not seen Manuel or Paul since their trip began.

Content to sit upon the deck and watch the flora and fauna of a foreign country, she had stayed for over two hours. It was now nearing dinner time and she was wondering what they had planned. The trip was at least another five hours up river and she desperately wanted to stay in a dry, cool bed tonight before rising early, performing the ceremony and then driving overland back to Bogotá. Her flight would leave the next morning and she would be back in Chicago by the weekend. Her friend Laura had some scheme to hook Claire up with her life insurance agent. Laura was never daunted, it seemed.

Claire often did not bother with detailing out every bit of her itinerary. She was paid by the job, not by the hour. This was considered hazardous duty, so her pay scale was significantly higher than going to Ireland or spreading ashes over the English Channel or in some remote town in Alaska. However, despite her laid back nature, she was curious what the next few days would be like.

Although she found Manny attractive, he did not represent an attainable or worthwhile pursuit. But, that did not mean she had to shut her eyes and ignore him. Something told her that this trip could be fun. Maybe she would have some juicy gossip for Laura when she arrived stateside.

∞

"When are you going to leave me alone about this, Paul?"

"You cannot expect your brother to come around just because it is you. Some leopards never change their spots, Manny."

Manuel put his hands on his hips, sweat beading up around his temples and soaking his cotton shirt. He was exasperated. He knew that Paul was right, but he wanted to push until he failed. He understood the danger in threatening his brother, knew keenly the results obtained from demanding ultimatums and forcing Domingo's hand.

"Paul, how can you give up on him? I don't get it. I thought you have this mission to save souls, save lives."

Paul looked serious. "I am saving lives. I am saving yours, my friend. Your idea is foolish and naïve. Certainly, you know this path is a destructive one. It is akin to suicide. You are trying to solve this problem on your terms. Your time. Your plans. Your way. These are not always God's. Patience. God provides ways to reach those who will serve him. This is not the time or way to win your brother to His cause."

Manny sighed and bit his lip. He wanted to throw something. Hit something. Cry. Yell. Something. Nothing productive came to mind so he sat in the resin chair and put his head down on the card table, his hands on top of his head. He could feel Paul come up behind him.

"I felt the same way about you, my friend. When you went into that jungle to get your brother back, I thought we would lose you."

Without looking up, Manny said, "You did. I did. I was lost Paul. And I knew it. That is my point. Domingo does not even know he is lost."

"He will. He will. Sometimes we are blinded by our own paths and all the paths that are before us seem to spring up with goodness. But we are mistaken. Domingo is searching for another path. Let us hope that he will find the true one."

Manuel scoffed. "Hope!" He looked up and turned to Paul, "What hope? My hope? I am afraid we will lose him forever if I don't do something."

Paul put a reassuring hand on Manny's back.

"Trust in God, Manny. Have peace. Look, a way will open up soon. We will pray. You will see." Smiling now, "But now, we have left our guest up there for too long. I am afraid she may just be a puddle when we retrieve her."

"She is not a delicate one. Hey, I think you like her!"

"You are perceptive, brother. She reminds me of Emily. Strong, eager, caring, clever. I think that Nina would fall in love with her."

"Too bad she'll be gone home before Nina meets her."

"Maybe it's for the best. Now, get up there and keep her company. I'm going to rest. By the way, find out a little about her. There is something sad about her and I don't want to pry too much. She is sensitive about being approached by 'religious folk.' I thought some

50

innocent probing by a young, handsome foreign photographer might make her open up."

"Sure, old man. I'm not sure what you want me to find out, but I will do my best to get to know her. By the way, chasing after all those kids must tucker you out. You don't usually take a nap in the afternoons."

"They don't make 'em like they used to."

"That's right. They don't."

∞

Through his binoculars Carlos could clearly see the cumbersome boat plow its way around the bend. The American woman walked--restless and bored--from bow to stern, glancing down into the hold from trip to trip. She was not aware of being watched.

Carlos was careful. He knew where the next landing would be and he could be there at least a half hour before the boat. He had not seen Manuel or the minister since they entered the boat over two hours ago. He could not fathom what this trip was about, could not even really care.

He had a job to do and it was simple. All he had to do was keep an eye out for Manuel Villarreal, former head of security for one of the most successful "honest" drug cartels in South America.

Simple. Nothing to it.

Maybe that was why he could barely control his shaking hands as he fished his keys from his pocket and hastily made his way to the Jeep CJ and jumped in.

He fired up the stubborn engine and backed up into the dirt road that led back to highway 45 and then on to Puerto Boyacá.

He glanced quickly into his back seat to check that the AK-47 was still there and earnestly hoped he would not need it. It was outfitted with a scope, which seemed out of place, and had an extra magazine taped to the barrel. At first, he thought that the extra ammo was foolishly optimistic, but he did not want to take any chances.

He knew with some certainty what his destiny would be. Carlos had made a deal with the devil when he was just a young man and now he was working hard to get out of that mistake. His hands were yet to be stained with the blood of innocents, but only due to his careful manipulation of the term "innocent." He convinced himself that anyone involved in illegal activities waived their rights to being considered pure or worthy. This had assuaged his guilt for years.

Now, at thirty he had come to face the truth that his life had been irrevocably sacrificed to the demands of his superiors. If he was not serving a crime lord, he was working as a snitch for the Americans. If not for the Americans, he would do mercenary jobs for the ELN or, ironically, for the FARC. His services were impeccable and his rates affordable. And everyone understood that he was a community pawn.

And that was the part that disturbed Carlos the most. He was not allied with any one particular group and so they all trusted him, yeah. They all harbored some hint of resentment, foreknowledge that he was doomed to someday cross the boundaries of the trust they naturally felt. Today, Alfonso--the prideful jerk--had come out and voiced this concern to his face.

"Carlos, what am I to do if you fail me one of these times? What am I to do if you run back to Don Domingo and cry and tell him his little brother will not be able to protect him from the coming storm? Huh? Cut off a finger? Blackball you from your work? I think you will like such punishments because I can tell you do not savor your work, Carlos. No, you would rather sabotage the reputation you have earned from your varied services! You would rather spit on the graves of your employers than to save the life of your own sister!"

And Alfonso was not wrong. He had considered these very thoughts. But, strangely, after hearing them expounded by his most hated ally, he could not bring himself to travel this road of destruction. It was better to continue down the condemned way to which he had already committed.

It haunted him even now, his hand slick on the steering wheel, his shirt soaked with jungle sweat and the salty ring already radiating out from the brim of his New York Yankees cap.

Lush jungle trees whipped by as he jammed the jeep into fourth gear, the grinding of the clutch echoing off of the walls of trees and the canopy of green above him. The wind was fierce here in this canyon. He could not hear the sounds of the jungle above the roar of the jeep's engine and the whistling humid wind firing through the canyon.

He raised an eyebrow as an ocelot skulked across the narrow road ahead of him. His mother had taught him that a cat, even an ocelot, crossing your path could mean bad luck. Of course, it was ridiculous, but in his heightened level of stress and anxiety, the superstition held onto his gut. He swallowed hard, not wanting to turn around, not wanting to fail, but fearing success as much as failure. Torn by his will to succeed and his desire to walk away from it all, Carlos continued his trek as the sun faded away behind him and the Colombian wildlife rose to gleefully meet the impending dark.

CHAPTER TEN

"Hey, it's going to get dark soon and there will be a chill in the air. Why don't you come down below and we will snack on some cheese and tortillas?" Manny had just poked his head out of the cabin and was leaning out by one hand and balanced on one foot. His hair was dark and curly, his smile wide, white teeth vivid amongst the dark olive skin of his sun-taut face. *Sheesh, he looks like he's right out of a Fern Michael novel!*

"I suppose I can join you two. I won't be interrupting or anything?"

"We apologize. Paul and I had some catching up to do. Now he is going to get some beauty sleep. Apparently, he needs it."

"And so now you come and visit with me because you are bored? You really don't like Americans, do you Mr. Villarreal?"

He put his hand over his forehead and then came out onto the deck and leaned against the paint-chipped railing. Smiling, he said, "Please. Do not mistake my jests for any real bias. I spent two years studying acting at the University of New York. I actually love America. Perhaps, my jests are meant to disguise my deep envy for your way of life."

"I see. Well, that would explain a lot. Acting?" She looked at him cagily, "I can't see you as an actor. Did you have to give it up, or did you have another calling?"

"No. I had to come back to my family. My father was struggling with his business and things had become...well, dangerous. My influence was needed here to keep the wolves at bay."

"What does your father do?"

"Before he was murdered, he ran a plantation: a large, prosperous organization in the mountains southwest of Bogotá. We grow coffee, bananas, and other famous Colombian products. He even owned some stake in oil in Barrancabermeja before the government had to step in and settle some trouble with terrorists. He said it was too risky to be in business with such a commodity. He sold that when I was younger."

"I've heard a lot about the violence. But things seem peaceful here. Normal. I have been all over the world. The Colombian people I have met so far seem so content and lively."

"It is not always so. We have a great many things over which to be sad or frustrated. Our people are resilient, though, and do not bear our burdens with bent backs and weeping eyes. We are as tough as the mountains and as patient as this river."

"I see. So, is there still violence?"

"Of course. This is a big country. What happens in Puerto Marco tomorrow may hit the headlines, stir up civil rights organizations, and even stop the flow of money from America to our government for a while

At the same time in Cartagena, people will surf along, oblivious to any wrong-doing, unaware that three women were raped, two children taken and four men brutally murdered all because they were the wrong race or were speaking their politics or religion too loudly or somehow stood in the way of the status quo."

"Wow. You sound angry."

"Like I said, we do not hang our heads shamefully. We know we have a nation rich in resources, overflowing with people with good strong hands and beautiful hearts. But, we also are a country that cannot shake the evils of an oligarchy, a protected minority that continues to hang the stone around our nation's neck weighing us down. We are drowning in our own blood, Ms. Eppington. That is not an exaggeration."

Claire looked down the river and considered this. Manny shifted uncomfortably.

"Claire, we've talked about me enough. Tell me something about you. What does your father do?"

"He is a county coroner. He has been a professor and a curator at different times. He is always dabbling in the sciences or history, sometimes both."

"And your mother?"

"She died when I was young."

"Oh. I am sorry."

"No. I asked about your father first. It was fair game. Besides, I barely remember her." She smiled wryly and reached down to get her backpack. She had no explanation why she was doing this. She just felt an indescribable temptation to share something special about herself. She extracted a small hand-bound book with glass beads and broken porcelain glued to the front.

"I haven't shown this to anyone before, but this is all I have to remember her by. It's her diary that she wrote to me as she was dying."

Manny stared at her for a second. She was mesmerized by the sun reflecting off of the beads, green and pink rays swirled around her eyes.

"Oh. Was she sick for an extended time?"

"Yes. She had a rare kidney disease. My father never forgave God for that."

"I can understand. My father was taken from me when I was a young man, and I was inconsolable for many months. I can imagine a prolonged suffering would test anyone's faith." An awkward silence ensued. Birds screeched noisily and a howler monkey swooped down to the river and watched intently for a second before climbing a mamoncillo tree growing near the muddy banks.

"Can I see this journal? It looks fascinating."

"Sure." She shrugged and handed it to him.

Manny turned it over and ran his hand over the cover, feeling the rough porcelain and the smooth colored rocks that studded it.

He admitted that he admired the craftsmanship of the cover and the ragged, thick parchment paper that graced the inside. He remarked that he dared not read the words.

Claire wondered why. Manny explained that he was afraid of its contents as if it were sacred. He noted, however, the dark pen strokes were written in a beautiful hand, the slanting p's, t's and l's punctuating the flowery capital letters and the dated notations at the top of each section.

"She wrote to me to comfort me. I haven't really been brave enough to read it more than to glance at a few pages and look at some of the photos." The edges of faded Polaroids and older photos protruded from the pages of the journal, the thick white bottom borders taped or stapled to the heavy pages.

Claire opened the journal to show Manny some of these photos. Claire's mother had provided captions below many of them. One had "Vienna Beach 1978" beneath a vivid photo of a bare-chested man carrying a small girl upon his shoulders, foamy waves crashing at his feet. The father was grinning and the child's eyes were wide and her hair tied in pigtails.

"So many memories. Why have you not honored your mother's gift and looked at it more fully?"

Claire hesitated.

She screwed her mouth up, one side rising up toward her ear, tilted her head and rolled her eyes. She held out her hand to retrieve the journal. Manny closed it and gave it back to her. She shrugged as she sat it on her lap.

She said, "I don't know. Always seem too busy. Dad didn't give it to me until I was out of college. That was fourteen years after she died. He called one day and asked me what I was doing for lunch. We went to a park near the county square and he treated me to a wonderful picnic of cheese and wine, fruit and my favorite muffins my aunt Beverly makes. Anyway, he gave me this journal then."

Claire straightened up and then let out a deep breath. She was not sure if it was a good idea to keep opening up to strangers. She held onto her composure, working hard to keep from getting emotional. *Death sure seems a lively topic this time around!*

"I love my dad, but I had never seen him cry until that day. I mean, I always knew he was hurt, but I remember the funeral and my dad was just stunned. You know, just walking around quiet and mad. I don't know: I was eight at the time. It's strange to see your dad cry for the first time when you are twenty-two."

"I see. So he gave this to you, this gift from your mother when he thought you were ready. That doesn't explain why you have left it alone."

"I guess that since it was so important to Dad, I just didn't want to mess it up. I mean, I feel like it is sacred and so special I can only diminish her memory by reading it. Dad was never a religious sort, so something that he held sacred was scary to me more than inspirational."

"Tell me about the way the cover is decorated. Is that something meaningful? Was your mom a crafter or an artist?"

"Uh. No." She shook her head and considered his question, staring at the baubles and pieces of porcelain as seeing them for the first time. "That was what my dad added. Another reason I can't bring myself to open it. If he held it in so high a regard, I am afraid to ruin my father's memories."

"I am positive that your father would be honored by you finally learning about your mother's love. It seems they had a special relationship. That is unique in this life to have a love that endures forever."

Claire was quiet. She stared into Manny's face, his eyes so serious, his hand resting lightly upon his knee, a slight smile playing at his lips. He was so friendly and relaxed. She wondered how she had come to share so much about herself so quickly. The spell lifted.

"Look. Manny. I don't feel comfortable. I barely know you and I'm not one to share intimate life details with just anyone. Don't take that the wrong way. I mean, you are already one of my favorite photographers and I haven't even seen your work. I need to get some rest. I think the long flight and this whole day has worn me out."

Manny stood up and turned a sad smile toward her. He took her hand lightly and gently kissed it. She felt her face flush as he looked up at her and released her hand.

"Pardon me. Of course. I am sure Paul has rested sufficiently. We all probably need to get some rest soon. We should be in Puerto Boyacá soon. We will stop there for the night and then head out again in the morning. We may be out another day due to the river moving so quickly. Our trip back will be much faster."

Feeling guilty now, and a little light-headed, she responded, "That will be fine. I apologize if I have offended you." She struggled to catch her breath for a second.

"And I apologize to you, Ms. Eppington. I am grateful for the opportunity to show my skills in photography. *La Republica* will only use a certain amount of my photos each month. I promise I will pry no more unless you are comfortable. How is that?" His eyes held such expression and compassion, but hinted at a more dangerous and hidden side that he held in check.

"Thank you. You are very kind." She stood up and crossed in front of him. She could feel her breath caught in her throat. Despite her sudden fear, she glanced back mischievously, "You may have just earned yourself a raise, Mr. Villarreal."

She ducked into the cabin. She could not tell until she reached the bottom of the short stairs that he had not followed her. She smiled absently. This trip was definitely becoming her favorite assignment so far in her career.

And Laura thought I needed a change of careers!

CHAPTER ELEVEN

Oscar finished with the lock assembly and began to put away his tools. The phone jangled its annoying song and Oscar quickly snatched it up as he wiped his brow with the stained cloth he had used to clean the oil from the new door fixtures.

"Hello?"

"Oscar? Is that you?"

"Yeah. Domingo?"

"Yes, brother. My assistant said you called earlier. What do you need?" He did not sound suspicious or upset. *Maybe this is my chance. Maybe God is opening a door for us.*

"Nothing important, I think. It's just Mom. Have you spoken with her recently?"

"No. Why?"

"Well, she seems different. She is keeping something from me, I can just feel it."

"Oscar, you are always worried about some conspiracy. Let Mom be. Let her live out her life. I offered her a place here last year and she just looked at me strange and changed the subject like I never said anything. Can you believe that? My own mother. Frankly, brother, if she wants to sweat away barely making by then it is her decision. I have offered her a better life and she can't stand to be around me."

"Now who has conspiracy theories? Domingo, it's not always about you, you know. The world does not revolve around the fourth largest cartel *Capo* in Colombia."

"Third largest, Oscar, and I know. It is just that Mom deserves better and it seems she is spitting on the memory of Dad when she refuses to collect on the riches that come from his labors. It just feels blasphemous or something."

"There you go again, Dom. Look, I don't want to argue--"

"Good, then let's don't. If Mom is acting strange, just ask her what's going on. She won't tell you the truth, but maybe something she says to you will discourage you from bothering her."

"It is amazing how accurate you are. That's exactly what happened today after I called you."

"So she cut you down, did she?"

"You know, Dom, we aren't little boys anymore. I can still kick your backside."

"Not until you kick my bodyguard's first, my friend." He sounded sixteen again, rebelling against everyone, befriending everyone, setting up the pins of the man he was to become. It sounded as though he never really grew up past the sudden responsibilities of a life of organized crime. "Take my advice, Oscar. Just let it go. I've told you this before about the family business and now I am telling you this about Mom. If she wants to tell you, then she…wait—did she mention Alfonso?"

"Alfonso? What's he got to do with it? I haven't seen Al in years."

"Don't call him Al to his face unless you want to lose two fingers. So Mom didn't mention him, though?"

"No. What's going on, Dom? What are you trying to say?" Oscar always felt that with Domingo there would always be some level of intrigue.

"I am just guessing. Alfonso may be looking out for himself. Or maybe I'm completely wrong. Sometimes he gets under her skin."

"Uncle Bolivar said once that Al was good with women, just not in a way they would like. Are you saying he's messing with Mom? Aunt

Rita moved to El Salvador four years ago because she couldn't stand to watch what Al had become, you know."

"Mom never forgave Al for running her sister off. But watch what you say about Al, Oscar. He's dangerous."

"Well, you should know, brother. He's your bulldog."

"Not for much longer. I think this dog is jumping fence soon. He's gotten too big for my porch and he wants to run. He'll be back tomorrow. Keep an eye on Mom, will you? I'll get back with you after I've had a little talk with Alfonso. I'm probably totally wrong, but I'd rather check it out than have you fretting over Mom like one of her gossip friends."

"For what it's worth, thanks."

"Don't mention it. Oh, and if you see Manny, let him know I said hi. I can't get him to call me back."

"He's busy right now. I am sure he'll call you back soon. Maybe we can all get together for a weekend. It sounds like you can use a break. Bring Blanca. We'll make a weekend out of it"

"As soon as I clear up my schedule, sure. The beach again, I assume?"

"Sure. Sounds great."

"Are you positive Manny will come? We're really not on speaking terms, you know?"

"Oh stop it. You two can't do this forever. We're family. Dad would want us to get along. Anyway, I gotta go. Mom will be back soon."

"See you Oscar."

"Bye."

Oscar hung up the phone. He had not felt that good for a long time. Domingo had sounded natural and like his old self again. He retained his bully attitude and his smugness, but beneath all that, Oscar believed he could hear his heart and care for his family.

It was their gift from their mother—an uncanny ability to care deeply while maintaining a level of aloofness as a defense mechanism. Dad had always just been straightforward and demanding, all hard edges and sharp points. He was as scraggly as his white wire beard and as rough as the wool trousers he wore.

Oscar thought again about his conversation with his mother. He had not detected any alarm, just sadness and maybe worry. *What did Domingo think Alfonso was doing? Maybe Domingo isn't telling me everything. And neither is Mom. I have got to get to the bottom of this.*

He pulled back the curtain in the living room and stared across the street. No cars were parked there. It was just after dinner and many of their neighbors were out. He felt lonely again; a sharp, but brief pain as he remembered Carmen.

He recalled her hair tied into a bun as they left the flat to get groceries, her laugh as they watched the children play in park, her sad eyes as they discussed their inability to parent. It was all so unfair and it all came back so quickly--and passed just as fast.

He knew it was foolish to hope that his life could be perfect. He had borne his share of grief and disappointment. He had at times stood on the brink of despair and loss only to turn back to "normalcy." Now, poised to bring his family back together again, he could only think of the obstacles that stood in his way. This inevitably introduced the failures and trials of the past, wondering what new enemy would rise up to bar the way to his happiness.

Cancer had taken his wife, a tumor the size of a grape had grown so quickly in a year that no amount of chemotherapy could slow its progress. Surgeries had left Carmen scarred physically and emotionally. After eighteen months of fighting for her life, she was a husk of the woman he had married.

He told himself that he could have dealt with the sunken eyes and the bone-thin fingers, her pallid skin and her bruised arms. It was her crushed spirit, her willingness to give in to the disease that was ravishing her that bothered him most.

He wanted to fight, to exorcise the demons inhabiting her body. He had urged her to have a positive attitude. He hired the best doctors in Medellin. He scoured the internet for information. He walked her around the house and soaked her feet. Priests and ministers and New Age healers all had their shot at her. At first, when he did these things, encouraging her to embrace the treatments and believe that she could beat the cancer, she would smile and placate him. But he saw early on the defeat that was in her eyes and he knew she had already given up. All the time, it was he who was the one standing in his own way. By August of that first year, she had come to grips with her destiny. She struggled on, faced excruciating pain, embarrassment and misery, for him: to give him more time with the woman he loved, but barely recognized.

He never resented this, but loved her all the more for it. He, instead, blamed himself. He could only imagine the anguish she felt as the cancer fed on her body and her mind. She never complained, never asked him to stop his foolishness. She only endured.

He let the curtain go and stared at the gold ring on his left hand. He remembered when he had asked Marchella, Carmen's father, to marry his daughter. It was strange how lately he had begun to remember more of their early life together. He had been wrapped up so much in those events that had led to his loss that he could not remember what he had possessed in the first place. He wondered at that.

He chastised himself for becoming distracted. It was happening more and more lately. He was tempted to blame it on being forty-one and still living with his mom, but he knew the truth. He still had not healed mentally. He had to get his head straight and in the here and now. A nagging feeling was telling him that people he loved would need him soon.

CHAPTER TWELVE

The view from his veranda was astounding. The vista of the Andes Mountains always humbled him. The sun setting against those same mountains to the south warmed his heart. Such natural beauty was not uncommon here as long as you could turn an eye away from the ramshackle huts that lined the valley, the guard shacks, the tin-roof barracks, the dark men in muscle shirts and fatigues.

Domingo exhaled the smoke from the Colombian Gold cigar, savoring its sweet, musky aroma. Blanca, his wife, was still in Peru and so he continued to sip the Merlot and smoke his cigar and watch the sun set without her. This was her favorite spot, watching her beloved Colombia's most remarkable sunset, but she could not stand his cigars or the wine.

He pondered his most recent dealings with Henry Fronçeau. He wished that Henry could be a permanent fixture in his organization. He was even more capable than Manny and had more connections. But, alas, Henry was a free agent and spent much of his time travelling the world, setting up mercenary jobs, handling contacts, facilitating assassinations, and generally funding leftist, communist, or socialist agendas wherever he could. He was a valuable asset that could produce a veritable army on command, all outfitted, regimented and ready to serve. Thankfully, Domingo had no need of such violent extravagances.

Domingo's plan was simple: protection and intimidation. With enough show of force he could easily open routes normally shut to those who were not aggressive. With enough training and the correct lieutenant in charge, the procedures could be carried out without bloodshed. Henry helped manage these projects and so far, only twenty casualties had resulted in over one thousand shipments.

Now, he needed Henry to set up an entirely different operation.

Instead of the usual route through Central America and then through the ruthless and thieving Mexico, or through contacts in the Caribbean into Florida and Texas, Domingo needed to re-route his supplies of coca into Europe via Western Africa.

First, he wanted to teach the Mexican cartels a lesson: do not try to duplicate what we have, do not try to siphon our product. Second, he felt if he could make just one or two large shipments without the usual casualties of product and profit, contacts and inroads, he could maybe change his operation.

His dream was to ratchet down the level of violence that permeated his organization. He was personally unfazed by it all, having been raised to accept it as necessary. However, the influences of Manny, his mother, Oscar and Blanca were beginning to wear on him. He felt if he could legitimize his business by leveraging his governmental ties, and seeking out newer, less trafficked markets with bigger profits, he could win everyone back to his father's business—his business.

He heard a knock at his door.

"Yes?"

The door opened and Maria Gallenes came out onto the veranda, carrying a notebook computer another bottle of Merlot and a wide, fluted wine glass. She smiled and walked briskly to sit beside him.

"Do you mind if I join you," she asked as she set the computer on the desk and the glass on the cedar deck.

"Of course not, Maria. Have you already eaten?" He gestured to a tray of chilled fruit and vegetables.

"Yes, thank you. I just want to update you on the agreement we have reached with Mr. Fronçeau." She opened the notebook and turned it around so that he could see the e-mail that Henry had sent as promised. It registered on the screen with his credentials and the security protocols engaged. As soon as he viewed it and Maria pushed "enter" it would disappear from the hard drive completely.

He looked it over and then nodded. Henry was efficient and had even taken measures beyond that which they had discussed this afternoon.

Not only had he secured protection and storage on the island of Ilha De Bubaque, three miles offshore from Guinea-Bissau, he had also made provisions for varied methods of transport to the mainland from the staging area with multiple security protections and fronts.

Henry claimed that Guinea-Bissau had only had sixty law enforcement personnel in the entire nation, and local police were so poor, they had no money for fuel.

Henry was still cautious. Breaking up the shipments and running them to Spain, France and the UK in one ton batches, was a first step in getting as much product into Europe as possible.

In addition, he had enlisted a secondary "dummy" shipment five hours prior to the actual departure on a ship with a similar name and two ports south of the shipment.

More than sixty percent of the shipment would make it at more than triple the profit of the same delivered to the US.

Henry had run enough attempts at smuggling drugs and arms that he had learned to think ahead of the national police, the foreign drug enforcement agencies and guerilla groups bent on stealing cartel profits. Plus, he was better staffed and better equipped than those attempting to stop him.

"You approve?" Maria tapped a manicured nail on the laptop impatiently. She was normally more composed. Something was bothering her.

"Yes. And I have the details here," he pointed to his head.

"Excellent." She turned the laptop around and pressed a key. A zipping noise accompanied the screen going black and then the computer rebooting quietly.

Domingo watched Maria over his raised glass of Merlot. She still had not poured the wine. He assumed she meant to join him but he had no idea why.

"Is there anything else, Maria?"

"I am waiting for it to reboot. I have other information I want to share with you. You want to see this, but I am not sure what you will think."

Now, Domingo was interested. Maria was not normally mysterious. He was not sure if it made him curious or nervous.

Something about the woman had always intrigued him. Domingo was especially interested in watching her failed pursuit of Manny. He could not understand why Manny had been so resistant. She was beautiful, capable and came highly recommended. Maria was educated, brilliant, driven and intensely attracted to Manny in a physical way.

The welcome screen appeared and a blinking envelope zoomed in at the top of the screen. Maria clicked on it and another e-mail popped up, this time without the security screen or protection protocols. It was a note from Carlos to an unidentified recipient with a cryptic address.

I am sorry for today. Alfonso showed up again this morning and I have another target. I cannot believe this jerk! I will make it up to you, sis. And I won't let that monster come near you again.

Stay at Aunt Hannah's for a while longer until I finish this one. At least he is paying me well for it. When I get the rest of my payment, I will stop by and make the arrangements to send you on to St. Thomas. Promise. Tell little Pete I said hi and I will bring him a treat when I come.

Love you,

Carlos

Domingo stared at Maria and then back at the laptop.

"Where did you get this?"

"We intercept all of Carlos' e-mails. Your brother set it up that way two years ago when Carlos did that hit for us in Mexico City. Ever since then, Carlos really worked for Manny, no matter which assignment, no matter for whom he thought he was working. Since Manny left, Carlos became more of a wild-card and now he is in over his head. You would be surprised at how he juggles these assignments—sometimes working for competing organizations in the same week against each other."

"I am aware of Carlos and his divided loyalties. He is like Henry— a free agent. He is welcome to work for anyone he wants. He accepts the consequences of his diminished role."

"I didn't know if you were aware Alfonso was picking targets without your consent."

"That is news to me. But why should I care? As far as I am concerned, Alfonso is independent, anyway. This isn't the Mafia, Maria."

Maria stared at him carefully and retrieved the glass from the deck. She put it on the table and poured Merlot from the new bottle. She lifted the glass to her full lips. She looked concerned.

"The 'target' is Manny," she said without a smile.

CHAPTER THIRTEEN

The boat drifted into harbor and Paul came up from the hold, rubbing his eyes. Manny was helping Gibbarda set the anchor and tie off the boat against the rugged dock. Claire leaned on the teak railing watching the bustle.

"Finally up, sleepy head?" she asked.

"What time is it?" he asked, stretching.

"My stomach says dinner time, but it appears it is coming up on seven."

"Oh. I must have overslept." He smiled. "I guess we are going into Puerto Boyacá and staying the night. Is that alright? Did you have a specific time in the morning to begin the ceremony?"

"No. I have not contacted the family yet. I will meet with them tomorrow and we will work out the arrangements with them. Katherine's mother, Jhoana, was very specific. She wanted time privately with the remains before having the public ceremony."

"Ah. Right. Jhoana is a good, gentle woman. But, being retired, she is very set in her ways. I believe you will like her. She has relied upon her art as an escape from grief. She is really a remarkable person."

"I look forward to meeting her," Claire replied.

Manny returned, rubbing his hands and retrieving his pack.

"You ready to go? John says the restaurants here close early. We need to hurry if we are going to get a dinner before we turn in."

They made their way down the dock and were questioned by township security. Paul and Manny showed their identifications and

Claire pulled out her passport. Soon, they found a taxi that took them to a part of town bustling with activity. The streets were full of young women in tight, immodest clothing and men laughing coarsely. Open bottles of alcohol were raised in loud, bawdy toasts and a throng of people surrounded a smiling young man in a white muscle shirt and put him on the shoulders of several of the men in the crowd. They lifted him high into the air, throwing green and white shirts, waving flags and yelling.

"OOO-AAA, OOO-AAA ! *Nacional!*"

Manny leaned closer so as to be heard over the din outside.

"Nacional beat Medellin. Juan there," Manny pointed to the man being hoisted into the air, "his brother scored the winning goal."

"When did you hear that?" Paul inquired.

"The guard at the station had the radio on. And he mentioned Juan was Barencal's brother. I just put two and two together. Besides, I knew I was going to miss the game when I took the assignment."

"I am sorry I pulled you away," Claire said.

"No, don't worry. I wasn't going to fight those crowds and be checked at the gate twice by the security goons. I had planned a quiet evening in front of the television, munching on momma's *arepa con queso.* I think the turn of events has been just as entertaining."

"*Arepa con queso?* What is that?"

"Oh. You must try some. This place up the street here by the neon lights makes some. There," Paul pointed up ahead and then directed the taxi driver to pull over.

Paul paid the driver several thousand pesos which Claire quickly calculated to be about five American dollars and they exited out onto the street. The crowd had moved farther south.

It was quieter here and the people milling about seemed more at home in a western. They wore boots and had bandanas tied loosely at their necks. The women wore boots beneath long flowing skirts, their dark hair tied into knots on their heads. Several men wore white straw hats.

Although the atmosphere was more subdued, a thread of excitement still could be heard among those conversing quietly. The game seemed to interest all ages. It reminded Claire of the fascination her father and his friends had with American football. It was one of his favorite past-times and he enjoyed taking her to watch the Bears. She could barely understand the game, let alone the passion and the obsessions that overcame the fans. She went to please her father, and always found one or two bits of interest—whether a cute fan, an interesting conversation or a funny story to tell Laura.

They were escorted into the restaurant by an elderly male host who set out glasses and asked questions in a quiet and modest voice. The staff could be heard milling around in the back, but the other guests were few and silent. The smells of frying onions and meat wafted into the dining room and Claire felt the pangs of hunger again.

"What should I order? I am not familiar with your language," she asked Paul.

"Um. Let us order for you. It will be our honor as you are our guest here."

Paul placed an order, and explained that everything would come out what Americans called "family style," meaning large entrees meant to be shared.

He ordered three separate dishes and tried to give Claire an idea of the difference between Colombian cuisine and what she may have been familiar with from Mexico.

Instead of *moles poblanos* and other heavy sauces, Colombians prefer light sauces, sweetened milk, and meats served simply with spices and grilled vegetables. The food was still flavored heavily with chiles and dried oregano, but contained less heat. Claire enjoyed the meal, and the company even more. The wait staff was attentive without being overbearing and soon Claire found herself getting drowsy from the long day, the flight and the humid trip up the river.

"Well, it is getting late and we should head to the hotel I have reserved," Paul observed after another hour had gone by.

Claire was barely holding together. Exhausted, with a full stomach and her head spinning from lively conversation, she smiled and said, "Please. I can't stand on my own. You may have to call an ambulance."

"You will find good rest, I am sure. I have arranged with a hotel nearby the wharf to be held until we arrive. The manager is a cousin to Katherine Borche." He indicated with a nod of his head the large bag she had carelessly left on the floor.

The bag held the remains of Dr. Borche's wife. She had not felt comfortable leaving it aboard the boat during their stay.

"Mr. Villarreal, did you know Katherine?"

Manny appeared uncomfortable as he glanced over at Paul. He wiped his mouth with the cloth napkin in his lap.

"Yes. We dated for a few months before I left for the US to attend New York University. When I returned, she had met the good doctor and had fallen ill."

Claire felt sad.

"I'm sorry I brought that up."

Manny smiled warmly.

"Don't be. Kate was a good friend. Our relationship ended amiably. It was never serious, really. But, I have a special place in my heart for her and her mother. In fact, it is yet another reason why I am here." He hooked his thumb at Paul. "Paul here recommended me because he knew that I would want to attend anyway. It seemed like a good fit."

Claire nodded. She could feel a heat spread across her cheeks. She must have eaten too much. She stared at Manny, her eyes glistening and her face flushed.

"I agree. It was a good fit," she managed, as she took another sip of her drink.

"If you two are ready, let us gather our things and get some sleep. I think we all deserve it," Paul said. He rose, placed some bills on the table and picked up his brown, worn luggage.

"And apparently, some of us need our beauty sleep more than others," Manny teased again.

"You really need to get some new material," Claire commented as they made their way out of the restaurant.

$$\infty$$

Paul tucked his luggage under the bed and sat down, bouncing up and down, testing the firmness of the mattress. It would do. He glanced over at Manny as he unpacked his gear and double-checked it. Paul was surprised when Manny pulled out a gun and began to check the barrel and dropped out the magazine, depressing the first shell down into the housing to ensure it was full. Paul took in a sharp breath.

Manny turned, serious now.

"Paul, I know what you're about to say. Don't say it. I know. There are just some habits I can't let alone. I don't intend to kill, just keeping it for defense."

Paul looked away. The intensity in Manny's eyes demonstrated his conviction in this matter. Any accusation to the contrary would only raise his ire. And Manny angry was not a man to be persuaded.

He decided to take a diplomatic approach.

"At least we will be safe in Yondo."

Manny scoffed. "Paul, do you forget so soon? Emily was taken in Barrancabermeja." He held up the Kel-Tec 9 and pointed it at the ceiling. Paul tried to ignore the anger that rose up in his chest. "This is necessary. I pray we will experience peace during our brief stay, but I will not become a victim."

"You are scared," Paul accused. He knew that he was intentionally aggravating Manny. He could not help himself.

"Nothing in Barrancabermeja scares me."

"But you are scared of losing your pride, your identity."

Manny stopped and his jaw dropped along with the Kel-Tec. It pointed toward the floor.

Paul waited patiently. He knew he had touched a nerve. The air was charged with Manny's shock at Paul's epiphany. Perhaps even Manny did not realize the truth of the statement until Paul had uttered it.

"You may be right. I don't feel comfortable either way. This is my way of coping, alright?"

"If you say so, but that doesn't necessarily establish good reason to carry firearms. When Peter took off the ear of one of Jesus' captors, Jesus reprimanded him, saying 'Those who live by the sword will die by the sword.' Manny, you do not need to bring this sin into your life when you have so successfully driven it out."

"I understand your concern. Let me assure you I do not intend to take life with malice. I only seek justice and peace."

"Bullets don't bring peace. Justice isn't vengeance."

Manny put the semi-automatic back into the case and slipped it into his bag. He looked up and considered Paul.

"I respect you and love you like a brother. I do not want to disappoint you, but I will keep this in a safe place for now. I cannot just leave it behind. It is a part of my former life that I cannot let go. Have peace in your heart about it and I will consider everything you have said."

Paul knew it was a stall tactic, but did not really have a choice. He had learned through years of service that people each had moments when they were susceptible to teaching and moments that teaching would not be received. Manny was shutting down.

Paul nodded. "So be it. Maybe we can talk about this when we get back to Bogotá."

"I'll consider it. Now, do you want to shower tonight or in the morning?"

CHAPTER FOURTEEN

Claire lay back on her mattress, feeling her muscles settle and stretched her toes and flexed her back. This was not the Carlton, but better than some American motels she had stayed in on road trips with her college friends. She could hear the quiet rippling of the waters of Rio De Magdalena and the hum of voices through the thin walls of the hotel.

Despite her full stomach, tired and aching body and the exhaustion she could feel in her very bones, she could not find sleep. It was too dark, or too humid, the blankets too scratchy. Everything seemed magnified. Voices in the halls, the clanking of the pipes, and the hissing of showers in nearby rooms. Even the clicking and plinking of the building itself would seep into her consciousness as it adjusted to the cooler temperatures of the night after a full day of the demanding Colombian heat. The cumulative effect of all this was that it prevented her from falling asleep.

After about an hour, at around midnight, Claire rolled out of bed and went to the bathroom to wash her face and to check her phone for messages. As she came back into the room, she noticed the large lump of her bag on the floor by the door in the dark. She paused and after some thought, retrieved her mother's journal and pounced back on the bed, turning on the light there.

At first, she just studied it. Looking at the pieces of porcelain on the outside, she tried to remember why they looked familiar. It was obviously something that had broken. Maybe it represented her dad's heart—broken. Maybe it was their lives, pieces that had been broken and then collected, preserved. She ran her fingers over the sharp fragments, the ends were dulled by sanding, she noticed, but some pieces remained pointed. These made a sort of landscape over which she could feel some of the love and the hurt that went into this gift.

She was stunned as she remembered Manny's words from earlier that day. Because, mainly, he had been right. As she closed her eyes and absently stroked the edges of the porcelain seemingly glued randomly across the face of her mother's journal, she came to realize that this makeshift piece of artwork by her father represented some deeper feelings he kept inside. Life is rough, life can cut deep, but over time, maybe, some of the hurt can be dulled.

It all came to her in a rush. Along with these thoughts came the realization of where the porcelain had come. She remembered with vivid clarity when she was nine.

A few years after her mother had died, her father had struggled to keep up her spirits. She only felt a vague ache and emptiness and she could barely understand her loss. But his loss was still a stark reality. One day, her father had made a wonderful meal, prepared the table in a fancy manner and invited her friend and some family over for a "Non-holiday meal."

It was her dad's little rebellion. No Christmas, no Thanksgiving. But, in the middle of October, he had decorated the house with fall colors, made a meal of pork loin and beef roast, vegetables and some kind of potato casserole her mother had made when she was young. Claire remembered the recipe was on an index card, yellowed with stains from cooking—grease and melted cheese and tomato paste. Her mother had put a green check mark on the top of the card and written "Frank's favorite—even his mom likes it," on the back.

Her uncle Jerry, his third wife Melissa, and their daughter Harriet had come, as well as Claire's friend from school, Julia. Julia lived at the end of their lane and wore bobby socks to school even when it rained. Also, Frank's co-worker, Bob, had come and talked to whoever would listen about his recent divorce or his new Pontiac.

Her cousin Harriet barely spoke to anyone. She only listened to her Walkman and chewed gum with her mouth open, which always seemed to be in a sneer. It was Claire's first experience with teenagers and the only positive thing she learned from Harriet was that bras were annoying.

The meal was a resounding success. Everyone seemed to enjoy themselves—even her father. He told jokes, laughed, and when it was time for everyone to leave, he smiled and walked them to their cars. Julia rode her bike home and Claire and Frank were left to clean up.

Claire remembered playing a game with her dad as they cleared the table, Frank marching like a band leader, the wooden spoon from the casserole dish his baton, the salad bowl his hat. She tooted and he made the sound of the tuba and bass drum—dads are good at those sorts of things, and Frank was one of the best.

That was when Claire had dropped the blue and gold etched dinner plates onto the floor. All six. They had swirls throughout them with gold flakes in the middle. Claire had thought them old and beautiful—family heirlooms cherished by her mom.

Her dad had stopped, the bowl coming off of his head into his hands, the wooden spoon placed hastily on the kitchen counter.He made a hurt, animal sound as he huddled on the floor on his knees, the broken pieces of plate before him, the salad bowl gonging its way across the tile floor.

Sobbing, he scraped up the pieces and looked up at Claire with sad eyes. She could remember the sound the broken plates made on the tile as they slid, like glass on glass.

"Honey, I think it would be best for you to go on upstairs," Frank had said, choking, his eyes brimmed with tears.

Confused and hurt, Claire managed to make it to the landing and turned. She watched as her father swept up the remains of the plates and deposited them not into the kitchen garbage, but a cardboard box that once held a train set. She stayed as he wept openly, oblivious to her presence on the landing. After a while, she had made her way to her room and cried the pitying cry of a nine year old who did not understand, but only felt lonelier than ever.

Claire remembered this day for the first time, lying in a hotel room deep in the center of Colombia. She remembered and cried and fell asleep with the light on and her mother's journal clutched to her chest.

∞

Downriver, the fog was beginning to clear. Around him, Carlos felt wrapped in folds of wet blankets as the warm, humid mists rose from the riverbank. He had not reached for his binoculars yet and had kept them capped. All of his gear was circa the 1970's, it seemed.

Bought from the black market, stolen from shipments, taken from victims, these tools of his trade were field-tested, duty worn and dependable. They would last him his whole career if he chose to keep them and to show them a little love and care.

His .45 caliber pistol with extended magazine and laser sights was his most prized possession. He was glad that he had not pulled it on Alfonso earlier. He was sure he did not want to part with it.

Carlos knew that he could not trust his decision-making when he felt cornered. He was liable to do something rash. He patted the side arm, snug against his left rib cage under his open cotton shirt. He had an arsenal of handguns, knives, smoke grenades, and surveillance equipment in a compartment in the rear of the Jeep.

His pits were stained with sweat. The day would prove to be hotter, but he hoped the humidity would cut back some once the sun cranked up full tilt. He sighed.

As far as he could tell, here at 0700 hours, Manny and his crew had not moved. The hotel was just out of eyesight due to the fog, but Carlos could hear everything despite the loud chirruping of the birds, the rustling of the underbrush and the quiet hiss of the river. Sounds from the hotel carried across the water and bounced off the tree growth on the opposite side. Delayed by several seconds, but clear, the muffled walk of the hotel manager as he checked the parking lot at 0500 and smoked his cigarette by the generator house had woken Carlos easily from his restless sleep.

With his face washed in the river, several shots of ephedrine taken for energy, and his bladder relieved, Carlos took back up his lonely vigil.

He had left the AK 47 in the jeep in order to not raise too much suspicion. He was not marked as belonging to any particular organization, so open hostility would logically breed aggression if he was spotted.

Carlos was foolish at times, but not entirely dumb. He was greedy and inconsolable, but not without a strong sense of survival. He squatted by the riverbank, listening, straining his ears and waiting for the chance to glass the hotel two hundred yards up river.

The sun was glistening off of the moisture in the air now and it would soon be time to uncap his precious Leopolds. He had paid a hefty sum for the German-made binoculars. They were heavy, old, reliable and sturdy.

However, when they were made, anti-fogging technology had not even been dreamt up.

He sat and waited with the patience of men and women who have performed the sacred ritual of the "stake out" all over the world. One learned that the concentration and mental adeptness that was required to maintain a stillness of body and mind also enabled time to be isolated. Carlos had been taught by a sergeant in the Peruvian provincial police that by keeping his body still, his movements to an absolute minimum, and by focusing his mind on this very exercise of inactivity, that time would "stand still."

Carlos recalled the lessons he learned as he served under Sergeant Berluvia for several months, training for his specialty: spying. Manny had connections in several South American countries as well as ex-SAS and Green Beret buddies he would fly in to provide training. Manny would tell these operatives that he was training a security force to protect the banana plantations from the FARC, which was not too far from the truth.

Alternatively, he would claim that he was planning on using troops to guard the oil refineries, which often elicited offers to perform the training free of charge.

He would tell them whatever he thought they wanted to hear: patriotic reasons, work "alongside" the Colombian army as vigilantes, protection of human rights groups and so on. Whatever would land their expertise.

It was a running joke among the men in the Villarreal organization that the Americans, Venezuelans, Peruvians, British, Spanish and Russians had all had a hand in the success of Colombian coca. The only country that was not still providing some form of assistance to Colombian cartels was Mexico.

Now, they had their own gig, such as it was. It was like they were boarding a sinking ship, though. They clamored over one another, killing each other to provide dirty drugs to a declining market.

In fact, Carlos was certain that the banning of drug travel through Mexico was probably the source of much of the recent upheaval that Carlos could detect among the Colombian cartels. They now had to find new markets, new routes and no longer had reliable "mules," who had thin excuses for traveling in and out of the country in droves.

He had cut ties with the Mexicans just two months ago, himself, barely escaping Oaxaca alive. Until the Mexican cartels got smart, killed each other off, or made some monumental mistakes, the usual route to funnel drugs into the world's largest drug market was seriously impaired.

Carlos mused about these things to occupy his mind. Another part of it, a part deeper in his subconscious, ground out the details of focusing on controlling his body's urges: the need to move, itch, twitch, shift, blink, breathe, cough, or swallow. This part of his mind slowed his heart rate, coated his mouth with saliva, controlled his breathing and stilled his nervousness. This allowed his surface thoughts to run through logistics, his ears to listen acutely, and his eyes to focus, and mind to stay alert. Of course, the ephedrine made some of these tasks easier, and so immensely more difficult, but his body had grown accustomed to the drug—his only vice besides the occasional beer. And, of course, the occasional assassination.

CHAPTER FIFTEEN

Claire woke with the journal beside her. She stared at the light coming from the window near the bed and tried to get her bearings. The bright green morning light blazed its way through the gauzy yellow curtains.

She was groggy. She was used to waking up in so many strange places; she often wondered why she had never gotten accustomed to it. It even happened to her in her own apartment.

Eventually, her surroundings began to clue her into her whereabouts. The low, soft bed, the cocoa-colored walls and the bright cinnamon accents throughout the room all reminded her that she was not in Kansas anymore, Toto.

She remembered falling asleep thinking about her father. She remembered crying.

Sheesh! I have got to get to the bottom of this funk I am in. I haven't had so many instances of plumbing leaks since the first time I had my period!

Claire rolled out of bed and tottered into the bathroom. She began preparing for a shower, thinking it possibly was now past eight, Paul and Manuel would be impatiently waiting on her. They were probably too kind to bang on her door after stuffing her to the gills at the restaurant.

As she checked her eyes and face in the mirror and began stripping for the shower, the water began to steam. She went over in her mind what she was seeking.

Or, probably more accurate, she thought, *what I am missing.*

Claire knew that ever since she had the conversation on the trip to Colombia with Nancy she had been dreading something.

Claire knew that she was good at hiding things. When she was fourteen, she had kept from her father the cigarettes that Janice Galleta had taught her to smoke. She had hidden them under the sink in her bathroom beside her "female stuff." That was what her dad had called it.

He never went to the store to buy it, either. Early on, after her mother had died, her father had taken to paying staffers and college students to do his shopping and occasionally do the cooking or the cleaning around the house.

Frank was busy and knew well how to buy into short cuts. Often, her "female stuff" would be put in a brown paper bag and left on the breakfast nook table with "Mistress Claire" written neatly with magic marker. He didn't even take it out of the bag.

It was easy to hide things from her father. She was equally adept at hiding things from herself, as well. When she was a sophomore at the University of Wisconsin, she had met Bobby Traber. He was a junior, a member of the wrestling team, and he was crazy about her. He would even skip practice and endanger his scholarship if it meant he could buy her a beer and a burger at Sammy's.

The problem was she was not attracted to him at all. But, every time she saw his roommate Alex Simmons, she got weak in the knees. Tall, with wavy dark hair and deep set eyes, he was the perfect match for her. And he did not scream "jock" like Bobby, who, despite his cleft chin and chiseled body, was short, thick and more than a little clingy. Alex seemed aloof, above it all, and "together."

It took her the better part of two semesters to understand that Alex was gay. She knew in her heart the minute she met him, but it was not until Bobby revealed Alex's secret to her that she knew for sure. When

Bobby announced it, seething and inglorious, Claire had slapped him and called him names.

What did that say about her? Her skill at disguising or ignoring the truth could not be construed as healthy. So, what was she missing? What was she in denial about? Her father? Her career?

As she splashed water on her face and stared into the gradually fogging mirror, a scary question edged its way into her consciousness.

What if I am looking for someone to replace my father? Or my mother?

Twenty-eight, she had been alone now for almost a decade. Was she prepared to always be alone?

She had been raised well by her father—fed, clothed, nice home, nice neighborhood, private school, university degree paid for, a new car on her twenty-first birthday. But, she knew that even as close as she and her father had become, he was always holding something back. Claire did not pretend to understand his motives.

She never really felt cheated or left out. Dad had been there for her softball games and her debate team matches. He had sat through an entire rendition of Macbeth when she was a freshman in high school just to see her arrange the sets in the dark between acts. Her dad loved her and supported her, even when he could not understand her. Maybe that was why her mom had loved him so dearly.

And that thought brought a sudden and unexpected result. She gulped, holding back a sob, holding back the urge to run back into the bedroom and clutch the journal to her breasts, hug it until the ceramic shards cut her. Tears rolled down her cheeks unbidden as she clutched the sides of the sink.

Here we go again, she thought.

There was a furtive knock at the door. Claire gathered herself, wiping her forearm across her nose, wiping away the clear snot that had begun to trail down her upper lip. She cleared her throat.

"Yes?" She tried to sound unperturbed—hard to do with the shower running and your body still wracked with barely-contained sobs.

"Just wanted to make sure you were up. Manny is taking the things on down to the dock and will come back and pick us up in a bit. We'll wait on you in the shop across the street." Paul sounded wide awake. Probably already had two cups of coffee, a morning devotional and called his wife Nina, Claire mused. She dropped a towel on the floor and checked to see that she had shampoo, soap and a cloth.

"Sure. Just give me a minute. I slept in, sorry. It's a real comfortable bed."

"Yeah. Ok. See you soon. No hurry."

She heard him walk off, his feet shuffling away on the wooden planks outside of her room. She stepped into the shower, cringing against the needling heat of the water. Soon, with the water cascading over her, she pushed thoughts of her father out of her head and began focusing on her job.

She needed to make sure this service was done according to plan. She had begun to really like Paul. Also, from all that she had gathered regarding Dr. Borche, she had developed a respect and admiration of him. Beyond doing her duty and finishing the job, she wanted get state-side so that she could concentrate on getting herself right again. Laura would know just what she needed.

CHAPTER SIXTEEN

Lucia reclined in the hammock and stirred her *aguapanela.* It was so fresh that the sugar crystals swirled around like a cloud. She liked hers with extra lime. Domingo had offered *aguadiente,* the Colombian national liqueur, but she had declined. He sat next to her sipping on his *canelazo,* a mixture of her *aguapanela* and *aguadiente* grown right here on their plantation.

"I am glad you have come, Mother. We should have arranged this sooner."

The sun was brutal, but the slight breeze brought with it the green odors of the plantation. Ripe fruits, blooming flowers, and dark, rich earth were carried on the currents and mixed with the clear mountain air. It was intoxicating. She had forgotten how pure it seemed here on their mountain.

"Yes, Domingo. I have always had my reservations. There are bad memories here, but I had forgotten how beautiful it is."

"Come, Mom. It is not so bad as that, is it?" His eyes were bright as he swept his hand out to indicate the lush croplands and vineyards in the valley below them.

"If I had not passed thousands of acres of coca plants to get here, perhaps I would agree, son."

His eyes were hard, but his smile softened his face. She had always thought that Domingo could be her most charming son. It was why being "Capo" suited him so well.

"I respect that concern. In fact, I have been considering our options. I cannot go into details, but I can say that in a year, maybe two, we will have a completely different operation here. One papa could be proud of." He sipped his drink, his eyes cool and dark.

"I think you overestimate your father's goodness. But, since you have broached the topic, I want to say what is on my mind."

"I know you had your reasons for finally accepting my invitation." He left it hanging there, his drink held aloft in his right hand, his left gripping his knee. His thin mustache twitched slightly. She knew that the pleasantries her son had shown thus far were cover for his displeasure that she and Manny had defied him.

"Yes. We all have our own agendas, I do believe. Mine is that I fear for your brother's life."

He turned his head and looked off down the valley. His mouth turned up in a wistful smirk.

"I have told you before, Mother, that I mean Manny no harm. I have already begun to replace him. It will be an adjustment, to be sure, but I love Manny and respect his decision."

"But you do not like it."

"I don't have to like it." His eyes were hard and his grip on his knee bunched the linen slacks he wore.

"I understand. But, it is not from you that I fear for his life."

Domingo smirked and took another sip of his drink.

"Manny has made many enemies, this is true. I cannot protect him from all of them, even though I do not want him harmed. My power is not what Father's once was."

"This is true. But what if I told you that the danger to Manny's life comes from within your organization?"

"You mean Alfonso, then?"

She was not surprised. She expected as much. Domingo had ears everywhere. He did not seem concerned.

90

"Yes. Alfonso seems to think that Manny should come back to work for you. He claims to be working for you to accomplish this task."

"Has Alfonso been bothering you personally, Mother? I will have his manhood removed if he has harmed you."

"You always were rash, Domingo. The only threat that concerns me is that Alfonso has ambition. Perhaps you can reign in your dog."

"Your nephew, Mom. He is a dog without a leash, I am afraid. He has become more independent of late. I have discovered that he has operations of his own, a warehouse, security, infrastructure all outside of my own employees and retainers."

"You speak like you have known of this threat. It seems that perhaps Manny isn't his only target."

"Father always said that you were the brains of his organization. I take you for granted. I will heed your warning Mom. As much for my own sake as Manny's. He is on his own, though. Even though he is my brother and will always be, he left my protection. He left ME unprotected. I will never forgive him that."

Lucia set down her *aguapanela*, half-finished. It left a wet stain on the wicker end table. She swung out of the hammock and placed her feet on the ground. She smoothed her cotton dress along her buttocks and looked down at Domingo, still seated in the cushioned chair.

"No. I suppose you cannot. You have your father's self-importance."

"I will arrange for your return via the helicopter. I don't want you to have to drive by those acres of coca on your way back and think poorly of me."

"Why, Domingo, nothing else is needed for that." She smiled and leaned down to peck him on the cheek. His skin was moist and smelled of cigars.

When she looked up, she saw Maria and her horned rim glasses. She stood pertly at the door holding a pitcher of *aguapenela*, its ice cubes practically suspended in the sugary gel of the drink. Her bright orange dress fit her slim figure, and her smile was warm and humble.

"More drink, señora?"

Her voice was familiar. Something about her made Lucia wary. She could feel her hair stand up on her neck. It was distracting and so she hesitated to answer. She stood numbly, staring at her glasses, contemplating the chiseled arms, the dark skin, the chocolate eyes and stylish but sensible hairdo. It was Domingo who spoke. There was a smokiness in his voice that belied his anger.

"Mother was just leaving, Maria. Please make sure that Walter Andrés has the helicopter ready to take her back home."

Maria glanced at her, her features guarded behind a crocodile smile.

"Of course. I will make arrangements immediately, sir." She looked at Lucia and said, "If you will follow me, señora, I will show you to the lobby where you can wait while Walter Andrés prepares your trip."

"I thank you. Please lead the way. Goodbye, Domingo. I must visit again soon."

Domingo rose, his full six feet towering over her. She preferred that he had stayed seated. He hugged her. She had forgotten what that was like. She had not been hugged by Domingo since he was a child. She felt a tear come, unwelcome. She wiped it away on his linen jacket.

She put her hand on his massive chest, the silk shirt beneath open to his hairy chest. She gently pushed him back and smiled sadly.

"Take care of yourself, Mom." Lucia could see Maria out of the corner of her eye. She stood at the entrance to the veranda, the pitcher still in her hand.

"Thank you, son. I will tell Oscar you said hello."

"I have already spoken to Oscar. We are planning a family gathering, once Manny returns from his most recent assignment."

Lucia stared at him. She could feel her hands shaking. He had spoken to Oscar?

"I am invited, I assume."

"Of course. We will invite you once we set the time and date. Oscar spoke of going to the beach." He held her hands in front of him.

"Good. The salt in the air there agrees with my skin."

"Until then, have my blessings. Safe travels, Mom." Domingo was more composed now and sincere.

She was glad they were leaving on good terms, but she felt worried. She could feel a bead of fine sweat on her lip. She resisted licking it and smiled, instead. A strong smile, a reassuring smile. Domingo returned it and squeezed her hand before sitting again.

She turned to go and caught a look in Maria's eye as she turned.

She did not trust this young woman. Something about her seemed familiar and foreign at the same time. Lucia had a keen eye and even better instincts. She was hard to shake and even more difficult to fool.

Lucia followed Maria as she put the pitcher down on a crystal table just inside the house. Lucia noted the younger woman's gait. Sensuous and controlled. She noted the hard calves, the simple but elegant shoes. She saw that the woman had taste and class. Domingo had good judgment when it came to employees. This one, though, was not his doing. Lucia suspected that Domingo's steward was more than she appeared.

She was so sure of it that she determined it was her duty to discover the truth about Maria. Perhaps Manny knew more about her. Maybe she had been one of his hires. It would not surprise Lucia if Manny had taken a liking to this young woman, so fit and beautiful.

She had noticed on her way in that the other members of the staff gave her a wide berth. She did not seem dangerous on the surface. She was small, unarmed, and with those glasses, she appeared as though she would fit in nicely at a library or an investment firm. Beneath the mousy exterior, though, lay a feline grace, watchfulness, and a sense that she did not belong here.

They descended the stairs and made their way down to the floor level. Lucia admired again Domingo's taste for art, décor, and architecture. The mansion had been improved upon, remodeled, refitted with new furniture, new flooring, and new window dressings. The modern décor was a huge improvement from her husband's penchant for 1970's island themes of wood paneling, thick carpets, dark tile floors, nautical themes, and heavy drapes.

Maria turned and smiled at her.

"I see you noticed the new art Domingo has purchased." She indicated a large, bright painting along the largest wall. It was hung with only a thin, dark frame. It appeared to be a collage of colors and shapes that represented a nude woman.

"It is one of Merello's new ones that Domingo picked up in Madrid last summer. It is quite striking, isn't it?"

"Yes. And much different than the dark oils my husband preferred." Maria nodded and continued on.

"We passed your husband's art on to the collector you had referred to us. Did he receive them?" She was all business: formal, pleasant, punctual, and sufficiently considerate. Something about Maria seemed almost *too* perfect.

"Oh yes. Thank you. It fetched a large sum from some American collectors from Miami at auction." She smiled politely.

"Excellent," Maria remarked as she strode confidently toward another veranda. "The hangar, such as it is, is just beyond in an attached alcove of the main house. There are refreshments there, if you are hungry. The flight back may be long. Sadly Walter Andrés does not stock food for the flight, so please help yourself."

"You are too kind. Thank you."

A wistful smile played across Maria's lips as she turned her head and continued through the sliding glass doors. The veranda was large with a banana tree growing in one corner and lush bushes separating the main house from the servant's quarters and the rest of the large complex. It opened onto a wide and long driveway paved with small white pebbles dotted with flat stones to denote pathways. The stones were cooler than concrete with more forgiveness for the movement of the dark earth beneath it.

Maria crossed the gravel drive with confidence despite her heels and the blaring heat of the day. Lucia followed. Soon they were among a grove of cashew trees. The shade beneath them was lovely; their fruit dotted the pure white drive.

"Through here," Maria commanded. She stepped through a stone archway with an emblem of a bird landing on a branch engraved in a wood plank above.

They entered a side door into a large metal building. The rush of air conditioning was welcome. The lobby was small, but pleasantly appointed. A glass wall provided a view into the hangar and large windows on the west opened onto a tarmac where several small planes sat, the heat rising from the tarmac in waves around their bellies.

She glimpsed, and then the bright green helicopter with red lettering proclaiming *"LOS CAFETAL BANDIDOS"* was visible. Its rotors began to move and she heard a high-pitched whine begin.

Maria turned and indicated a low table with trays of food.

"It is not the season for *el dia e las velitas,* señora, but the *boñuelos* are fabulous. As are the pineapples and coffee. They are all products of our lands here. If you prefer, there is also fried cassava and yucca under a heat lamp, if Walter Andrés has not eaten them all yet."

"It all looks very appetizing. Would you join me?"

"Of course. Allow me to pour us both some coffee. Cream, sugar?"

"Café negro, por favor."

Lucia seated herself in low, long white leather couch. Maria placed her coffee between them on a mahogany coffee table and sat opposite.

She crossed her legs and sipped her coffee. She raised a *boñuelo* and took a nibble.

"The chef sometimes makes *arepas con salmon y aguacate.* Walter and I fight over them, even though Christiana makes them by the dozen."

"I did not come here to discuss food with you, Maria. I want to know how you came to work for my son and who exactly you really are."

Maria raised her eyebrows. Her smile was gone.

"Pardon me, señora. I do not know why these things concern you. I am merely Domingo's steward."

"That is not true. The truth is written in your walk, your careful insightfulness and your eyes. Did Manny hire you or Domingo?"

Maria almost dropped her *boñuelo*. She caught it deftly between two manicured nails. Lucia smiled.

"I see why you do not carry a weapon. You have the reflexes of a cat to match your stride and your balance."

"Manny hired me, yes. Domingo has seen fit to employ me in a different capacity than Manny had intended."

Lucia had lived a life dedicated to being bold. She pushed forward, using her instincts and her experience.

"You were Manny's spy, weren't you?"

"I was many things to Manny. I am now Domingo's steward, and that is all," Lucia did not miss the implication.

Lucia drew herself up, stiffened her back and stared at Maria.

"Do you love Manny Villarreal, Maria?"

She laughed. It was a nervous exhalation, an unexpected outburst.

"Who does not love Manny? You are his mother. Surely you understand at least that about your son."

"He rejected you, didn't he?"

Maria smiled sadly and placed the *boñuelo* on a plain white plate beside her. She glanced outside.

"It appears that Walter Andrès has all the preparations ready for your departure, Señora Villarreal. I will escort you to the tarmac. It was a pleasure to visit with you." She stood and grabbed Lucia's satchel.

Lucia tried to smile back but could not.

"The pleasure was mine, Miss Gallenes."

They exited the glass doors together. Neither spoke another word until Lucia had settled into the helicopter. The rotors whipped her hair about and she struggled to straighten it with her fingers as she clutched her satchel to her lap with her other hand.

Walter Andrès nodded to her from the front. He mouthed something to her and hooked a thumb over his shoulder. She could not hear him over the roar of the helicopter's engine.

The door opened and Maria stood outside, her dress riding up her athletic legs, her hair blown to one side. She did not smile, but her features were soft. Forgiving.

She leaned in and put her mouth close to Lucia's ear. Even this close, she had to yell to be heard over the whine of the helicopter.

"I will protect Domingo like I protected Manny, Señora. Do not worry about your sons. They are in good hands."

With this she grasped Lucia's hands in hers. They were warm and soft. She stared at her with piercing chocolate eyes and nodded. She leaned back, shut the door, and Walter Andrés began his ascent above the coca fields of the Villarreal plantation.

CHAPTER SEVENTEEN

Manuel Villarreal knew when something was not right. Most people had a sense of it when they made a mistake. Sometimes a sense of dread could overcome them or they would have a prescient moment. The way that Paul had explained it to Manny was that the Spirit of God moves in each person and manifests itself as guilt, prophesy, regret, or action, among other manifestations of the Spirit.

Whatever the explanation, Manny knew without a doubt that something bad was about to happen. Mostly he could attribute this sense of dread with a dream he had.

Initially, he had chalked it up to the heavy meal they had consumed together before they retired last night. It was not a premonition. It was a memory. This was not the first time he had experienced this dream.

He had dreamt of Domingo and his father. He remembered the dream so vividly because it called upon his memory, not his imagination. Often, when he had this dream, it foretold of pending trouble.

He recalled the dream again in his mind's eye as the boat drifted in port and he awaited the arrival of Paul and Claire. He closed his eyes and let the dream take him back to that time ten years ago. The gentle rocking of the boat in the moors allowed him to drift, to go back, and to experience the past again.

He moved through the jungle with four others. They were all shadows. Dressed in black with dark paint on their faces, their rifles were charcoal black, their painted bayonets black, and their knives at their sides a flat black, even the blades. They were murderous, black-clad devils, their movements graceful and deadly. Their purpose—dealing death—was awash upon their stoic faces, the set of their feet upon the lush forest floor, the urgent breathing, caught in their throats, ragged and full of expectation, revenge and regret.

They stole through the undergrowth toward a rise. Cesar, the tall one, took the rifle from his back, a Russian Dragonov sniper rifle he had stolen from a Nicaraguan militia. He stooped in the tall grass at the top of the hill and unzipped his carrying bag in the dark.

They gathered around him silently as he pulled out a large pouch. From it, he extracted the PSO-1 sights. He fitted it quickly on the side rail of the rifle. Then, he pulled from the bag a suppressor that fit on the barrel just past the flash reducer already there. He chambered a 7.62mm bullet from the ten round magazine with a sharp report.

Cesar looked up at them and nodded.

Manuel gave him a "thumb up" sign. They all hunkered down or lay prone on the grass. Cesar crawled forward; the sling wrapped around one hand, his elbows digging into the moist soil.

They managed this way until they could see the cabin less than two hundred yards away. Bright yellow light spilled from its windows and illumined the four guards standing near the front. The Venezuelan guards chatted quietly, their voices carrying in the night.

Manny checked his watch and then resumed his vigil. The men eyed him anxiously, their rifles at ready. He could hear their nervous movements as they checked extra magazines and the maps that each carried in their belts.

He looked for each of them, knowing their shapes by heart, knowing the gleam in each of their eyes. Miguel Santos, the wiry explosives expert from Cali. Luis Guilliermas, a French nationalist who had worked for the Villarreals for a decade. Mateo Chaguala Espanoza, the largest and strongest of the group. They called him The Santa Martan Bull. He carried the light machine gun, a Belgium-made FN MAG 10, with two metal boxes of ammunition.

They each had a role to play. Cesar was to quietly eliminate the guards so they could breach the perimeter. Miguel's role was to plant explosives to cover their retreat, taking out a bridge, an armored personnel carrier, and two guard towers about a click away. Luis and Mateo were to breach the compound with Manny as Cesar covered them from this rise.

Once Domingo was removed from the compound they would rendezvous at a truck they had stashed just over a kilometer to the north. Cesar would drive. It was a farm truck with Venezuelan tags. Cesar was known more as a farmer in these parts than a rifleman. Only Manny knew the truth.

Without warning, the grass in front of Cesar snapped as he fired the SVD. One man who had bent over to get a drink collapsed quietly into the dark surrounding the house.

Everyone held their breath and watched.

The other three guards in the valley below continued to talk.

One wandered off to the north.

Just as he was almost swallowed up by the night, they saw him lurch forward. Cesar had adjusted his rifle so that the grass would not give away his position. The night sounds remained uninterrupted. Birds chirped. Insects hummed.

Manny could see Cesar's smile, cold and satisfied in the gloom. His teeth were gritted together as he swung the rifle to the front again.

"Perhaps now would be good, Miguel," Manny said as he tapped him on the shoulder.

Miguel nodded silently and blinked. He gathered a satchel and his silenced FAMAE S.A.F. submachine gun. His face was grim and set as he moved stealthily toward the bridge below them.

Soon, the other two guards were down. Cesar moved off to the north, closer to the truck and in a better position to cover the others. Manny led Luis and Mateo down the path. They searched ahead for signs of more guards. There were none.

Manny glanced behind them, satisfied that he could not spot Cesar on the ridge, even though he knew his exact location: left of the large boulder before the tree line. He scanned the creek and watched as the silent silhouette of Miguel stalked toward the ditch on the opposite side of the road where the APC was parked, silent and hulking in the night.

The cabin was before them, its light casting the long shadows of the corpses littering the grounds. Manny could see inside past the glare. Several heads were visible, some seated, some pacing the room.

He placed his hand on the ground, pointed to Luis, and gestured to his left. He looked at Mateo and patted his back. Luis moved off to the left, his black boots crunching in the gravel of the drive. Mateo nodded and took up a position ten feet behind Manny and to his right as they approached the front door.

With eight armed guards and two officers inside, Manny didn't want to take too many chances with crossfire. They had Mateo for suppression, Luis using his shotgun from the side door and Manny's deadly aim with his folded stock AK-103. Theoretically, they would subdue the captors quickly, despite being outnumbered.

Before they reached the door, a shout from behind them pierced the gloom. Short, muffled bursts, signaled Miguel's submachine gun at work. A low groan emitted from near the ditch. The noise had alerted those inside the compound.

Movement from within was Manny's cue to hurry. Before he could clear the porch, though, Mateo began firing through the window. The light machine gun bucked in Mateo's hands, his face lit with effort and glee. His smile radiated through the night.

Manny leapt to the porch and to the left to avoid the spray of bullets whipping by him. They echoed in the night, ripping the rotten siding of the cabin to shreds and mowing down two guerilla captors.

He kept his back to the wall, glancing inside the only remaining intact window. He saw someone coming toward the door.

Manny fired from the hip, taking out a mustached officer as he slammed the front door open, an automatic pistol in one hand and a flashlight in the other.

The flashlight was torn from the officer's hand as his chest exploded in a rain of gore. Manny swore under his breath as he desperately searched for his brother inside. He could see him through the dirty glass of the window. Two men had Domingo between them. His head was slumped down, unconscious.

Manny heard the loud report of Luis' Franchi SPAS-12 tactical shotgun exploding inside the confines of the house. Someone screamed. Someone cursed. Blood splattered windows, wood splintered and Manny continued to move and fire in bursts. Two more guards lay dead.

"Reloading!" Mateo yelled.

Manny could see him squat down and hear the coil feed drop clinking to the ground beside him. Mateo opened the metal box and pulled a new chain of ammunition out and fed it into the huge rifle. Without suppression, without surprise, and without numbers to their advantage, Manny began to worry. He could see concern etched on Mateo's face as well.

Seasoned soldiers, they understood the risk they had taken following Manny into this folly. The Villarreal family would not allow their father's murder to go unpunished and they would never allow the family cartel to be taken from under them with violence. Retribution was necessary.

Manny felt a pull in the air near his shoulder and watched as a high-velocity shell tore out the eye of an officer who had flanked him while Mateo was reloading. Mateo glanced to the knoll and offered a silent nod of sincere thanks to Cesar. The officer snapped his head back and lay across the doorway.

Manny ran for the door, and hurdled the body, firing a round off as he entered. It penetrated an overturned couch and he heard the satisfying cry of a voice from behind it. He checked his left briefly, seeing Luis slumped near the side door, blood covering his pants and boots, a grimace of agony on his haggard face.

"You alright?" Manny asked.

"They left through the back." Luis responded, pointing with his eyes.

Manny heard the shuffle and clink of Mateo running while lugging the machine gun and ammo outside. Manny glanced out the window and saw him pursuing someone to the west, back toward Cesar's flank.

They would get away if he didn't move quickly. He patted Luis shoulder and exited through the back door.

The man he had shot behind the couch rose up, a long combat knife slashing the air. He stabbed out, missing Manny by a scant inch. By reflex, Manny smashed the man's cheek with his rifle. He felt the stock crunch against bone and watched out of his peripheral vision as the man slumped lifeless into a heap amid the overturned table. He rushed through the door and continued into the night, pursuing the plodding guards as they drragged the unconscious Domingo through the tall grasses west of the cabin.

Manny didn't stop to consider why they were running in the opposite direction from the APC until he saw the headlights bounding through the grass towards him. A truck skidded to a stop, illuminating the retreating guerilla soldiers. Then shots fired, bullets arcing blue and white fire into the darkness, flinging dirt and spraying grass all around him.

A white hot pain struck his arm and spun him around as he ran. He lost his balance, dropped his rifle and felt the earth come up to meet him roughly as he fell. He heard Mateo shout and fire at the truck as the men pushed Domingo into the back.

Another bullet tore into his ankle, shattering bone and tendon. He grasped the grass in front of him and tried to lie lower, crawling desperately and fighting the pain in his arm and leg.

He reached for the .45 at his waist and brought it up with his good hand and fired off several shots, knowing he was firing too high and too wildly.

The same was not true for Mateo. His shots rained across the hood of the car, pinging off the engine, flattening the front tire, caving in the passenger door. The door flew open as the truck hurtled past them and one man fell out limp to the ground. Mateo began to fire at the truck as it fled back toward the bridge.

"NO! Domingo is in the back! Mateo!"

He fired high, stopped suddenly, and fell forward, face first. There was a moist smack as his gun hit the ground. Manny blinked. Mateo was dead.

Manny struggled to his knees and crawled over to him. Just as he reached him and saw the large exit hole in his skull, he heard the truck stop with a loud screech, and a scream of the engine. Manny looked up in time to see it flip over, end over end. He felt a sickened knot develop in his chest.

He tucked the .45 into the waist of his slacks and grabbed Mateo's weapon. He used it as a crutch to rise to standing. As he did, he glanced again to the ridge. He saw a glint of light off the optic sight of Cesar's SVD. Suspicious, Manny *grimaced as he limped forward to the truck immobile and on its side two hundred feet away.*

As he neared the durable personnel carrier, he could see flames licking the underside near the engine. He knew time was crucial. Two bodies lay to the side of the truck, one the driver and the other the final guard. He was dead. The driver groaned and turned over onto his back.

Manny stepped on his hand, which held a .45 Colt revolver. A classic, American Wild West revolver like his cousin Al liked to play with. Manny shot the man in the center of the head with a single shot from the FN MAG.

He heard footsteps and looked up to see Luis struggling across the field. He stopped and looked at the truck, his eyes sad and his right arm hanging limp and dripping blood down his side. He was dead, standing.

"This was a mess," he admitted. He collapsed to his knees on the grass.

"Yes, Luis. A mess. Stay here a minute. I will be back. I have to see if Domingo is alive."

"You'll die trying."

"If I must," he said, not looking at Luis. He stared at the truck as the flames raised higher, lighting the grass around it in a smoky blaze.

He staggered forward, limping on his destroyed ankle. His arm throbbed mercilessly. He trudged on inexorably and lifted the canvas cover over the rear compartment of the truck. Domingo lay there, his leg at a sickening angle beneath his torso, his arms splayed over his head in a sort of bizarre dance pose.

Manny got on his knees, feeling the heat of the fire licking at his clothes. He crawled, it was easier than walking. He grabbed Domingo's collar and dragged him out from the back of the truck.

He didn't examine him closely. For all he knew, Domingo was dead. His body certainly felt stiff and heavy.

"Come on, brother. Wake up," he whispered hoarsely. The smoke was filling his lungs, burning his throat. His eyes watered. With all his strength he pulled. He could feel the muscle in his arm tear more. He could feel the crunch of the shattered bones of his ankle.

Pretty boy Manny would never look the same. He smiled despite the pain, despite the fear and grief that grasped at his heart. Father, and now Domingo. He pleaded with God, a God he had never believed in. A God that he had denounced. Now Manny needed Him, would do anything.

The tears in his eyes streamed down his face, etching the soot there in moisture, leaving a dark trail. Through the smoke and the tears, Manny saw the figure of Luis lying in the grass now where he had left him. His breath came in shallow spurts and rasps.

Luis looked at him from the ground, turning his head. He smiled at him sadly and blinked slowly.

"You found him. He looks as dead as me."

"You both will be fine. Cesar will come get us in the truck soon."

"No. Cesar killed Mateo and shot the driver. He is working for them, too. Manny, be car—" he coughed, blood splattering the grasses near him. He swallowed with a grimace. "Be careful, Manny. They will kill all the Villarreals."

Luis' face and his words haunted his dreams ever since. In those next few years after he had rescued Domingo, avenged their father's death, and re-established the Villarreal family legacy, Manny had taken a great amount of pride in his efforts to never allow Luis' prophecy come true.

Many times as danger lurked, he would have this dream. It was a dream to remind him that enemies were everywhere and that even the most innocent had an agenda.

He opened his eyes, taking in the vista of the mountains ahead, the river cutting a wide brown swath through the forest and the fields. He wondered what threats were at hand and if maybe he was in the wrong place, if maybe he had made the wrong decisions.

The past beckoned him, his guilt called him, a sense of responsibility pulled at him.

He regretted speaking to Paul the way he had last night. Deep down, Manny knew that Paul was right. He could not ignore the influence of the dream and the warning it held. At the same time, he could not submit to the man he had been. He had to focus on the man that God wanted him to be.

He felt sad and wary. He had left his brother alone with wolves at his door. If only he could convince Domingo to put it all behind him and begin a new legacy. Maybe it was too late, maybe that was why the dream had come and why his gut was telling him something bad was going to happen soon.

CHAPTER EIGHTEEN

Alfonso rummaged in his credenza, searching for the document he had left there a few months before. The news that some American CIA agents had torn up a bar in Cartagena had spurred his memory.

Sweat poured down his sideburns and tickled his ear lobe. He could feel it going down his back and soaking his cotton shirt under the jacket. Dark stains marred the grey fabric.

He fumbled with discarded mail, bills, notes from Domingo, a box of cheap cigars from a dancer he had picked up one night at *Vasados,* a bar in Bucaramanga.

He found a faded yellow paper stuck to a green sticky note. He wiped his brow with a white handkerchief from his breast pocket and dabbed his temples while staring at the note. Alfonso wanted desperately to gain control of the Villarreal cartel, but one thing was still in his way.

When Manuel turned in his resignation, he had left Alfonso with a chest full of information. It was mostly dossiers on Villarreal enemies. Names of Venezuelan mercenaries, Mexican assassins, files full of old family feuds dating back to the late 1800's.

Alfonso had considered it mostly paranoia and Manuel being overprotective of big brother.

But, this note was different. It had stood out from the rest of the information because it was one of the only hand-written pieces. Manny had taken this note on the back of a hotel receipt. His writing was neat, his letters precise and compact.

Uribe and his cronies are dangerous. They create lies within lies and cover them with the truth. They would make excellent cartel Capos. *Even agents like Buecher and Gomez are caught up in their act. It is amazing what cold hard pesos can get you. The "treaty" or agreement with* FARC? *They merely bide their time and lay in wait for the next opportunity.*

On the surface, this note was just some mental ramblings of a paranoid and deluded man. Buecher and Gomez. Both were US agents assigned to assist Uribe's Drug Task Team. Agent Alvarez had mentioned that Gomez had been re-assigned about the time that a drug bust had interrupted the flow of traffic through Buenaventura. The Americans had discovered one of their greatest secrets: submarines.

That was the first of many submarines that the Colombian Navy and Coast Guard had found in the last two years. They even had a parade of them in Bogotá. The authorities called them "narco-subs," and Ecuador, Guatemala, Mexico, and even Italy had confiscated several. Most were scuttled before the crew and captain were caught.

The days of the crew of a sub scuttling it, sending it to the bottom of the sea or river, and then waiting as they were rescued by the authorities in international waters was over. New international regulations attached as much as a twenty year prison sentence for this crime, whether caught in the sub or in international waters suspected of transporting cocaine.

The subs were not what interested Alfonso. It was the contact. Manny had agents everywhere and counteragents overseas that kept the Villarreal organization out of headlines, off government desktops, and in the good graces of organizations who wanted quality materials from a professionally run manufacturer. One of these organizations, the 'Ndrangheta from Calabria, Italy, had ordered the manufacture of a sub capable of carrying over ten tons of cargo and a crew of six.

Manny had overseen its manufacture, deep in the jungles bordering Ecuador. Alfonso had assisted him in acquiring the sophisticated

108

electronics and sonic equipment as well as the second diesel engine required to propel the monstrosity. It was a beauty, cold Kevlar and fiberglass, with a large observation deck, a working periscope, and the ability to submerge over forty feet below the surface.

The sub was seized in international waters near the Caribbean on its maiden voyage. The crew was still in custody in America for their crimes, the drugs confiscated. Manny had shrugged at the time with a sad smirk on his face.

"I guess today we make a new enemy. The Teganos do not forgive incompetence. Now we must watch Sovarato as well as Sicily. Get in line, boys," Manny had said. His manner had been jovial. Manny had always been brave and confident. *Fool.*

Giovanni Tegano. Alfonso had forgotten. The note brought back the memory, if only after some mental gymnastics. Italian shoes with a high shine, even in the middle of the Colombian jungle. A deep olive face with a fat upper lip and a rumpled suit. He was the grandson of Pasquale Tegano, named for his great uncle who was one of the most wanted criminals in Italy.

He had smelled like coffee, cigars, and sweat. His handshake was limp and his eyes were hard. Giovanni hated Manny. He thought the submarine was a foolish idea, something concocted by his father. When it had failed, Giovanni was the first to visit the Villarreal estate and demand that their investment be returned—all forty-five million dollars. Domingo refused, and had shipped another twenty tons the same week, instead.

The cocaine was what they wanted, not the stupid submarine. Giovanni, however, never forgave Manny's impudence and arrogance.

Alfonso was proud of himself. He felt like a detective. The note had opened up his mind to remember the contact: the name that could possibly be the solution to his great problem. He needed someone to kill Domingo. He knew Carlos would not do it even for his sister, or all the millions of dollars Alfonso could eventually offer him. Alfonso could not do it. He could not even be linked to it.

By sending Carlos to chase after Manny, he had created an excellent diversion. Carlos would take the fall for Domingo's death, but someone else would have to do the deed. Assassins were too risky. They left trails, asked too much, and had difficulty keeping their mouths shut. Carlos was the only reliable assassin Alfonso had ever met. But, he was too loyal to the Villarreals.

If Giovanni could be trusted, could be coerced, then the 'Ndrangheta mafia could be his meal ticket. In exchange, it would be easy to let the Teganos in on exclusive European action. Action that Agent Alvarez did not want. However, it was action on which Alfonso was depending.

He thought that perhaps Domingo's greatest stroke of genius was to make friends on the African continent and to bypass their Mexican "friends." America was coming down too hard. Now, with a new President, they were providing even more pressure and even more money being dumped into Uribe's pet anti-drug programs.

By getting more product to Europe there would be less competition, less regulations, better distribution, and less product lost on the trip. The way Alfonso understood it, the difference would be that in under a year, they could double their production for any five years of moving product to North America.

Agent Alvarez would get his wish, though. If in charge, Alfonso would not be foolish enough to allow the routes to North America to totally dry up. There was no reason to burn that bridge. He had spoken to farmers throughout Arauca and Meta-Guaviare. Production could easily be doubled and perhaps, with enough pesos, tripled.

Alfonso's idea was to establish a new way of transporting and paying for cocaine. In the twentieth century, with "legitimate" businesses at their fingertips, drug trafficking did not need to be still stuck in the 80's and 90's. For sure, the Villarreal organization was nothing like Escobar's. It was vaster, for one. They maintained control of "independent" traffickers, and "independent" farmers. These thousand farmers, called *cocaleros*, scattered throughout the mountains of Colombia, Venezuela, and Ecuador and the hundreds of trafficking agents had a sense of freedom and profit that was uncharacteristic of drug smuggling. In addition, they worked in conjunction with both militia groups through a "taxation" agreement.

To this infrastructure, Alfonso had dreamed of establishing call centers and websites, cells of labs located in the States and in Europe that were disguised in modern warehouses, legitimate places of business: in plain view. He knew it could be done. He had disguised his labs in downtown Bogotá for almost three years now, right under the nose of the government, Domingo, and Manny.

Planning had always been his best trait. He had been planning this coup since he was a teenager. From the day he had met Manny struggling out of the forest dragging Domingo around his shoulder with a look of victory on his face, Alfonso had thought of nothing but this moment. He needed to take action now, though, he realized.

He flipped his phone open, crumpled Manny's note and dialed his office.

A girl, barely twenty, answered pertly

"Get me Giovanni Tegano. He may still be in Bogotá. I need him to call me promptly." He calmly repeated the name and spelled it and gave country of origin and profession. Finished, he snapped the phone closed and lit a cigar.

He sat on his bed. He realized he had not slept in two days. He did not need rest. His destiny was upon him now. It weighed him down. It was magnetic and gravitic.

Alfonso pulled on the cigar, feeling its warmth enter his throat, the smoke filling him like a force.

He sat like that for several more minutes, filling his lungs with the killing smoke, enjoying the peace of his dwelling, the silence of his home. A knock came to the door downstairs. He waited as his staff answered. A booming voice announced his guest.

"Ah, Henry. My old friend," he murmured. He rose, picked out another cigar and his lighter and left the room headed for the stairs. He checked his side pocket of his jacket to make sure the pistol was still there and descended the stairs with a smile. Plans were in motion.

CHAPTER NINETEEN

Claire watched as the village came into view. The jungle parted, the river widened and became shallow. Several villagers gathered, speaking in a quick melding of Spanish and another, more foreign language. Paul had explained that the mixture of Wayuu and Spanish immigrants had produced a broad mixture of the two languages so that some villagers of Yondo would interject a word from the Wayuu amongst their Spanish. Partly this was because of a high level of illiteracy among the villagers.

In the distance, Claire could see the smoke rising from the oil derricks of Barrancabermeja across the river. Yondo had a hospital, schools, a cathedral and a small police force.

They were in the shadow of the metropolis downriver, the oil barons, barrios, and "civilization" of Barrancabermeja. Yet, of Colombia's ninety-one percent literacy rates, very little of that number resided in Yondo.

The cacophony of voices echoed across the river. The rich tones of happiness and good nature were mingled with sobs and crying. A crush of people gathered around the dock and scattered out in a fan shape on the embankment.

Claire took in the beaming smiles, mothers cradling babies, old women fussing over toddlers, and middle age men scrambling to tie the boat and greet their visitors. They were expected, she saw. A woman with a deep complexion, almond eyes with deep crow's feet, and a simple dress came forward. The crowd parted for her as she walked upon sandaled feet. Claire saw sadness and wisdom in her eyes and noted that she wrung her hands.

Claire watched her carefully; she was positive this was Katherine Borche's mother, Jhoana. Claire had gathered the metal box that held the remains of Doctor Borche's wife. She held them now, cradling them against her breasts as if to protect them.

Many of the faces watching turned to her, even as they greeted Paul and Manny with shouts and what Claire understood to be friendly ribbing. They were the stars here.

She was the oddity, the outsider. Paul jumped down from the deck of the boat to the pier as if he were fifteen years younger. He seemed energized by the excitement.

Manny smiled sadly. He seemed more somber than Paul. Something had been bothering him since Puerto Boyacá. She had sensed it as soon as she had made her way back to the boat. Manny had been less engaged, and had spent the better part of the final leg of the trip trying to get his cell phone to work or fiddling with his camera equipment.

Claire tried not to intervene. She was not sure what was bothering him, but after giving him a cold shoulder earlier, she did not blame him if he wanted to be alone.

Manny, Paul, and Christian scampered to tie up the boat and Claire took the opportunity to grab her things. She wanted to disembark carrying the ashes so that the village could see. Her instructions from her employer were to hand them over to her mother in Yondo, and then to perform the ceremony in the afternoon. She was not clear on any other traditions, but Paul had mentioned a banquet and a ceremony tonight in Katherine's honor.

Her mind was on these things as she returned. Paul had already joined the men at the dock and was jovially inserting himself in their conversations. They seemed to enjoy his company.

Manny, however, stood apart, his camera bag over his shoulder and his Nikon digital camera around his neck. She watched him for a second, curious. Paul told her that Manny had worked with him here last year in the school. They had taught Spanish for a week while a teacher was recovering from gunshot wounds from a guerilla attack at an outlying family farm.

Then, Claire's vision was on the mother again. Her eyes were brimmed with tears, and her dark dress was stained with them. She had beautiful eyes, full lips, and had retained a youthful appearance. She did not seem old enough to be a grandmother. Her illness was only evident in the pallor of her skin.

Then again, the grandchildren were in the States. Yet another straw to break the camel's back, as her father would say. It would not be a simple thing, adjusting to the death of a child. Having the rest of the family so far away would only make it worse. Her heart went out to this woman, who looked so regal. Even under duress, grief, and frustration, she seemed above it all.

Claire was suddenly nervous. Her palms were moist and she was aware that she had an unexplainable grin. She desperately worked to turn it into a sad, respectful, and sympathetic smile. She was not sure it was working.

"I am Jhoana Esuella Sanchez. You may call me Jhoana. It is so nice to meet you," she said, extending her hand. She was not smiling.

Claire held out her hand, her left clutching the edge of the steel box with Jhoana's daughter's remains tucked neatly inside a chrome tube within the box.

"I am Claire Eppington. I am here to deliver your daughter's remains and the love of her family."

Now Jhoana did smile, still holding Claire's hand. She realized how clammy it was. She wanted to take it back, but Jhoana held it firmly in both of hers.

115

"We are her family, Miss Eppington." Her tone was as firm as her grip. It was flat, devoid of emotion, blame, or accusation. It still stung, its meaning not lost upon Claire. She had practiced that greeting, not realizing how formal and assumptive it was.

"Come, let us celebrate your daughter's life," Paul interjected, grabbing Jhoana's shoulder gently.

She turned towards him, still holding Claire's hand. Her gaze was colder, but her voice was measured.

"Yes, *pater*. Let us celebrate. I am glad you have come, despite the circumstances."

Paul nodded silently. His face was grim.

Claire was amazed at Jhoana's proficiency with the English language.

Paul had related to her how Katherine had come back to her village and taught English, Spanish, and World History to many of the villagers. Katherine had a big heart, a beautiful soul, and an American husband, Clay, who was determined for his wife to spend her final days receiving the best care in the best situation possible.

Of course, Jhoana never approved. Her daughter belonged in Colombia. Paul claimed that she did not blame Clay or Paul for Katherine's death, but she would never forgive them for taking her daughter away from her at such a delicate time.

Claire had worked under more difficult circumstances. These awkward situations were common in her line of business, and she had become sort of a specialist in clients just like this. Invariably, she got emotionally attached to the situation. Perhaps that is why she had such success dealing with the families. They saw her as sympathetic and caring rather than cold and calculated and just doing her job.

That was also what she was bothered by most on this trip. She seemed to be losing her grip on her objectivity. Something about death in general, and the death of a family member specifically, struck a chord with her.   Deep down, she was dealing with emotions, thought processes, and a lack of faith that scared her.

She had not admitted it, yet. She had not defined it as such: fear of the unknown, fear that she had missed out on something that would complete her, fear that she could not handle dying.

Instead, she buried the feelings, ignored the thoughts that sprang unbidden into her mind like now.

Moved inexorably on by the momentum of the moment, Claire cocked her head and listened intently to the rhythms of Jhoana's cadence as she talked. It was musical.

The woman was engaging, for sure. She could see why the entire village showed up for this event.

"It is good to be here among her family. I am looking forward to meeting all of you," Claire said.

Jhoana raised her brows.

"Good. But it will be a short visit, I am afraid. We need to have the ceremony this afternoon. The weather will turn on us before nightfall."

Claire glanced at the sky, noting the clear blue hue and the blaring heat of the early morning sun.

"Jhoana is a crack meteorologist. Trust me. She is rarely wrong."

"I assume you are complimenting me. You know not to mock a grieving mother, Paul."

Paul bowed, a serious look on his face.

Manny diffused the situation by taking Jhoana's hand and dragging her off across the tall grass towards the entrance to an alley close by.

"Come on! I want to see your new stuff. Show me what you have done."

She blushed and shrugged. Claire could see she liked the attention. The crowd parted for them. Children and dogs ran at their heels as they walked briskly back toward the center of the village.

Paul looked at Claire as she stood, perplexed.

"Manny knows the way. He is a friend of the family. Katherine and Clay actually were responsible for converting Manny after I had been working with him for years.

"Oh. I see."

"Come on. You should see her paintings. They are marvelous. Manny promises her that he can sell them to a gallery in Medellin, but she won't have it. She is modest to a fault."

"I didn't know that was possible," she teased.

"Perhaps you are correct."

Paul led her, but it was not necessary. They merely had to follow the crowd. It seemed the whole village was headed to Jhoana's home. It was at the end of a narrow street, parallel with the river.

The house was surrounded by large trees. Birds chirped, easily louder than the crowd gathering in the street. As she and Paul neared, the crowd began to fan out. Tables and chairs were set up at the neighbors' homes.

All the houses were built rough. None were painted. Roofs were corrugated tin. The houses were low, built in a "U"-shape with a courtyard in front or back.

The atmosphere was festive. Claire wondered if that was why she felt the pall of sadness most. She carried Katherine's ashes with her. She realized with a jolt that this was a marked contrast with a funeral procession in America.

A sense that mourning was a part of the atmosphere was hard to define. It was intermingled in the celebration. She watched as people hugged, pushed, teased, and played. She saw some with tears, some with laughter, and others morose and jovial, respectively.

Claire saw Jhoana ascend the stairs to her home, Manny fumbling with the door. People cheered as a soccer ball sailed out into the street. Two young men chased it down, bounding across someone's lawn. Laughter and clapping followed them as they raced away.

Paul walked beside her. He was quiet and seemed deep in thought. She glanced over at him and she watched him perform the nervous tic she had noted when they first met.

Soon, they entered Jhoana's home. It was simple, but clean. The walls were washed white, the knots of the wood showing through. The furnishings were cushioned rattan. A long, low table dominated the entry. Framed pictures of family were displayed upon it as well as a diploma and a large, decorative tribal mask.

Claire could hear Manny and Jhoana in the next room. They were laughing. She could smell coffee and flowers. Bouquets were arranged everywhere. Many were dry and brittle. Paul took her arm and directed her gaze to a picture by a shelf along the wall near the kitchen. In it, Jhoana, Manny, Clay, Katherine, and Paul stood at the entry to El Campin stadium in Bogotá.

"That was in 2001, just before they crowned Colombia the South American Champions. Manny, Jhoana, Clay, and Katherine are like family. It makes my heart ache to know that Jhoana feels I betrayed them."

Claire could see the pain in his eyes.

"Is that your wife?" She pointed to a picture with Paul, Jhoana, and a woman in jeans and a loose blouse standing on a boat. She had short brown hair with a flower in it. She had a farmer tan and a smile that radiated even through the grainy photo.

Paul beamed. "Yes. That was our first year in Colombia. She is from Kansas. Total culture shock. She loves people more than I do, so she adjusted better. Jhoana is her best friend and the only reason Jhoana still speaks to me."

"Quite a bonus to have a wife that is a peacemaker."

"Funny you say that. It is true. Even after Emily was..." Paul coughed, rubbed his face, and sobbed quietly. He composed himself quickly.

"I am sorry—" Claire started.

"No. Even after all that happened to Emily," he continued, his voice husky, "it was Nina who kept me together. She kept me from losing my faith in God."

"Many people lose their faith when they feel God has failed them."

Paul nodded. "I was angry with God. I stood in judgment of Him in my grief. It was Nina who helped me. She reminded me of God's love."

Claire looked at the picture because she did not know what to say. Paul's eyes were red and swollen and his words stuck in his mouth. She had to admit that she was no help in moments like these. She just did not know what to say in the face of death or grieving.

"I'm sorry," escaped her before she could pull it back.

Paul looked at her with eyes full of gratitude.

"Thank you, Claire. I apologize for getting emotional. It's just that Katherine was like an aunt to Emily. And now, with both gone, I have a large emptiness. I fill it with God when I can, but I sometimes I feel lonely."

"From what I can see, Paul, you are far from alone. Besides, Nina sounds like enough woman to fill your life."

"You are right about that. I wish she could be here today. But, Claire, I am glad I came with you. It is good to get to know you." He patted her on her shoulder. Claire glanced around the room nervously.

"Is there somewhere I could change before the ceremony?"

Just then, Manny entered with Jhoana. His hair was pulled behind his ears as if he had been combing it back with his hands. He seemed flushed and his eyes were red.

"We can change later. Please come see Jhoana's work first." He was beaming and beckoned them to follow.

Paul took Claire's hand in his and led her into a large room with windows looking out onto a small courtyard crowded with statues, planter boxes with beautiful exotic flowers, and a large tree in a raised planter box surrounded by more flowers. It was a peaceful place. It was a gorgeous place to relax.

Despite the view, she couldn't concentrate. Manny's hands around hers felt right. She could feel his pulse at the base of his palm. She didn't want him to let go.

She struggled to keep her attention on the art Manny was showing them. The world seemed to coalesce into light-filled room washed in bright colors. She and Manny held hands in the middle of the maelstrom of beauty. She shook her head to clear the image. She hadn't daydreamed since she was in college.

The image didn't recede because the room was exactly the way she had imagined it.

The light in the room was perfect to expose the brilliant colors of the paintings hanging on the walls. A canvas with oil paints, towels, trowels, and other art tools sat in the corner. It was a blank canvas, but those on the walls were wonderfully finished. They were vibrant with color, texture, and life. Jhoana's favorite subject was flowers. Her second favorite was her daughter.

Claire could see that Jhoana remembered best her daughter's smile, her youth, and her strength. The portraits of her daughter were as full of life as even the vibrant colors of the flowers that jumped from the canvas. The flowers' beauty rivaled their living counterparts in the garden outside.

She heard Paul's breath escape in a rush. She sympathized. She felt something special here. If she had a relationship with Katherine, she would probably be struck with the incredible power behind the love and beauty of these portraits.

"Wow. These are all so lovely. Which are the recent ones?"

Claire panicked for a moment as Manny released her hand. She was a little ashamed at herself for feeling cheated.

Manny sat on a white leather sofa, his eyes brimming with tears and hugged Jhoana. She smiled and hugged him back, leaning sideways while addressing Claire's questions.

"The paintings that are striking our soft-hearted friend here are against that wall. The paint has recently dried on the one closest to the window. I just finished it early this morning."

The four paintings were remarkable. Two depicted a lush garden with a young lady reclining in one and walking in another cradling a small dog or puppy. She looked sad yet content. The other two were portraits of a mother and a daughter holding hands on a beach, the waves white at their feet and the sun bright along the expanse of the ocean.

In the one closest to the window, the mother seemed to be saying goodbye, her face turned halfway, and her long dark hair spilling out in the ocean breeze. The young lady had a playful smile and a one hand held out almost searching for the waves crashing at their feet.

All four pictures were vivid in their imagery and full of emotion, memory, and pride. Claire could barely take them all in at once, so great was their power. It was raw, unbridled talent meeting grief, joy, and anger all at once.

The paintings spoke of Jhoana's love, her frustration and sadness at her loss, but most of all, the art was a chronicle of how incredible a human being Katherine had once been.

Perhaps that is why both men in the room sniffled, dabbed at their eyes, and sobbed quietly. Jhoana's love was so strong and her form of art so adept that the person that Katherine had been in life fairly jumped from the paintings. They were poetry. They were song. They were the words and images and emotion all contained in the swatches of color, the play of shadows, the promise of light, and the blankness of that final unfinished work.

Jhoana rose and interrupted the reverie.

"Come on, all of you and let us get something to eat. You must be famished from your trip. Besides, you two must get your act together before the ceremony. We cannot have these dabbing of eyes coming from those who are performing the ceremony, can we?"

"I wish I had your strength, Jhoana," Manny said. He rose as well and straightened his slacks.

"All my strength went into those paintings. I have a little left, and I am reserving it for the last one."

"I cannot wait to see it."

She took both his hands and looked up at him. Manny looked down at her as if she were his mother.

"It makes me so happy to know that all of you appreciate my work. This is my life now, remembering her. Knowing that she is somewhere with no pain gives me peace. Let it do the same for you, Manny. We celebrate her life."

"You are right, Jhoana," Manny said softly.

"It has taken me a long time to get to this point of grief. To accept what has happened. You will be relieved to know, I am sure, that I have even forgiven the doctor."

Claire looked at Paul who wore a chagrined look. Claire realized that she had not said she had forgiven Paul. Her heart went out to him.

Manny watched out the window as Claire played soccer with some village youth. Laughter filled the air as much as the dust and the sweet smells of the blooming flowers in the neighborhood. He saw Paul sitting on a low bench with some old men, all trying to talk at once. A Bible was open on Paul's lap. He looked radiant.

Manny continued to watch Claire running around the lot, her hair tied on her head, rings of sweat under her arms, and a willful smile upon her face.

"Are you falling in love, Manuel Villarreal?" Jhoana rested on a comfortable white sofa, a frozen drink in her hand and a playful smile on her face.

Manny scoffed, quietly.

"She really is quite remarkable. I have never met anyone like her before. She has a sense of humor and a gentle soul. However, I sense that something is bothering her."

"Perhaps she is damaged goods, has a past she would rather forget. Why else would a young woman choose a career path that takes her all over the world?"

Manny allowed the drapes to fall back in place.

"Hmm. I never thought of it that way."

He caught Jhoana looking at him intently.

"Speaking of baggage, Manny. What is this I am seeing in your eyes? A sadness? Concern? Are you still grieving Katherine, or is it something more?"

Manny paced in front of her, hoping to keep her from looking into his eyes. She was perceptive. She knew him better than anyone. Certainly, better than his own mother.

"I don't know. I suppose I am worried about Domingo."

"Domingo can take care of himself. If nothing else, maybe he should retire. He certainly could do anything he wants now. Not many men in his position have as much general popularity. It is because you, Oscar, and Domingo are good men at your core. You have not always acted that way. It is your destiny to do something great, Manny. I know your mother has told you just such a thing. You should listen to her, you know."

Manny had his back to her now. It was a good thing, too.

He did not feel special, did not feel that his destiny was great, and definitely was not proud of his past. In fact, he wished he could do it all over again.

He hated feeling guilty. His past was not something he could change. What he was accomplishing now, that was an improvement? He protected his mother. He tried his best to influence Domingo. He assisted Paul in his ministry. He helped give Oscar a peace of mind and much-needed companionship since his wife died.

So much death. With perspective, he now knew the impact of his past actions. Every hit he authorized, every assassination he had planned, and every execution he had overseen bore down on his consciousness. That did not include the lives he had personally extinguished.

He remembered Paul relating the story of Saul and how he had persecuted Christians. That was how Manny usually got through his day, remembering that he was a sinner, but could be forgiven.

"Mother says a lot of things, Jhoana. Since I have come to live with her and Oscar, I have learned so much about her. So much more than I did as a child."

"Your mother was burdened by your father's legacy, Manny. Give her some credit."

"You are right. I believe Domingo still lives in fear of him. You know, of his memory, the expectations, the paranoia, the greed."

She got up and crossed over to him, resting one fragile hand upon his shoulder. Her hand felt like a bird's wing, light and hollow. Manny had not realized how sick she had become.

"What is truly bothering you, Manny? I know you don't want to look at me. Just tell me. It might help to get it off your chest."

"I feel helpless." *There. I said it.*

He did not feel any better, though. In fact, he had to fight at the clawing in his throat, the feeling that threatened to overwhelm him with anger, fear and self-loathing.

"I see," was the only response he got. He wanted to turn and hug her. He knew the tears would flow and he would be wracked with self-pitying sobs. He had to be strong. He was former lieutenant for the Villarreal cartel! He was a man of action.

She was turning him gently, her hands grasping him by the shoulders. The forcefulness of her gesture belied her weakness. She stared at him with eyes daring him to cry.

He felt like he was being reprimanded. A misbehaving child. A proud mother, prepared to drive home an important life lesson.

"You aren't helpless, Manny. Death is beyond us, sometimes. Katherine, your father, Emily. Did you not know, Manny, that every week another young person from this village is lost to either drugs, the rebels, the river, or to gangs in Barrancabermeja? You are not alone in this.

"You are not unique in this way. If you think you can go back and be who you once were and it will bring even one of them back, or protect those you love, then you will find yourself a fool." Manny could feel the heat in her voice. She was a force of nature. She was hard love personified. "You are not a fool, Manny. And you are not helpless."

He stared at her. Direct, firm, but loving, Jhoana's lecture gave him hope. It did not completely remove the burden, but it gave him the courage to stand firm in her sight.

"You are right, of course," he managed, suppressing a lump that had formed in his throat.

She looked up at him, her eyes moist. He loved when she smiled at him. She could make him feel more at home than he felt in the presence of his own mother.

"I am so proud of the man you are becoming Manny. It is a shame you and Katherine did not marry. I would have been proud to have you as a son-in-law."

She released her grip and her hands fell weakly to her sides.

Manny could see the illness in her eyes. He could see the ravishing effects of the disease in color of her skin, the deep set of her eyes.

Sickness and sadness weighed down her delicate shoulders, bowed her once elegant neck.

"You are right, Jhoana. I am glad she met Clay, though. He is a good man. He made sure she was comfortable."

"There is that, yes. Come. We must join the others. Soon, we'll have to make our way down to the river and perform the ceremony that you came to photograph. I believe you left your equipment in the hall."

"That reminds me, Jhoana. Claire wanted to know if there was a place she could change her clothes before the ceremony."

"There is a room just off the main hall here," she said, a mischievous look playing upon her face. "Right next to yours, in fact."

"You are incorrigible, woman," Manny said. Despite his protestation, her teasing set him to thinking of Claire.

Her laughter and her inner toughness tinged with vulnerability were making an impact on him. He had to admit, she was the best employer he ever had.

CHAPTER TWENTY

Oscar sat across from Lucia. The restaurant was almost empty. This time between lunch and dinner was a slow time. It was perfect for a quiet conversation. His mother had arrived less than an hour before and had been mostly silent. She seemed thoughtful and distracted. He sipped his drink, played with his food, and waited patiently for her to come back to Earth.

"Who do you think Alfonso works for," she asked out of the blue. Her eyes were dull, her mouth turned in a frown. Oscar swallowed his mouthful, and tried to look unconcerned.

"I have no idea. I thought he worked for my brother."

"That's what I thought, too." She ran her fork absently through her *sudado de cerdo*. He glanced down and bit his lip. "Oscar, I have been keeping secrets from you."

"Really? I never suspected."

He tried to keep his response light and teasing, the sarcasm innocent because it was obvious.

"Alfonso has come to visit me frequently since Manny left your brother's business. He doesn't threaten directly, but he claims that Domingo has set him to watch after Manny. He says Domingo expects Manny to come back to work someday and give up his new life. What do you think?"

Oscar did his best to control his angry response. He wanted to lash out at Alfonso. He never did like his cousin. He was too ambitious, too crooked, too caught up in what was best for Alfonso. Oscar remembered him as a child. He was brutal, conniving, and quick to get upset when things did not go his way.

Oscar was older than Alfonso, but he recognized the fine line between envy and idol worship that Alfonso held for his cousins. He suspected that much of his service to the Villarreal organization was self-serving as it was duty. That could be dangerous.

His response held some danger as well. His mother was a powerful woman. Though removed from the business directly, she still held sway over many of the political strings attached to the cartel that allowed it to exist. Some of those contacts were high ranking officials in the Defense Ministry and worked directly under Juan Santos Calderon. Lucia could flex her considerable political muscle when it came to fundraisers, social issues, and public relations, mostly. It was rare that she influenced direct acts of violence on behalf of her family.

Oscar knew that she was capable, though. Following the death of her husband, Lucia had ensured the safe return of Domingo. Her deft ability to recruit a small rescue force to be led by Manny into the jungles of Venezuela had kept the cartel intact.

"I don't know what to think, Mom. Why does this mean that Alfonso is working for someone else, though?"

"I feel strongly that Domingo has accepted Manny's change of life. He said so himself. It makes sense to me because he has always had a big ego. He gets it from your father. Plus, Alfonso is a little rat. I think he wants Manny out of the way. He always was a jealous one."

His mother was perceptive. He had to be careful how he answered. She was on the verge of being furious. That was not a safe place. Bad things could happen. Above all else, Oscar wanted peace. He wanted his family to forget the past and move forward into the modern world behaving like civilized people.

"Yes. But that doesn't necessarily mean that he intends to harm Manny. That would be ridiculous. I don't know much about the family business. I don't want to. But, I would think that Alfonso is just being an obnoxious punk."

"That is what I thought at first as well. I know this may bother you, Oscar, but it is my experience that a man like Alfonso lacks the discipline to act according to what most people think is proper behavior."

"What do you mean?"

"Alfonso is plotting something. He is obviously going behind Domingo's back running his own operations. That is just a step away from a coup. Domingo is too pig-headed to see it."

"It's a business, Mother. There is nothing wrong with Alfonso going out on his own and creating his own destiny. That would be uncharacteristic of him, but certainly not out of the ordinary."

Lucia took a bite of her soup.

"This needs some *ali*," she said, gesturing with her spoon.

"Mom, you still aren't telling me everything."

She looked at him, her age showing in the lines on her face. Her silver hair framed her ice blue eyes and her thin lips. Her fingers sparkled with the brilliance of a half dozen flawless two karat and larger diamonds.

Her visage was grim. He could always tell when his mother had made up her mind. He would not be able to make her budge. In her mind, Alfonso was a "bad guy."

"What do you want from me?"

"You have always had a bad taste in your mouth about the business. I let you say things about your father that most mothers would never have brooked. You deserved to be turned across my knee or slapped in the mouth."

It hurt him more than it should have, these words. She had never spoken to him this way. He wanted to retaliate, to defend himself. He was right, wasn't that obvious?

"I will not apologize for being right," he said quietly.

"I don't want your apology, Oscar. I want you to listen to me carefully. Manny has gotten his hands dirty more than I care to know. It haunts me at night, and God knows that I have never given your brother the type of love he deserved or needed. Domingo, up there high on that mountain surrounded by guns and men that tell him what he wants to hear, is no angel, either. You, though, have been able to keep your distance from corruption, evil, and the ills that come from being a Villarreal."

"Not without my own scars, Lucia."

She looked at him sternly. Lucia had never been kind to self-pity.

"What you experienced was unfortunate. But, you are not alone in your pain and your baggage, son. You have to put that behind you. Besides, I am speaking of your soul, Oscar. You are unstained, your intentions pure. You have love in the center of your being. That is why you have not cursed God for your loss, did not accept the mantle that your father would have gladly put upon your shoulders when the time came.

Oscar, you are the eldest of the Villarreal sons and to you falls the burden of the family. Manny has already showed you the power of your influence. The family needs you to be strong. I will not be here always to remind you of this."

Oscar fought back the tears that wanted to flow from his eyes. Not since his wife died had anyone been as frank with him. As he stared into his mother's eyes, he realized that he was missing something. He was not asking the right question.

"Why are you telling me this now?"

Lucia looked down and cut up a large piece of yucca. She looked back up at him, her eyebrows arched dramatically.

"The proud will fall. I am afraid more for your brothers now than ever. I have seen things, Oscar. Do not be surprised when the news comes that Domingo, Manny or both have fallen. You have been warned."

Oscar sat in disbelief. His food sat in front of him, forgotten. His mother sat across from him, calmly taking lady-like bites of pork and yucca from her bowl of stew. Oscar's calm, slightly melancholy world came crashing around his ears as he processed what his mother was saying. He read between the lines: what Lucia was saying and what she was not. Oscar had a deeper appreciation for his father's colleagues who had complained jokingly for years that Lucia was the actual brains of the Villarreal organization.

"Are you warning me to be more cautious? Or, are you asking me to finally take action in place of my brothers?"

She carefully sipped some red broth from her spoon.

"You can take it however you want. I am just telling you what I feel in these bones of mine. If you want to be a hero, then that is your call. All that I know is that you are looking for something. You have been ever since Carmen died." Oscar winced. "You can keep hiding away and denying what we both know is true, or you can stand up and become a part of this family again."

"Don't use that against me," he said, seething. He felt his face flush. Was it embarrassment or anger? Both, probably. He understood immediately that his mother was manipulating him. He vowed quietly not to fall into her trap. He would not let her railroad him, either.

"Being the oldest is a heavy responsibility, Oscar. I always thought that someday you would shoulder that responsibility and be a man like your father."

"Really? My father was a murderer and a criminal. I am confused. Do you want me to be pure and upright or do you want me to be like father? Those are two different things."

"They are the same, Oscar. Your father was a good man that made my life worth living. He needed me as I needed him. Despite what you think you know about your father, he made this business into what it is through sheer will and love for you boys. Now, I need you to choose. Are you going to stand with me and help your brothers or are you going to sit in the house like a maid and nurse your pride and honor?"

"Mother, I don't know what you expect me to stand for? Murder? Human trafficking? Drugs that kill people? Government corruption? Dealing in weapons that kill? What is it you want me to do?"

He realized that he was creating a scene. Lucia glanced around the restaurant.

"Why don't you eat your food, Oscar? It's getting cold."

He seethed. He had never completely understood his mother, had never connected with her ability to be hot and cold. She was calculating and yet loving. She could tear you down just as easily as she could build you up. She was maddening to him. Now, she was challenging him. She had never done that before. He had always skated by doing what he wanted, independent and willful.

He was sulking. He was too old for that. He took a deep breath.

"I am not telling you I have decided one way or the other until I know what it is you have up your conniving sleeve, old woman."

She smiled and took another bite of pork. She chewed it slowly.

"Your father used to say something very similar. I knew you would be interested in what I have hatched."

CHAPTER TWENTY-ONE

Paul had never been to a ceremony like this. He had served at several funerals over the years. More funerals than weddings, sadly. He became even more impressed with Claire as the evening moved along. She was a natural "people-person." Children gravitated to her, older people could not keep a grin off their faces, and Manny was completely smitten.

He had to admit that her charm was elusive. She was not outwardly gregarious or flirtatious. She was not showy or gaudy. She was just genuine, compassionate, engaged with other people, and sweet. His heart sank when he realized that she reminded him so much of Emily. In some ways, he was glad that Nina was not here. She would be in tears, for sure.

He did not regret breaking down in front of her earlier this morning. It was cleansing. It allowed him to open up to Jhoana's friends, Xavier and Consuela. They were receptive to his message mostly because he had dumped the baggage of his grief at the feet of Claire earlier. His praise for her had reached new heights.

He watched her now as she carried out the ceremony with professionalism and compassion. She was genuine as she addressed those gathered there in memory to Katherine. One of the teachers from the school had been asked to translate. She worked hard to not only communicate Claire's words, but to give a sense of her deeper meaning. It was not necessary. It was evident in her voice, in her eyes, and in the tears that fell as she delivered her introduction.

"I have been honored to meet all of you today. It is refreshing to know how deeply you all have loved Katherine. It makes me wish that I had gotten to know her myself. I have officiated almost a hundred ceremonies such as this all over the world. I have never felt as welcome, never felt as much love and admiration from a community as this.

I suppose you all know who I am now. For those of you late to our party this afternoon or just now able to join us, I am Claire Eppington from the United States. My company, Cremation International, has been hired by Dr. Borche, Katherine's husband, to return her remains to the place of her birth. Yondo is Katherine's home. She was born here and she and her family wanted her to return to be here forever.

Before we perform the ceremony of releasing her remains upon the ground and the river that she called home, I would like some distinguished people to join me here. They have more to say and can speak more clearly about Katherine and about coming home. I would like Brother Paul and Jhoana Sanchez to come up."

Paul was not surprised by the sudden change in the proceedings. Manny had warned him that Claire would do this. Jhoana, though, seemed surprised. She held a white handkerchief to her bosom and looked around her as villagers urged her to make her way to the front. A path cleared. Paul approached as well, touching people's arms gently and looking in their faces with a warm smile.

He loved these people. He knew so many by name. As he passed to the front, he noted the tears, and the sad smiles. He noted Manny near the front, never taking his eyes from Claire. Paul smiled, despite himself.

He had prepared a short devotional. The village had participated earlier in recognition of Katherine's life with pictures, story-telling, tearful farewells, prayers, and laughter. Everyone had seemed upbeat. Most had already said their goodbyes and had managed to contain the grief that was related with the loss of a loved one. It had been almost three months since Katherine had finally succumbed to her illness. The grimaces of pain, the downcast eyes, the sobs, and sniffles in the audience of over three hundred villagers was sporadic. Just as many beaming faces greeted him.

Jhoana reached the small platform that had been built near the dock overlooking the Rio De Magdalena. She looked around her, seemingly at a loss. She tried to smile and it failed. She looked desperately for him, and then saw him. He grinned and nodded to her. She looked frightened. She smiled nervously and shrugged.

He climbed the stairs and took his place next to Claire and Jhoana. Claire put her arm around him and gave him a little side hug. Then she kissed Jhoana on the cheek and placed the black box she had been carrying on low table covered with a red satin sheet. Jhoana leaned over to him and whispered in his ear.

"I don't know what to say!"

"Let God lead your words. Tell them why you loved Katherine. They know, but they need to hear it from you. Paint with your words, Jhoana. You are a mother; it is what you do best."

She pulled away from him with a sad, thoughtful smile. She grasped the handkerchief as if it was a life buoy and she was drowning. Paul noted how the setting sun shone on her silver hair. It reminded him how in French, sunset is *coucher du soleil,* which literally meant that the sun goes to bed. It was appropriate for this moment. The sun was setting on Jhoana's life; the sun had set on Katherine's. He knew better than to bring that up in his devotional, but it gave him a sense of personal peace.

The crowd was quiet. They seemed almost as nervous as Jhoana. Claire took a place on the opposite end of the table, a confident smile on her face and her hands crossed. He followed her gaze and saw her staring at Manny.

Oh, they've got it bad.

He was not surprised.

Paul had seen the mutual attraction the moment he introduced Manny and Claire before going to the market. The air had fairly crackled with tension.

Jhoana steeled herself, and with a glance at Paul, she began to speak quietly.

"I am so humbled. So many people." She laughed nervously and the crowd tittered with her. "Katherine looks down with a big smile tonight. She is so happy with her Father in heaven, I am confident. We will miss her. That is a good thing. Where she is there is total joy always: no hurt, no sickness. We are here grounded in our humanity, grieving our lost ones, with regrets, guilt, illness, pain, and suffering. We are caught up in our selfish little lives." She looked at Manny, her head bowing purposefully. She swallowed hard and shifted her body painfully. She wrung her hands around the poor handkerchief, squeezing the life out of it.

She is preaching a better sermon than I ever could!

Paul watched as the puppy dog smile on Manny's face disappeared. It appeared that Jhoana was taking this opportunity to preach a personal message as well as remember her daughter.

"I am clear in my conscience. I can see that my days on earth are short, and that soon I will join Katherine and my beloved Chavez. I know that many of you have lost loved ones. I am not unique in that. As long as we are on this earth, we will experience loss. What are we to make of this plight? How are we to continue on in the face of such a cruel, evil, unfair place?"

She gestured behind her, wildly, indicating the lights of the city behind her teeming in squalor, corruption, death, and greed. Her eyes showed none of the sickness that ate at her body. Her voice was strong.

"I suggest that we go forward with our lives with as much love in our hearts for each other as we can muster. Put away our differences with each other and live as a family. Cherish the times we have together." She paused, then, scanning the audience.

Her face was sad, but it held a power. It was the power of conviction and love, of determination and the rush of realization that she could open up to these people. Something that she would say tonight would resonate with someone and change that person's life. It was the same effect she had with her paintings. Jhoana was a punch in the gut, a slap in the face, a not so gentle nudge into an icy pool of realization that you are not as important as you think you are.

"It is together that we have power. Alone, we are weak, pitiful, disgraceful, and unproductive. Together, we are strong, glorious, beautiful, and effective. We can conquer worlds together. The power of the individual is multiplied in a family. We are family.

When I think of Katherine, I think of the times we spent together, the memories we made, the things we accomplished together. Even through our struggles with health, loss, and frustration with the lot we were dealt in life, we triumphed. We were victorious because we did not quit.

So, don't quit. If you have a heart beating in your chest, thank God and embrace someone close to you. Love each other and lift each other up every day. This is how we live."

Finished, she nodded to a stunned Paul and stepped down from the podium.

The crowd gathered around was silent for two seconds after she joined them. Then, a thunderous roar of applause, shouting, and wailing erupted into the growing gloom. Jhoana stopped, her eyes big with surprise. Manny was shooting pictures with his camera, the flash sending bright rays of light echoing across the water.

Claire grabbed his elbow and leaned toward him.

"How are you going to follow that, Brother Paul? I am not a Christian, but she just gave the best sermon I ever heard."

Paul smiled at the irony.

"I agree." He nodded, smiling.

He watched as the crowd chanted "Jhoana!" and waited his turn. After a full three minutes, the crowd began to settle and soon Paul was staring into the audience trying to remember the words he had prepared.

He almost panicked and told a joke about following such a great sermon. Instead, he listened to the night sounds: birds, the water of the river rushing by, dogs barking in the distance, insects buzzing, and the low buzzing of the crowd before him.

"Most of you know me for a man of many words." Gentle laughing. "When I remember Katherine, I think of Yondo. I think of Jhoana." He gestured toward the place where she had entered the crowd. He could not see her. A smattering of applause. He waited patiently until it died down. He was a professional speaker, after all.

"Some words are most encouraging. Words we can all understand. Words that we can all agree matter. Love. Family. God. Faith. Duty. Home. Yondo was Katherine's home here on earth. It is a temporary home. As Jhoana eloquently reminded us, we are here for just a little while compared to eternity. It is our home. A place we can feel some level of security, acceptance, comfort, and a sense of belonging, community.

The same goes for our eternal home. This is the home to which Katherine has gone. She returns here to Yondo to be with us, but she was already here. Her home is here." Paul pointed to his chest.

"Her home is here." Paul pointed to his head.

"Her home is here." He pointed heavenward.

"Rest in peace, Katherine. Welcome home. We love you."

CHAPTER TWENTY-TWO

He was not the most patient man. In fact, it was sort of his calling card. His lack of patience, his ability to snap at a moment's notice was why people feared him, why they respected him.

Alfonso knew that one of those people was not Henry Fronçeau. Henry could not be impressed by anyone. He was unflappable.

If Alfonso was any other person, he might have been intimidated by Henry. First of all, he was almost seven feet tall. His height and his athleticism combined to make an imposing figure. Paired with his attitude and his reputation, Henry should have scared Alfonso more than Agent Alvarez.

Instead, he felt more comfortable. He had known Henry for years. He had worked alongside the large man for over a decade as Henry developed his status—a reputation much grander and darker than his father's.

Henry lounged on the leather sofa, an unlit cigar rolling in his fingers, the end wet. His eyes were droopy, and he looked up at Alfonso as he entered. His gaze showed that he was unimpressed. Alfonso would change that soon.

"You call me here and make me wait, *monsieur*. It is not good manners," Henry said, his speech slow, deliberate and with only a hint of malice.

"I am glad you have come. I was on the phone with an overseas contact. Someone with whom you are familiar, Mister Fronçeau. Do you remember Giovanni Tegano?"

Henry raised his eyebrows and his cigar drooped in his hand slightly "Gimpy Tegano? Why on earth would you talk to him?"

Alfonso lit his own cigar and pulled his jacket aside. He was smug and he knew it. He puffed out and blue smoke rose over his head and encircled him.

"We have a deal," he said, gesturing with his hand.

"A deal. You deal with the devil, Alfonso. You call me here to tell me of such foolishness? You waste my time, *monsieur*."

He did not appear to be as upset as his voice indicated. He stared at his cigar, rolled it in his huge fingers and put it back to his mouth. He dragged on it, unlit, and it made a sucking sound. Alfonso could not resist his disgusted grimace.

"I respect your position, Henry. Señor Tegano and I have an agreement. It is time for me to push away from the big table. I am going out on my own. With Tegano's help, of course."

Henry considered this for a moment, staring down his cigar at Alfonso. Alfonso removed his jacket and placed it on the back of a chair nearby. He left the pocket with his gun out toward him just in case.

"I remember you when you were young. You may not remember, but my father used to visit your mother from time to time."

"Father was always gone." Alfonso shrugged.

"Your father was a womanizer and a cheat. I remember you in the yard, snot nosed and crying for the papa who kicked you and left you to your uncle."

Alfonso did not like Henry's version, but he remained stoic.

"I will concede that I may have missed my father when I was young. My uncle was a rich man. Not a bad situation for a young Colombian boy considering I was raised as a bastard."

"Hmmph. Yes. I suppose you were that. But, I remember the boy who liked to play with fire." Henry leaned forward, his meaty hands out in front of him. He made a motion like he was striking a match. He held the imaginary flame up to his cigar and puffed.

"I remember the Alfonso who would take a burning stick and poke the dogs in the yard. He would scream murder if the dog chased him and the soldiers would be ordered to put the dog down. All because Alfonso didn't know that when he was playing with fire, it was he who was getting hurt, not the poor animal."

Alfonso watched Henry through a haze as he took the cigar from his mouth and put the cigar into the palm of his hand and made a hissing sound.

"I will try not to be offended by what you are suggesting, Henry."

"Be offended. And stop calling me Henry."

He had made Henry mad. *Good.* He had hoped he could get Henry to aid him in his endeavors. Knowing where he stood was helpful, even if it was not the response he had expected.

"I thought that perhaps we could work together. We have known each other for some time now, as you admit. I have come into a fortune and I am willing to share it with comrades who have talent and...loyalty."

Henry actually smiled. He scoffed.

"I do not partner with people who play with fire. I do not wish to be burned." He showed Alfonso his palm, a dark pink stain where a burn scar marked his hand. "This I received from your father when I was ten. I do not wish to repeat this."

Alfonso did not believe him.

"You can't possibly say you will not work together with me before hearing what I have to offer, will you?"

"Oh yes." He stood, his hand on the hand gun at his side.

"I am offended. You disrespect me."

"You disrespect your family. The Villarreals have treated you with respect. They have looked the other way as you play your games. You think you are so smart. Domingo knows all about you. He gives you leash, like the dog on the porch. He just waits for the day you try to leave or bite his hand. He will put you down."

Alfonso saw through a red haze over his vision. Henry was scared. Alfonso was often more brave than wise. He reached for his jacket and grabbed the collar.

"Allow me to escort you, Monsieur Fronçeau, to the exit. It seems our meeting bears no fruit. I am glad you have come at least to hear my proposal."

He slipped on the jacket and reached out his right hand to shake Henry's. Henry looked doubtful as he extended his hand and reached for his cigar with his left.

As Henry reached forward, Alfonso wrenched his pistol from his jacket pocket and pulled the trigger as he extended the barrel under Henry's right armpit. He fired twice.

Henry jolted and squeezed Alfonso's hand. Alfonso pulled Henry toward him with a quick jerk and their shoulders collided. Alfonso switched the gun to Henry's gut. He could feel the hard muscles there against the gun barrel. He pulled the trigger two more times, the shots more muffled this time. Faintly, as if in another world, he could hear the servants moving, hear his soldiers yelling orders and feet coming closer.

He felt Henry's body tense and then slump; he could smell Henry's sour sweat, his moldy cigar on his breath. He realized then that he was covered with blood and bile. Alfonso's slacks were coated with the contents of Henry's bowels; his hand was covered in blood all the way to the elbow.

He allowed Henry to fall to the table. His torso lay in a pool of blood and he breathed raggedly for a moment. Then he stopped. Alfonso stood there, no longer smug and triumphant, his mind reeling.

He was alone.

How was he to win with no allies? He could see now that he had been a fool. He had panicked and now his plans were crumbling. The pressure was immense.

Agent Alvarez was correct. Perhaps he should just defect to America, using his information to gain immunity, perhaps make a living as a consultant.

He had bitten off more than he could chew.

He saw Henry's logic and was already regretting his hasty decision to partner with the Tegano's. They were foreigners. Mafia. What did he think he was offering them? Access? Material?

He put his hands to his face, the pistol pointing to his hairline. That is how his soldiers found him, crying on the floor on his knees, a gun to his head, and splattered in the blood of Colombia's largest supplier of arms.

He had just effectively committed suicide. He was desperate now, seeing his dreams flowing through his fingers.

After ordering his men to clean up the mess and calling on his attendants to start a bath, he had his assistant procure a prostitute, took a line of coke and made a call to Carlos from the blood-frothy waters of his golden whirlpool. The American woman was his ace in the hole. Perhaps, he could get Alvarez involved and he could salvage this.

CHAPTER TWENTY-THREE

For the first hour he had felt comfortable in the crowd. After all, he was one of them. He was not from Yondo, but Carlos had grown up in a village very similar to this one. He could fit in, could blend with the others. Several people glanced at him curiously, but the scene on the dock held the crowd in sway.

Now, though, Carlos felt like an outsider. He did not know the deceased. As he watched, he did his best to push away the emotions that threatened to overtake him. He had a job to do. He could not allow the words coming from the elderly lady on stage to affect him. The crowd reacted with open mouths that followed her every word.

She was a force of nature. He found himself staring at her, watching her nervous energy that belied her age and her illness. He had overheard others talking that she would soon be having a similar ceremony.

But not tonight. She was radiant, her eyes sparkling, her neck strained from speaking loud enough to be heard at a hundred yards. A sheen of sweat sparkled on her brow, her silver hair blew gently in the wind and reflected the dying rays of the sun. Behind her, the city sat across the river in its dingy, illuminated squalor. Carlos concentrated in order to remember his mission here.

New orders had been relayed through an independent contact. Alfonso did not want Manny. He wanted the American woman.

Unfazed, Carlos had adjusted. He had called ahead to a guerilla leader stationed in the jungle nearby. Arrangements had been made for transport. Carlos needed only to perform a simple "snatch-and-grab" and deliver the package to a remote farm twenty kilometers away. Timing was the only issue.

He tracked the path of the sun, thankful that the ceremony had been held at dusk. Soon, he would have the cover of darkness, the assurance that the long, emotional day would drag these spectators to an earlier bed than usual. He glanced around the crowd. He could see only two officers, both carrying CZ 75s in shoulder holsters. He noted their motorcycle parked by Calle 50. They wore the blue uniforms of Barrancabermeja Police. The Army had mostly abandoned outlying villages like Yondo and San Luis.

Less than a decade ago, this region had been perhaps the most violent area in all of South America. Hundreds of people were killed during skirmishes between right-wing paramilitaries and left-wing guerillas, between international mercenaries and insurgents wanting control of the billions of dollars that the oil industry represented. The working class was hit hardest. The union fractured during the five years that the region was under military control, a corrupt local government, and personal attacks by guerillas. These attacks occurred in areas where liberal outcries, humanitarian endeavors, or plain outrage was rewarded with small-scale massacres in the working class barrios of Barrancabermeja.

Carlos had lost friends, family, and fellow workers in that violence. Thousands of people had been displaced—most forcefully. They had left, had found new lives in the central parts of Colombia, where international efforts to suppress the violence had found the quickest acceptance.

Here in the eastern edges of the Santander Department beneath the apparent calm, was uneasiness. No public violence had occurred recently, but an attitude of neoliberalism and the suppression of the unemployed who had been connected with liberal parties in the past decade created a division among the people that could not be reconciled with class, race, or religion.

It did not surprise him that even the mayor of Yondo had shown up for this ceremony. It did, however, seem strange that only two law enforcement personnel were present. It was for the better. They would leave soon after the ceremony dispersed. This area along the river had rarely seen this many people.

Dust rose around them, swirling in the half light of the departing sun and the gas-powered lamps that had been set up along the perimeter. The small docks jutting out into the river were in bad shape, the rusty boats tied to their moors a testament to the poverty here.

All around him, women in bright blue skirts cradled children, wiping sweat from their brows. Men squatted on the ground, or wrapped arms around their wives, large pools of wetness staining their white button-up dress shirts. Tears etched the faces of several of the older ones. He suppressed a yawn. He supposed it was restlessness, perhaps the lack of sleep.

He was almost done. He anticipated getting a long rest. Exhaustion ate at his attention and chipped away at his resolve.

He heard the mother of the deceased pause and he looked up. He noticed Manny along the edge of the platform they had built for this occasion. He had a camera in one hand, a bag draped across his shoulder. Carlos knew he should be concerned, but he was disappointed that he would not have a chance to test his abilities against Manny. He knew he would probably lose, but in some ways, that would come as a relief to Carlos. He was tired of this life. He was tired of the feeling as if his life was a series of concessions made for the dead or the dying, the corrupt and the innocent.

He studied the American woman. She was tall and blonde and dressed in a light dress that looked as though it was purchased locally. She had a confident smile and she touched the black box on the low table beside her as if it was something that gave her comfort. He supposed Alfonso wanted to keep Manny occupied finding this woman. It made some sense, but it seemed a waste to Alfonso. Why keep your most capable enemy at arm's length when you could pull him near and kill him if you must?

So far on this mission he had not seen any reason for his involvement. Even the abduction could have been carried out by a small team of insurgents for half of his fee. If this alone brought any suspicion to his mind, he pushed it away. He did not need the distraction of doubt or analyzing the motives of his employer. These sorts of things were what got a man killed.

Circular logic always led back to the fact that you could not trust anyone—not even yourself. Once you started on the road to discover the meaning of these things, you guessed wrong, exposed yourself, got caught up in self-doubt, and distracted yourself from your goal.

The last thing Carlos wanted was a surprise. He had trained himself to be one of the best in the business and charged accordingly. He did not make it to the ranks of the elite by being sloppy. That was why he noticed that Manny's bag was still heavy, even though he had his equipment removed from it. He guessed that Manny had taken precautions, possibly falling back on his old habits and fears.

Carlos remembered the stories of his daring rescue of Domingo. Many of them were blown out of proportion, but the one thing that stuck out to Carlos was that four men had gone on that rescue, entering into an army of Venezuelan militia and hired mercenaries and only Manny and Domingo had returned. That was enough to convince Carlos that Manny was someone to be feared and respected.

It was this respect that enabled Carlos to see clearly that Manny would not brook the kidnapping of this woman without getting involved personally in her return. Carlos smiled bitterly. Perhaps then he could have the opportunity to test his mettle. Carlos wanted to avoid contact until he delivered the package, but once the chase ensued, Carlos was hoping his expertise would be called upon to dissuade pursuit.

The minister stepped forward. Carlos had never liked the man. He spread dissension like wildfire. Where ever he went, people would rebel, people would stand up for their rights. This is why people died. They should just stop fighting the inevitable.

His eyes were cold as he took in the figure of Paul upon the hand built structure, the gloom closing in around him. As far as Carlos was concerned, this man was just as responsible for the death of hundreds of farmers, women, children, and politicians as Carlos was. His hands were just as bloody. The irony was that this "man of God" thought that he was spreading peace and love.

All that came of his preaching, the crop from the seed that he was sowing, was that people died. Surely, they could all see that. Some people understood and resisted. They continued to languish in their cathedrals, practicing their blind religion as their forefathers had: the bare minimum. But, Paul's disciples still multiplied, like vermin.

Just over in Barrancabermeja, hundreds of workers who had formerly been involved in the union for *Refinera Ecopetrol* were now forming churches and organizations that outwardly opposed the local government, the military influence and the political discrimination in the workforce. All it would get them was death, Carlos was sure of it.

He knew how the men in charge thought. He had witnessed their greed, corruption, blood lust, and violence. These men and women who wanted equality, who wanted to live life on their terms, were doomed. Until they stooped to the means and methods of their oppressors, they would get nothing but sorrow. The paramilitary groups on both sides understood this. Although the conservatives denounced violence, they still carried guns, still killed innocent people in their crossfire. This is what Carlos thought Hell would be like.

The minister was speaking of "home" now.

What a joke.

These people were proud and obstinate. Why else would they remain here in the face of squalor, death, and torture? They called this home.

Now this "man of God" was telling them that their unhealthy infatuation with this so-called home was a good thing. Carlos almost could not control his rage. He wanted to punish these people, wanted to hit them over the head with reality.

He was desperate for the ceremony to end so that he could get out of here.

The people around him seemed to close in, stifling him. He could not stand the smell of their complacency, their hysteria, and their grief. With all the death that had been administered here, they were mourning over someone who had done the smart thing and had gotten out. She had not died from violence, she had died naturally. That was something that Carlos knew would never happen for him. He wondered briefly what that would be like.

The American woman came forward as Paul finished his sermon. She carefully opened the black box and extracted a chrome cylinder. The mother was summoned to the platform and she and the minister took the chrome cylinder. They walked together to the end of the platform near the river.

Carlos had never seen a ceremony like this. He liked the idea of being returned to the earth. He approved of their methods.

He watched, his breath coming in shallow gasps. He had no idea what to expect. He could feel his heart beat harder and wondered why he was reacting like this.

A tear fell and he became angry at himself. It was impotent anger, because the tears continued to fall and he could feel himself losing control. A hand rested on his shoulder. An elderly woman was staring at him.

"It's alright. She's going home, now," she said. Carlos could see her missing teeth, could see the genuine concern on her face. He nodded and turned back to the spectacle on the rickety dock.

Paul was saying some words. They were lost in the gentle breeze and the rush of the Magdalena. Carlos watched, caught up in emotions he could not understand. He berated himself and struggled to concentrate on his duties. Duties he did not want to carry out, a life he no longer wanted, a career path that had led him to these dirty banks of a brown river in the shadow of Hell.

CHAPTER TWENTY-FOUR

Claire watched as Jhoana and Paul held the canister aloft. The breeze was perfect, the lighting perfect. The gray and white crystals of Katherine's remains glittered in the gas lights and the yellow glow of the lights illuminating the oil refineries north of them.

"From dust we were created, to dust we return. We give our dear Katherine to our maker, our Father in Heaven. We have faith he will hold her close in his care. He will care for her even better than we did. Our dear Katherine is returning home," Paul intoned. Jhoana sobbed.

Claire was sure that Paul had prepared more to say, but she could hear his voice choke and he cut his message short. A calm silence overtook them. She could hear the shuffle of Manny's feet behind her as he positioned for a better shot. Several video cameras had been set up to record the event.

One camera she could see out of the corner of her eye, its light shining in the gloom, creating swirls of color across her peripheral vision. Another camera had been installed in the tree above them, looking out toward the crowds over the head of the speakers. Paul had surmised that Dr. Borche would be pleased to see the audience's reactions and more clearly hear the speaker's words. The third camera was being operated by Eduard, a young man who Katherine had babysat as a child.

Manny was taking shots with two cameras: one digital, one analog. She could feel him behind them, could sense his eyes on her back. She liked the feeling.

She was not sure where this was heading, but she knew every time Manny was present, she had a hard time not staring at him, hanging on his every word and hoping like a teenage girl that he would return her stare or say her name.

His presence had even repressed some of her fears of death. This ceremony she had performed over a hundred times and she invariably went home shaking and in tears. She did not feel that way now. She was confident, she was comforted. Partly, she understood, it was due to the affection she felt in the community for this woman and the confidence that they displayed that she was going home.

Home. That was a concept that eluded her. She loved her father, but his emotional distance was difficult to penetrate. She found it hard to feel homesick.

She noted the juxtaposition of Paul's serenity and the turmoil within him. He stared at the ashes still pouring out toward the river. His eyes were illuminated. She could see the pools of tears there and watched as he swallowed hard. He noticed her watching him and smiled sadly.

"Good job," she said.

"It's what I do."

Paul handed her the empty canister with a solemn look. She put the lid back on the cylinder and they turned together toward the crowd. Jhoana stepped down from the platform with Paul's help. The crowd erupted in applause.

Manny smiled at her and took a quick photo. She loved the way his shoulders rippled under his shirt as he brought the camera up. She was not sure of the look on her face just then, but tried hard to smile.

"Thank you all for coming to the ceremony. It has been a long, emotional day. Please pray for the family and have a good night everyone," Paul said.

He was still on the platform moments later, his hands at his side, his face drawn, and the color high on his cheeks. She had said her goodbyes to her new friends and had gathered her things to take back to Jhoana's where she was to be spending the night. She looked up at Paul, curious.

Manny was beside her.

"Come. Let him have some time to himself," he said, drawing her away gently. He had both of his bags over his shoulders and carried two heavy lengths of electrical cord in his hand. He smelled faintly of sweat and the river.

She responded by taking his arm and removing one of the bags.

"Here. Let me help," she said.

"Thanks."

She glanced back at Paul, still standing motionless on the stage as the gas lamps were turned off with a loud snap. People continued to mill around, gathered in small groups, walking slowly back toward the village.

"Why is he so sad?"

"Emily died near here."

"Oh."

"Actually, it was over in the city. She was killed in crossfire between a paramilitary unit and the FARC."

"That is tragic. I suppose if Nina was here, she could console him." He shook his head sadly.

"Nah. No one can console him but God. He is praying. But, he does miss Nina. It would have been good for him if she were here. It just would not have been good for Nina. She has a hard time keeping her concerns to herself. She would be over in the city in the morning stirring up trouble among the workers before breakfast was over."

"Sounds dangerous."

"That is Nina for you. She is passionate and loving, but she has a hard side to her that does not tolerate the persecution of the innocent or the exploitation of children. She is a fiery one, Nina. It is why Paul and

154

most of Colombia loves her so much. She is a rock star among the humanitarian groups. She is a force that is for sure."

"I can see some of that in Paul, too."

"He feeds off of her: that is true. Paul is foremost a man of peace, a man after God's own heart. That is why he has remained in Colombia. For people like me."

Claire could recognize the emotion welling up in Manny and it touched her. She had not experienced this much genuine love in one place in all her life. It was strange how raw and deep it was.

She was astounded at the irony. Here, where there was death, corruption, and such widespread hatred, there was also some of the most powerful love she had every witnessed.

Perhaps that was why her feelings for Paul had escalated as quickly as they had. She had never really gravitated toward someone in a forty eight hour period like this before. It was exciting and scary at the same time.

"I am glad I came."

"Me too."

"Honestly, I have to say that I have never had an assignment like this before."

"It makes me happy to hear you say that," he said. His voice was husky with emotion. She glanced over at him. He had his head down, the long locks of his dark hair hanging forward, his olive skin glistening in the gloom.

They walked a little further in silence.

"Can I ask you something?" She blurted this out. She did not know why. She was not even sure what she was going to ask.

But you do know, silly!

"Sure." He did not look up, just kept trudging along the dirt road back toward Jhoana's.

"Why don't the women in Bogotá speak to you?"

He laughed, a sort of surprised grunt. She loved the sight of his teeth glimmering in the dark. His smile was genuine and remarkable. She was smitten.

"Well. That might be more truth than I am willing to reveal at this moment. Maybe a story for another time."

She nodded, understanding.

"I...well, I just noticed that the children think of you as a hero or something, but the women avoid you."

He never looked at her, but his smile disappeared.

"You are very observing, Claire. You are not wrong." She did not want to say anything more. She could see he was brooding. It was not fair. Claire wanted to know this man better and she only had another twenty four hours before she left. She felt some desperation. She silently cursed herself. She was acting like a junior high crush.

"I can understand that you don't want to talk about it." She scuffed her feet and adjusted the camera bag.

His silence was his answer. Men could be so closed off. It was always ironic to her that men could open up and be such fools at times, but when asked to tap into deeper emotions than humor, sex, careers, sports, or cars, and they clammed up.

The sounds of insects enveloped them. The hum of the generators faded and the men working to shut them down came to them echoing against the waters of the river. One of them was addressing Paul. She glanced back in time to watch him climb down slowly.

"You think he will be alright?" He finally looked at her again. He seemed relieved to change the subject.

"Paul? Sure. He just needs to get back to Bogotá. This place depresses him," he said.

"He needs time alone right now," Manny continued. "He will be a basket case for a while. He is exhausted physically and emotionally. The trip takes a lot out of him."

"I see." The lights of the houses illumined the road before them. Villagers scuffled between the trees, going through fences, and around shops to get home.

Claire wanted to say something else. She knew her time was short and if she wanted to make a connection with this man, she needed to be assertive. She was always too quiet around men and she understood that was part of the reason she was still alone.

"You still play soccer?"

Stupid!

"What? Uh. Yeah. I actually coach some now. Some of my old buddies still get together for a game now and then, but my legs aren't the same."

Silence again. She could ask him about coaching. He knew she was clueless about soccer. That would be a short answer, a patronizing answer. She was terrible at small talk. She was terrible with men.

"Look. I was thinking. You want to go have a drink or something?"

He gave her a sideways grin.

"Are you asking me out, Claire?"

She shrugged.

"Call it what you want. I just thought we could grab a drink before we head off. I won't see you again after tomorrow."

There it was: the truth. It was out there, floating in the humid night air between them. She was two thousand miles from home and on some of the most violent soil she had ever stood upon and she was coming on to what was in essence a stranger.

Manny smirked and nodded.

"I suppose you are right. I don't think any place here is open, though. We would have to go into Barrancabermeja."

She did her best not to appear disappointed. He didn't exactly turn her down, after all. She shrugged, noncommittally.

"I understand. Maybe I will be back this way sometime. We could get one then," she lied.

He put his hands behind his back and bowed his head.

"I tell you what. Why don't we stop by Jhoana's? She doesn't drink but she has some *aquadiente* in her cupboard for guests. I can mix some together and make a very sweet *canelazo*. There is a clearing nearby we can sit in peace and talk, if you like."

She blushed. She liked Jhoana. Claire began to think of the circumstances of the public pursuit of Manny. In the end, she decided that she had to take chances if she wanted to get what she wanted. Right now she wanted as much time with this man as she could get. All else was immaterial.

She could feel her skin creep in anticipation. She blinked slowly and took a deep breath. The air was as thick as soup and heavy with the scents of the surrounding fields and trees.

"What is *aquadiente,* anyway?" She put a teasing smile on her face. "You aren't trying to get me drunk or anything, right?"

He smiled back.

"Furthest thing from my mind. You will want to take it easy on the *canelezo*, though. It tastes so sweet with the lemon and cinnamon, you don't really realize how fast the alcohol gets to you. Drink it slow and in small amounts. I will make a small batch and see what you think."

He let her slip her arm in his as they walked on. She liked the feel of his hips swaying against hers, the warmth of his arms and the feel of his skin. She noticed scars along his forearm and at his bicep. She wanted to touch them, to ask him in a whisper how he got those scars.

At Jhoana's they came in giggling. Jhoana sat in a chair at the bar, a housecoat on and a tall, older gentleman standing in the bright light of the kitchen.

"Oh. Hello, you two. I knew you would arrive together. Meet Jhon Jairo Ruiz. He is a special friend."

"Hello."

Jhon waved, his dark wrinkled skin showed years of hard work in the sun. His smile was warm.

"Hello," he said, his mouth full of gleaming white teeth.

"We were just going to get something to drink and head out to the park. We will leave you two to visit."

Jhoana smiled brightly and took a sip of her coffee. She nodded.

"I will be in bed by the time you get back. Jhon was just leaving."

Jhoana got down from the chair delicately and practically floated across the floor on bare feet. She embraced Manny and whispered in his ear. It made him smile. Claire loved her for that.

The next hour they spent under a street lamp on a bench, sipping the sweet distillation of Manny's favorite drink and visiting. They never got around to the scars or the reasons for the women in Bogotá avoiding him, but Claire still learned enough about him to know that she wanted to learn more.

The drink ran out, and with her head reeling a little from the *canelezo* and from the effects of too much Manny, too little sleep and too little time, they made their way back to the house. They stood in the hall, whispering to each other. She could tell he did not want to go. She did not either, but reality was, she needed to sleep and to dream on these things.

He held her hands in his and traced her knuckles with his fingers. His hands were strong, but he was gentle. He looked at her deeply and sighed.

"I really do want to open up to you and tell you everything. Claire, you make me want to confess more than any priest ever could."

She scoffed.

"Glad to know I bring out repentance in you. Paul would be proud of me."

She expected Manny to grin. He didn't.

"It's not just that. I have been alone for so long, it is hard for me to open up to anyone but Paul. I can't even talk to my mother or brothers. I know that sounds strange. I just met you. I hardly know you."

He pressed her hands together. She felt herself leaning toward him, her face turning up to meet his.

She closed her eyes. Trusting he would respond, she parted her lips, waiting for him to kiss her.

He did not disappoint. Their lips met briefly and she felt the warmth and sweetness of the *canelezo* on her mouth and tongue.

He pulled her closer and she felt his body shiver for a second. She smiled and let him go.

"I know," she said.

He pulled her close. She could feel the muscles of his chest and she buried her head there, smelling his skin.

"I don't want you to go yet. Could you stay longer?" Manny whispered. She could feel his breath hot on the nape of her neck.

She wanted the same thing. Reality was, she had to be back. Her next assignment was the following week. She had a client debriefing and her visa was time and job sensitive. Her job was finished. It was time to go home. As much as it pained her, she knew it.

"Yes. I will make some calls tomorrow," she said, her breath moving the fabric of his shirt. She looked up at him again, hoping to look confident. All she could think of was how she did not want this to end.

"That makes me feel better," he said. "I can go to sleep now."

"Me too." He grabbed her hands again and brought them to his lips.

"It is odd to say this on a day like to today, but I enjoyed myself more than I have in years," Claire said.

"I had an incredible time as well. This is a special place."

"Special people. Like you," Claire replied. She searched his eyes.

She swooned a little, then. The florescent lights from the kitchen made a halo effect in his dark hair. His lips were pursed lightly. She wanted to kiss him again. And more.

Ok, now you are drunk on Manny!

"Thank you, Manny. You are so kind." Steeling herself, she kissed his cheek quickly and released his hands. She was glad for the brief look of disappointment that flittered across his face.

"I suppose we should get some sleep. We have a long trip back tomorrow."

"Yes. I will make the calls once we get back to Bogotá. I think I can extend my time by a week. No promises."

"No promises," he repeated. He smiled mischievously.

She laughed nervously.

"I think I am a little drunk. That doesn't explain this, though," she said, rotating her hands in front of her, palms down. "You understand, right?"

He nodded.

"Definitely. Sometimes the best things are unexpected."

She agreed. She liked the way his eyes lingered on her. They held her captive.

"We both need some sleep," she said, willing herself to break his hypnotic trance.

"I could just stand here and watch you all night." She would let him.

"We can't. We are adults. Come on." She pushed him down the hall.

"Go to bed, you two. This old woman needs her beauty sleep," Jhoana crowed from the attached bedroom.

Manny grinned, his smile lighting up the dark hallway. As she laughed and tried to push him again, he darted downward and kissed her once more.

It caught her off guard and their teeth clacked together. He reached behind her head and kissed her with a different tactic: gentler and more passionately. And then his mouth departed and she was left standing in the hall with her eyes closed and her lips parted.

She recognized the heady feeling of dizziness. It was a powerful mixture of alcohol, passion, and something deeper. She reveled in its glow for a moment, a sly smile slowly wending its way across her face. She tucked her chin to her chest and took a deep breath.

When she opened her eyes, she caught a glimpse of Manny quietly shutting the door to his room.

She just shook her head.

The weariness of the day descended upon her. She entered the little room adjacent to Manny's and listened to his furtive movements as he prepared for bed. She lay on the bed with her clothes on watching the ceiling fan and wondering if she could ever fall asleep. She was still wondering moments later as she drifted off to the sounds of Manny's soft snoring next door.

CHAPTER TWENTY-FIVE

Carlos watched them from behind a bush. He could have easily removed her now by ambushing them, but he did not like to take chances like that. He knew where they were heading. If they did not end up in bed together, this was going to be easier than he had hoped

In the meantime, he decided to head back to the house and get prepared there. He had already entered through the courtyard and watched the old man leave, the mother of the deceased had cried as he held her.

Old people were strange, Carlos thought.

She had retired to bed after his shadow had rounded the bend at the end of the neighborhood.

Even in the dark he could tell the woman had some talent at painting. The art on the walls there was powerful enough to speak even to his hard heart. It reminded him of his sister.

Just a few more hours and he could return, perhaps.

He knew better, though. He was a fool if he thought he could just walk away and have a normal life. They would never let him alone long enough to enjoy it anyway. He decided that running would be his best bet. He knew people who could forge passports. He knew English well enough to communicate; he could read and write. Maybe he could live in England, or hole up in the Caribbean. He had friends there, friends who thought he still worked at an oil refinery.

He trudged back down the road, not bothering to hide in the shadows. He was just another villager stumbling home after a long, emotional day. Carlos made his way around the back of the house and waited in the bushes surrounding the statue in the courtyard.

About a half hour later, he was almost dozing when he heard the front door creak, and two people entered the home, closing the door behind them. He listened to their footsteps, their furtive movements, and their hushed conversation. He could not make out what they were saying, but he could guess. He did not hear any passionate moans or bodice ripping. He did not expect that with the old woman in the house.

He heard the old woman shout something about sleep and then two doors closing. Carlos prepared himself. He put on the black long sleeved shirt made from stretchy cotton and the black ACU tactical pants with the foam inserts already sewn in. He extracted two sets of plastic "flexi cuffs" from his gear and threw the bag over his back.

He decided to wait twenty minutes before entering. He pushed it to thirty just in case. Carlos was usually more cautious, but he wanted to get this job finished.

He moved stealthily inside the patio door. He had oiled it earlier to ensure that it worked quietly. The hall was dark, but his eyes were adjusted. A faint light came from the kitchen and living room beyond. The only questions were: which room, and was she alone? He had heard two doors, so his guess was she was alone.

He listened at the first door on the right. Light breathing emitted a deep tenor to the inhale. Probably just Manny sleeping off the effects of the alcohol he had consumed. Carlos knew Manny rarely drank. He was thankful that Manny had finally let his hair down. It made his job easier.

Easy money, as his friends in the Irish Special Forces had liked to say.

He crept over to the next door and entered. He allowed the door to remain open as he let his eyes adjust to the darker gloom of the little room. A day bed was against the wall, the small form of the woman lying across it. He had a moment of panic as he realized that she was lying across the bed in her clothes. Then, he saw her chest rise slowly. This was almost too easy. She was out cold. He may not even need the restraints.

No sense getting too cocky.

He retrieved the bottle and the cloth and applied them to her nose and mouth gently. Because of the angle of the bed and how the American woman was laying, he struggled to keep his body arched over her so that they would not touch. It was crucial that this part was done without a struggle.

She arched her back for a second and tried to moan, caught between a dream and what was actually happening to her. She relaxed suddenly and slumped back to the bed, her head turning to one side and her mouth hanging slack as he removed the cloth.

She was beautiful. Not in the movie star type way, but she had a firm jaw line, a perfect nose and her mouth was delicate with a cleft in the center of her upper lip. He could certainly see why Manny found her attractive.

Still, it was strange that after all these years, Manny was finally smitten…by an American stranger. Manny had been pursued by some of the most attractive and available women in Colombia. He had never shown an interest.

Of course, that was just fuel for the fire and made them want him even more.

He waited for her breathing to return to normal and then grabbed one wrist gently and brought it around in front of her body. He checked the door with a glance and then slipped the flexi cuff over her hand and brought the other wrist across and repeated the process. He wanted her hands in front so he could see them.

Most abductors seemed to think the risk was decreased by putting their hands behind their back. When they needed the prisoner to do something for themselves like climb a ladder, get down behind cover during a fire fight, or raise their hands over their heads, the abductor found they were forced to get within reach of the prisoner to help them.

Besides, if they wanted to escape, the oldest trick in the book was to get out of the cuffs behind their backs; pretend they were still secured and then plan an ambush. With their hands in front, Carlos could see exactly what was going on, lead them by the hands, and give them the ability to defend themselves when he needed them to.

Once he had her secured, he grabbed her legs and pulled her forward until only her torso was on the bed. He bent over and draped her hands over his back and took the weight of her torso over his shoulder. With a little jump, he adjusted her weight. She never stirred. *Good*, he thought. He hoped the drugs did not react with the alcohol too much.

He turned carefully, to avoid tripping over anything. He saw her bag near the bathroom door. He stooped down and grabbed it. He left her suitcase. She would not need it. Most of her personal things should be in the small satchel he had the presence of mind to obtain before he left. Sometimes, demands for personal items could help when trying to handle the prisoner. They also came in handy in the blackmail process.

Of course, he was not sure what Alfonso had in mind for this young woman. As far as he knew, Alfonso needed another prostitute. *And another hole in his head.*

Maybe he was looking for some more funds, or a way to blackmail Manny. Either would be plausible. Carlos did not care. The motto was simple: *a job is a job*. Carlos did not care how often Alfonso offered him a position in his "organization," he would never be more than a work-for-hire merc. What had kept him alive so far was that he had no allegiances.

As he made his way toward the door, he managed to keep the woman's feet from hitting the frame by hooking the handle of the satchel through her ankles and pulling her legs closer. Again, she did not stir, even though her body was contorted. He could feel her try to shift. He made his way into the faintly illuminated hallway, turned and closed the door quietly. His biggest fear was the old lady. He kept imagining that he would turn around and there she would be.

As he had drifted off earlier in the courtyard, he had a nightmare that the woman in the painting with the dog had stepped out of the painting and set the little dog after him, the yapping little mutt waking the whole neighborhood before he could escape. He pushed these fears to the back of his mind and tried to control his breathing. She was not heavy, but she was tall and her weight was spread out, making the transport difficult.

He padded across the threshold and down into the room with the paintings and remembered that he had closed the patio door. He had to set the woman down. He did not want to do that, so he struggled with the latch on the sliding door and closed his eyes as he pulled it across his body, hoping that the oil would do its work, and hoping that he did not drop the woman.

He managed and he was in the courtyard. He propped the woman against the statue, her bare feet squashing the plants below.

Bare feet. She would need shoes.

Women needed shoes!

How would she run when he needed her to? She would complain. The incessant complaints of a prisoner were enough to wear a kidnapper down. He needed to make sure she had only one complaint: she was held captive.

She would be fed. She would be allowed to sleep comfortably. She would have her personal things: soap, makeup, feminine products, freaking diary, and a pen. AND SHOES!

He sighed deeply, cursing his stupidity. His comrades would laugh their backsides off. This would be a funny story to tell around the bar after a few beers. He had forgotten the shoes.

He stomped his foot, got his temper under control and reached into his bag on his back and pulled out his Chinese Type 64 handgun. It had an integrated silencer and fired 7.65 mm, specially made, ball-type ammunition. He only owned one magazine of ammo, but that would be all he needed if he could find her shoes without waking anyone.

He checked her one last time, slumped against the statue. Her head was tilted. Satisfied, he stepped back in the patio door, remembering to leave it open and went back to retrieve the stupid shoes. No one woke and he found three pairs of shoes.

Women, he thought.

When he returned, he noted that the dew was beginning to cover the yard. He would leave marks across the grass, an easy trail to follow. He looked for a solution. He was not in a hurry. If he hurried, he would make a mistake. Finally, he decided that the only way to avoid leaving an obvious trail was to go back through the house and out the front door.

He sighed. Nothing was ever easy. He chastised himself for being fooled into believing that all was going better than planned. He was confident that he could make it through the house unscathed. The light snoring was almost in stereo when he had returned for the shoes. He tucked them into the American's satchel, one sandal poking out of the zippered top. He put her over his shoulder again, grunting. He was getting tired. He could feel it in his legs.

Just get it over with, Carlos, he encouraged himself.

Soon, he was in the hall, trying not to breathe hard, trying to walk on padded feet. He was going slowly, half expecting a door to open and someone poke their head out. Suddenly, he remembered the minister. Where was he? He had followed these two back to the house and Paul had still been at the docks.

Was he not staying here tonight? The others had not been concerned. He tried to put it from his mind. If the others had not worried about him perhaps that meant that they knew he was elsewhere. Maybe he had stayed with the boat. It was in dock not far from where the ceremony was held.

He padded through the living room, fighting the urge to turn and make sure he was not being followed. His nerves were frayed, his head was pounding and his knees hurt from crouching with all the extra weight. Still, his captive never moved, never groaned, and never woke. He opened the front door, remembering the noise it had made when the couple had entered. He eased it open, shifted his burden through, turned, and shut it with as much care as he could muster.

He turned and started to leave, a sense of relief that a loose gravel path led to the road. He could avoid leaving an obvious trail. He started to smile.

That was when he missed the step down and tumbled onto the gravel, dumping his load over his head as his knee gave out. He heard a pop and watched in horror as the American woman toppled completely off his shoulder. Her head hit first, then her bottom. She made no sound, but he yelped as he landed to her left, skinning his knee and lodging small gravel in his palms. The pain in his knee was the worst.

He closed his eyes and tried to concentrate. He saw flashes of red and black behind his eyelids.

Irrationally, he was embarrassed. He hoped in the back of his mind that no one had seen him. That was his first indication that perhaps he was not as mentally balanced as he should be. He chalked it up to being tired. He got to his knees and tried to stand.

He had pulled something in his right knee, but he could bear through the pain. Remarkably, the American woman lay on the grass, unmoving. He kneeled down, wincing at the pain. He gritted his teeth and reached for her carotid artery. A strong, slow pulse.

Good.

He brushed the gravel out of her hair and checked the wound at the top of her head. It would bruise, but he was sure she had not suffered a concussion. He cursed his luck. He was fortunate that he had another five hours before dawn. He lifted her up again, fighting the urge to just drag her. He picked up the satchel and trudged off into the waning night to find his vehicle parked about a kilometer away.

No one stopped him. He saw three stray dogs, got his wits scared out of him by a cat jumping from a metal trash can, fell once more and ripped a fingernail completely off of his right index finger. He made it, panting, sweating profusely, and cursing himself for not bringing a wagon or dolly.

He threw her in the back seat of his Jeep, checked his watch, and sat in the front seat smoking his last cigarette. It calmed him some.

He sat there, smoke rising around his head as he managed his breathing and heart rate. He had some harrowing experiences in his life, but never one like this. He understood that on some levels, what had just transpired was comical.

He chuckled softly at that and tapped the ashes off of his cigarette.

He tried to deconstruct the evening, fighting the feeling that he had forgotten something. He could not remember. He was so tired. Even the nicotine barely touched his exhaustion.

He glanced in the back seat at his captive. Her form lying there reminded him of his sister. He wondered if it was his sister who had been abducted, how would he react? He thought back to the funeral earlier. He knew that his emotional breakdown could be attributed to his fear of losing his sister. However, he thought that the best explanation was that he envied the deceased. He wanted to escape.

Despite his longing for the release that death offered, Carlos found that the best he could muster was a pathetic attempt at putting himself in as much danger as possible. Of course, if he continued to sabotage his assignments like this for much longer, he might get his wish sooner than later.

Carlos put the cigarette out on the dash and stared at the plumes of flame coming from across the river. He sighed.

After a few more minutes, he started up the engine and motored out of Yondo for the last time.

CHAPTER TWENTY-SIX

"I am not afraid of Alfonso," Domingo insisted.

Maria stared at him. Her eyes bored into him, searching for a weakness. She made him uncomfortable. She appeared to know something he did not. He chalked that up to her education. He usually was not intimidated by having more talented people around him. It was one way to true power.

"I am sure you are not, Domingo. But, Henry was a friend as well as a colleague. Perhaps this is more than a threat. Maybe it is a warning." Maria could be so cryptic, sometimes.

"About Manny? Manny can take care of himself."

"A warning regarding you, Domingo," she said, her head tipping forward. "Henry was capable of taking care of himself and look where that got him. I'm recommending very strongly that you call in some of your highly trained muscle and protect yourself."

Domingo sighed deeply and turned from her. Her advice was not unreasonable, but he had to be careful not to send the wrong message.

"Henry had a partner in his organization that can carry on his duties, does he not?"

He heard her hesitation and understood.

"Of course. But, as you can imagine, Monsieur Durand is being very cautious. He has disappeared and is not answering my correspondence. You cannot blame him."

"No. I do not." She managed a comforting smile.

Domingo sat down on his leather couch. Maria continued to stand near the glass table that dominated the room.

"What am I to do with Blanca? She will not feel comfortable here if there is to be any violence."

"I have already arranged for Blanca to travel to Morocco. She has reservations there and money transferred for her to shop and stay for a week. She was grateful. She hasn't been to Morocco in two years. She is looking forward to returning."

Domingo looked again at this capable, stunning, and highly intelligent woman. He barely knew her, he realized.

"You are so considerate."

"Don't thank me. She only agreed to go because she has a lover there."

"Oh." He was surprised. Stunned, actually.

Maria did not appear sympathetic at all.

"I thought that would be better than having her here at this time. Because of the situation there, she was more than eager to comply with my arrangement."

"I see." He wanted to be jealous. He just could not muster it.

"The good news is that you don't have to worry about her health."

"Of course," he said, nervous. He knew he should be upset now. He looked down at the high shine on his leather shoes, the perfect crease in his gabardine slacks, and the tight, expensive weave of the rug beneath his feet.

Domingo wondered why he was devoid of emotion. He looked up again at Maria. She waited.

"I am glad to see you have accepted this with such calmness," she stated. He huffed.

"I am more concerned about my life. About Manny's. Mom's." Again, he was struck by how odd it was that he felt little other than fear for himself. "Oscar. God, I never even thought of Oscar being involved before today. Alfonso is considering taking this away from us, isn't he?"

She said nothing for a moment.

"It appears so. The question isn't 'why?' but rather 'how?' And, I think we should be more concerned about what our response will be."

"Yes. It is a wonder that I have not been visited by our friends from AFEUR."

"The Major General's special forces for anti-terrorism called this morning with inquiries into Henry's whereabouts. His passports had conflicting information. We claimed no knowledge of his whereabouts. No links to arms or evidence of his presence exist here. They were merely gathering intel blindly."

"You are very thorough."

"It is why you pay me, is it not?" She smiled, her eyes showing no mirth, no pride.

"Who are you?"

She did not answer. He could sense that she wanted to say something. His suspicions mounted.

Is this why Manny had kept his distance? It certainly was not because she was unattractive.

"I am simply a servant of the Villarreals, sir," she said carefully. "Now, if you will excuse me, I must make some calls to get your security force together."

He nodded, dismissively. He leaned back in the couch and picked up a magazine. He wanted to appear unfazed.

"Do what you must, Maria." She bowed politely and exited the room without another word. Domingo listened to her heels tapping purposefully on the tile floor as she distanced herself from his presence.

"If that is really your name," he mumbled to himself.

He wanted to believe that Maria was what she seemed, but something about her set alarms off in his head. He had not gained his position without being cautious. Since Manny left, he found himself trusting no one.

Domingo tried to apply this caution to Alfonso and his reckless murder of Henry. If reports were to be believed, Alfonso had performed the assassination himself. Surely, he did not think it was wise to try the same with the Villarreals.

No matter what he did, he could not get Maria out of his mind. It bothered him more than Alfonso, more than his cheating wife, more than the danger to his family. Domingo's instincts told him that Maria was more than anyone knew. Perhaps she was the key to his troubles. Not that she was to blame, but the answer he needed.

What more could he ask from her than what she was already doing? The secret to the Villarreal organization was that it ran smoothly without Domingo micromanaging it. Deliveries were made, labs moved, crops abandoned, and payments counted without his approving or declining every action. Maria was just another cog in that wheel.

Even though Maria was a part of the machinations that was the Villarreal cartel, Domingo could not underestimate her. He had to discover if she were an asset or a threat. Or, as he suspected, she was somewhere in between, serving a third party.

In many ways, she fulfilled Manny's old position. Maybe he had underestimated Manny's importance.

Domingo struggled with his emotions where it concerned Manny. He wanted to feel abandoned, betrayed. After Manny had saved him in that jungle, after he had served him directly, protecting him for all those years, it was hard to muster anger or disappointment in Manny's decision.

In some ways, Domingo understood. Just as he had understood Oscar all those years ago.

He still remembered Oscar's heated argument with their father. At first Domingo had considered Oscar to be a coward. It was only after their father was murdered and the weight of the organization was upon his shoulders that Domingo fully understood that Oscar was braver than all of them.

Domingo put the magazine back on the table, unable to concentrate on luxury boats and three thousand dollar-a-night penthouses in America.

He did not want to sit back and do nothing. He had personally grown weak as his organization had grown stronger. He had not shot a man since before his rescue.

The thought of putting a bullet into the traitor, Alfonso, did not appeal to him. It would be better for someone in his organization to do that. As fond as he had been of Henry, he was not desperate to avenge his death. Despite his reluctance to seek vengeance or defense, Domingo refused to cower, refused to feel trapped.

He shoved thoughts of Maria from his mind and focused on the problem at hand. He needed to make sure his family was safe and that the Villarreal organization remained in the hands of those who had built it with blood, sweat, and coca.

CHAPTER TWENTY-SEVEN

Oscar was distraught. The news of Henry Fronçeau's murder was not front-page news, but Oscar had known him since they both were young. Henry's father had been an influential man and a great friend of the Villarreal family.

His mother had told him. Her role in breaking the news to him was purposeful.

His mind went back to the conversation at the restaurant. His mother had been correct. Oscar was concerned for Domingo.

Lucia was in the kitchen drinking tea and ostensibly reading from the Bible that Manny had given to her. She had seemed calm. He understood that she wanted him to do something. Instead, he sat on his bed, his hands numb, and his mind churning.

The light from the window dimmed as the sun set. He did not get up to turn on the light. The dark enveloped him. He stared at the dresser and the picture of Carmen. She would know what to do. She would support him.

But now he was alone and he did not know if he had the strength to do what he needed to do. He was afraid that he would give in to his mother and fall into the corruption that had scarred and condemned his family. It was why Father was no longer here, it was why they were fractured and vulnerable.

He knew that he should resist the temptation, should ignore the insults to his manhood and his claim to the family name by his mother. His stance was not of inaction or fear, but of principle and moral righteousness. He refused to believe that anything about the cartel was wholesome or redeemable.

Lucia was asking him to take it over. The prospects of that were conflicting to him. He could change the culture, re-plant the coca as coffee or bananas, disband the security personnel, sever ties with the guerillas and paramilitary groups, and turn them into the government to receive justice. He feared that plan was idealistic.

Whichever direction he turned would be dangerous. He was torn between making the safe decision and possibly going against his principles. He so wished that Carmen was there.

When she had first passed away he would hallucinate that she was in the room with him. He would carry on conversations with her, hold her in the bed, and cry. It was comforting for a time. Now, all he had was his mother. Lucia was loving, but cold, hard, and demanding. He would get little sympathy from her. In fact, his temptation was to stay out of it all to spite her. He knew that sins of omission were as damning as sinful action.

Finally, he wiped his mouth on his shirt, got off the bed and trudged down the hall to the kitchen with a heavy heart but a mind clear of purpose.

"I am going to see Alfonso," he announced to his mother.

She looked up at him, her mouth slack.

"That's not an option."

"If this is going to stop, then it is the only option. Even I know what his intention is. He is fooling no one."

"This is not what I meant."

"It has nothing to do with your manipulations. I cannot sit by idly while my cousin plots to kill my brothers."

"You don't know that." Lucia's mouth was set, her hands shaking. Oscar took them and looked his mother in the eyes.

"I can do this. Maybe I am wrong, but I can stop him."

Lucia began to cry.

"You are not a man of violence, Oscar. You intend to threaten Alfonso?"

"My intent, Mama, is to convince Al that it is in his best interest to let this foolishness go."

"Let the law take care of it," she begged.

Oscar fixed his mother with a scolding glare.

"What law? No one will come near Alfonso. He hasn't even been listed as a suspect and Henry was murdered in Alfonso's house! Shots were heard, the body was found, and no investigation has been issued. The fact is, Henry was still a citizen of France, and yet no one in the global community seems to care. No, Mom, I will not let the law take care of it."

"You seem to have become a bigger cynic than when you were a child." She was trying to hurt him, but he was beyond her manipulations now. He smiled.

"Maybe so. I do not trust in man. I trust in God. He will see us through this."

Lucia narrowed her eyes and pulled her hands from his. Anger and pain flashed in her eyes.

"Where was God when my husband was murdered in his own bed?"

A tear formed in her eye. Oscar could tell she was as concerned as she was angry.

"We all die, Mom. God is there always."

"What if it is your time to die?"

He waited to answer. He did not want to sound flippant.

"Then it is time. Maybe this is what I have been waiting for. I have been searching for something to commit myself to ever since Carmen passed." His voice choked at the end. He swallowed the lump that formed in his throat and held his mother's hands to his chest.

"I don't want you to go," Lucia said in a hoarse whisper.

"I have to." He let her go, and walked out the door.

His feet were heavy as he descended the stairs. He noted the van parked at the curbside across from their apartment. He nodded to the driver, a small man, slumped back into his seat. He seemed to be half asleep.

Oscar crossed the street and he could feel his mother's eyes on his back. He knew she had pulled back the curtain. Oscar walked right up to the dark grey van and knocked on the window. The driver lurched forward, his eyes registering fright and surprise. He was alone.

The man's eyes flashed as he noted Oscar.

"Take me to Alfonso. Now." The man shrugged and then reached over to the passenger side to unlock it. He motioned with his head for Oscar to get in.

CHAPTER TWENTY-EIGHT

Something was wrong.

Paul woke like most men his age. He lay in the bed letting the aches of his back, his joints, and his mind to subside before he swung his feet out onto the floor. He was used to waking up in strange places. From his surroundings he got subtle clues that dawn was an hour away.

The nagging feeling that danger lurked, played at his mind. He lowered his head, listening to the ticking of the house as it cooled. He closed his eyes and formed a prayer, asking God for insight and wisdom.

As usual, he got nothing. He had waited all his life for a miracle or some special calling.

He grinned in the dark of his room. He never actually thought he would get a direct answer. Paul had followed God's will in his life for so long and seen His love in so many ways, he would never doubt.

He rose slowly from the edge of the bed, anticipating the crack in his knee. He was not disappointed.

The thorn in my side, he thought.

A light from a neighbor's porch illuminated the yard out front. He saw fresh dew on the yard. The blue glow from the alarm clock on the mantle lit the modest room.

It was four-thirty.

Surely, everyone else was asleep.

Maybe Jhoana was milling around the house. He had heard Claire and Manny in the kitchen earlier and knew where that conversation was heading.

Paul was surprised at Manny's openness with a stranger, but from what he had learned of Claire, she was a jewel. God worked in strange ways.

Paul crossed the room and leaned out of the door. He checked the door to the living room. It was closed. He looked out into the kitchen. It was lit by a lamp. By its light, Paul could see nothing wrong. Some tumblers sat unwashed on the counter, a dish towel was draped over a chair. He listened closely, but only heard a gentle wind blowing and curtains moving.

Curtains. He remembered the curtains in the room with the paintings. Maybe Claire and Manny were in the courtyard having a discussion. He considered for a moment joining them and urging them to go back to bed. These were their last hours together, perhaps, so he hesitated.

He retreated to his room, gathered his socks and some slippers and slipped into a warmer shirt. He had forgotten to bring his robe. He padded his way to the hall. He heard Jhoana snoring. He smiled. He saw the curtains swaying in the room ahead, but he paused to listen at the doors across from Jhoana's.

He could hear Manny's distinct breathing pattern. Paul had spent many a night listening to Manny's snoring. He was puzzled. He heard nothing from the other door. He wanted to open the door to Claire's room. Just to check.

Instead, he turned and moved down the hall toward the courtyard, his mind turning. Maybe Claire was out here to clear her head.

She had been drinking *canelezo*, according to Jhoana. Perhaps it did not set well with her. Paul wished he had brought his flashlight. The courtyard was darker than the front of the house.

Paul wrestled with his irrational fears. It was not the first time in his life that he had woken to strange things in a house that leant themselves to mystery. Of course, these events were easily explained with a level head and a mind that was fully awake. Despite realizing how his thoughts were racing through worst-case scenarios, he continued to dwell on the feeling in his gut that something was wrong.

He grabbed the curtains to keep them from swaying. He noticed his hands were shaking. Paul imagined finding blood, or a wild animal.

Maybe he would find a mercenary looking to loot houses or maybe another defector from the FARC. He had heard that many of the members of that organization were beginning to seek protection from the government in exchange for information. Several of the units had become disorganized after the recent attempts by the Colombian government to cut the head from the serpent.

These situations drifted into his thoughts, his fears freezing him in the patio doorway, the curtains held bundled in his left hand. He stared into the night, his eyes searching the shadows surrounding the statue and the flower beds nearby. Dull light shone from the dew on the grass of the yard, and nothing moved.

Then he saw the sandal. Thinking at first that perhaps Claire had ventured here tonight inebriated, he began to relax. He realized the truth of it.

He released the curtain and sprinted to Claire's room, throwing the door open without announcement. He knew it was rude. He was prepared to apologize, thinking that maybe he had been foolish, old, and scared.

Her bed was empty. The sheets were scattered on the floor, spread out as if they had been dragged from the bed. He saw that her bag was gone as well. He stood there, his hands held up near his ears in anticipation for an apology, and his mouth forming an "O."

He almost screamed. He slapped his hand over his mouth.

Paul did not want to worry Jhoana. She had gone through so much. Something like this happening in her house might be too much for her to handle. Instead, he turned and went to Manny's door. He and

Manny had dealt with their share of friends who had experienced abductions, kidnappings, and murders. Manny would know what to do and who to call.

Paul was afraid that Manny might react badly.

Manny had struggled to put his past behind him. It was possible that Manny would regress, would fall back into the cesspool of sin from which he had climbed. Paul felt weary just thinking about it. There was nothing he could do but pray.

Paul moved quickly across the room to the bed and roused Manny from his sleep. It did not take much. Manny rubbed his eyes and sat up with a start. He had a puzzled, almost perturbed look upon his face.

"What?"

"Manny. Claire is gone." Manny blinked.

"Gone? What on earth do you mean, Paul?" He glanced around the room, orienting himself to his strange surroundings. "What time is it?"

"It's not yet five in the morning. Claire is gone." He said it slowly, enunciating the words clearly. "I think someone took her."

Manny looked incredulous.

"You have to be kidding!" Paul could hear Manny's feet hit the floor. He could also hear the accusation in his voice.

"I am not."

Manny's eyes narrowed in the dark of the room. The light from the hall illumined the room enough for Paul to see Manny grip the sheets with his hands, bundling them in anger. He could see him set his jaw.

Manny leaped from the bed, naked from the waist up. His muscles rippled. Paul was quickly reminded of who Manny was and of what he was capable.

"Who?"

"I hoped you would know."

Manny slipped on some shoes, not bothering with a shirt and socks. He rubbed his face with both hands and pushed back his long, dark hair.

Paul stood, waiting to follow Manny.

Manny nodded. "Let's go then, and see what we can." With that, he walked briskly to Claire's room.

Paul followed, his mind racing through possibilities.

"I didn't want to wake Jhoana," Paul whispered ahead to Manny. He nodded.

It was all surreal to Paul. Whenever he was faced with tragedy or danger, it seemed time slowed and he felt like he was outside of his body. It was as though someone else was controlling his body, saying the words coming from his mouth.

Manny inspected the bed sheets on the floor. He rubbed his hands across the pile of the carpet slowly. On his hands and knees, Manny looked under the bed, and then knelt and checked the bed itself, turning the mattress over and looking in the corners around the bed posts. He put some small items on the bed, lining them up carefully. Paul stood back and watched quietly.

He understood not to interrupt Manny when he was like this. He was hunched over, the muscles of his back flexing, his jaw working as if he were chewing gum.

Paul could see Manny's eyes in the lamp light. They were flat and flicked back and forth as he searched for clues.

Manny turned away and asked, "Do you know which way he left the house?"

Paul blinked. "No, but the back patio door is open. I guess he could have left that way."

"No. Carlos wants us to think that was the way he left. I think that is how he came in."

"Carlos? The Carlos?"

"Yes," Manny responded, his mouth clenching, his teeth bared.

"Oh." Paul wiped his mouth with his hand. He tried to not say what was on his lips. He hoped to God that Claire was alive. He had heard stories about Carlos for years.

Manny turned to him, his eyes vacant.

"We have to hurry, Paul. You won't be able to come with me. Please tell Jhoana goodbye for me."

"Manny, you don't have to—"

"Stop it, Paul. You know I do.

"But, how do you know it is Carlos?"

Manny rose and held out a white handkerchief. Paul did not understand.

"It is sort of a calling card. Carlos isn't just a killer, Paul. I know his sister has told you that he has assassinated dozens of *capos* and government officials. That part is true. He even worked for me a few times. Paul, he also performs snatch and grabs for the cartels. He does none of this on his own. He is hired to do them. I think Domingo hired Carlos to do this."

"Domingo? I don't believe it. Manny, he would never do something like this…" Paul motioned to the mostly empty room.

Manny raised a questioning eyebrow.

"Really? You can't believe Domingo capable of kidnapping someone to get me to come back to work for him?"

Paul felt chastised, but he held his ground.

"This has to be someone else. Could a military group have done this for ransom money?"

Manny shook his head.

"Claire isn't rich. She doesn't know anyone rich."

"Dr. Borche is rich."

"Dr. Borche has no interest in Claire. He barely knows her. She is only here because you were able to convince Dr. Borche to bring Katherine back home."

Paul did not know what to say in the face of the truth. He fumbled for something. He did not want Manny storming off to Domingo's villa with blood on his mind.

Revenge was a powerful emotion and difficult to maintain a moral standard in its midst.

It became a moral code of its own. He feared for Manny's soul. He feared for Domingo's life.

He scrambled for the right thing to say to diffuse the situation.

"I know what you are thinking, Paul," Manny said quietly.

He crossed past Paul and walked back toward his room, his hands wringing in front of him.

"You want to protect Domingo and you don't want me to run off doing something I might regret," he finished.

"Something like that," Paul said.

He was careful to guard his emotions.

"Don't worry. If Domingo wants me back, he can have me. I just won't be the Manny he remembers, that is all. I have been considering this for a long time. Maybe it is time that I pushed harder to take Domingo's place."

Paul was surprised. He followed Manny into the other bedroom. He tried to keep his voice down, but he could not contain the panic in it.

"You said you didn't want to ever be in control of an organization that corrupt. Have you given up your faith in order to gain control of your brother? That is revenge, too."

Manny picked up his suitcase and began to pack his clothes. Paul saw the machine pistol Manny carried.

He knew not to mention it. Manny was focused now. Any accusations or pleadings would just solidify his position. Paul felt his best course was to allow Manny to think about his actions logically.

He understood why Manny was conflicted.

"Paul, I will not be able to live with myself if Claire dies. I cannot allow my brother to continue to control me, to use people in my life that I care about to keep me in submission."

"Do you mean like Maria?"

Paul knew he had made a mistake. Manny stopped packing and turned slowly to face Paul, anger and shame flashing in his eyes.

"I am absolved of those sins. I no longer have to answer for mistakes in my past. Isn't that what you try to convince me of?"

"Yes. You are right. Forgive me. I spoke out of concern for you. Nina says I never fight fair."

He tried to smile, but found it harder than he expected.

He felt his emotions rising up to engulf him. He struggled to maintain his composure. Manny needed him right now.

"Is that what you see this as? A fight for you to win? Give it up, Paul. I am going to see my brother. Pray that he had nothing to do with it."

"What about Carlos? What about Claire? Don't you want to find her?"

"Of course I do," Manny said, his voice choked with emotion. "Which is why you have to find her. I will find out who hired Carlos to take her and where he was heading."

"I can't take on Carlos!"

Manny smiled.

"I would never ask you to do that. Stay clear of Carlos. He will only drop Claire off somewhere. He probably already has. I need to find out who hired him. I think it was my brother, but maybe….I don't know. I can't think right now."

"Where do I start?"

"Ask around in the villages. It is more likely that Carlos left her with a militant cell like the ELN or probably one of Henry's groups in the FARC. Be careful Paul. You don't have to rescue her, just locate her. I will take care of the rest."

Paul sat on the bed, dejected. His fear for Nina welled to the surface and he could not help sharing his concern with Manny.

"I haven't seen Nina in almost two weeks. I haven't heard from her. Do you think…"

Manny looked at him with compassion. He sauntered over, his backpack slung across one shoulder and hugged Paul with the other.

"Is that what has been worrying you?"

Paul nodded, his head down on his chest.

"Well, maybe we will have two mysteries to solve. I think Nina can take care of herself, Paul. She is as tough as nails."

"I know. I 'm just worried, that's all."

Manny stood in the doorway, his back to the hall.

"Jhoana's going to be upset. Console her as much as you can. I know you can't lie to her, but try not to tell her too much."

"It doesn't matter, Manny. She will guess most of it anyway. She will know you went to see your brother."

"I suppose you are right. Look, I am going to get a ride to Barrancabermeja and get a private flight out by helicopter to Domingo's."

"Do you really think he has anything to do with this?"

Manny set his jaw and his eyes roamed the dark room.

"I sure hope not. I won't do anything rash, but maybe Domingo knows who does. I will try to call Henry and test the waters while I am on my way there."

"Good idea. Henry can be trusted."

Manny cringed.

"It is sad that I have to trust in an arms dealer to get the truth. I don't even know if I can trust my own brother."

Paul looked grim.

"You can trust Domingo. Go on. I will break this to Jhoana when she gets up."

Paul could see a softness come to Manny's eyes. He saw him relax his shoulders and could tell from his body language that Manny was distraught. They had become close friends. Manny was like a son to him. Paul enjoyed the feeling that Manny was concerned for him.

"Goodbye my friend," Manny managed through his grief.

"It is not goodbye, Manny. It is farewell for now. I will see you soon. Get this business with Domingo over with so you can have peace that your brother is innocent. I will follow Claire's trail as best I can and keep you informed. Do you have a cell phone?"

Manny shook his head.

"I will get one before I leave. I have your number. Be careful."

Paul moved closer, hugging him and clapping him on the back with one arm. Manny was strong.

"You, too, my friend."

Manny turned, sadness weighing his body. He made his way down the hall silently. Paul did not hear the front door close.

Paul was left to wonder how he would break the news to Jhoana. He decided that the truth would hurt, but Jhoana was strong and the truth clearly spoken would be less jarring than truth being obviously concealed. It was opposite from the wisdom of the world, but Paul had found himself rarely thinking that world's wisdom made much sense, anyway.

CHAPTER TWENTY-NINE

"What you have done here jeopardizes my entire operation. You have no idea what you have done. Are you stupid?"

He had never seen Alvarez this angry. He held his tongue. Alfonso did not want Alvarez to suspect his larger motivations. It was better that he continued to seem meek.

"I reacted. I didn't intend to kill him," Alfonso whined.

"What do you mean? Henry Fronçeau would never have threatened you without being threatened himself!"

Alvarez composed himself, wiping the spittle from his lips. He turned, putting his sunglasses back into his wrinkled suit jacket.

"Look, I know what you are trying to do. You call in some favors, ask around for some help, you want to see if you can do this without me," Alvarez said.

He was being deliberate. This scared Alfonso more than anything else. The agent would not draw a weapon on him directly; Alfonso was secure in his immediate safety.

As Alvarez went through the motions of getting his cigarette out of his jacket pocket and putting it to his mouth, Alfonso could easily imagine his plans for taking over the Villarreal cartel crumbling on his thirty thousand dollar Persian rug.

"I never intended to circumvent your operations. I was merely drawing in other resources to complete the task…to cover for you."

Alvarez snorted

"Cover for me, huh?" His American accent was thick now. He smirked, his mouth turning up on the right side.

"Yeah. You know, with all the mess going on with Plan Colombia, I thought it was best to, you know, keep your hands clean in this whole thing. I guess I botched it up," Alfonso said, shrugging.

"I don't need you to cover for me. Do you know who I am? Do you not understand who you are working with? I thought you knew, you stupid piece of---"

Alfonso was prepared for the insult, but his phone rang loudly. He glanced down and held up his hand.

"Just a sec. This is one of my guys in field surveillance."

Alvarez just shook his head and put the unlit cigarette to his lips. He sucked on it, his cheeks pursing as he began to pace, giving Alfonso some room.

"Yeah, Vic. Who? Oscar? Why?" He looked up at Alvarez, worried. Alvarez hated smoke. Had he driven him to take the habit up again? That could not bode well.

"Well, I am kind of in a meeting. How far out are you?" He looked down, trying to think. "Fine. Bring him in. He can meet my friend, here."

He snapped the phone shut and looked up at Alvarez. He could feel his face flush with embarrassment. He prepared himself for the onslaught and the insults.

"Well? Who is our visitor?" Alvarez asked, inspecting the cigarette. The end was wet.

"Oscar Villarreal."

Alvarez arched his eyebrows, looking interested. He smiled broadly.

"Really? So, big brother rides to the rescue."

"That's what it seems. He approached one of my surveillance teams and demanding that he bring him here."

"Someone more stupid than you are."

Alvarez walked back to the table and grabbed a handkerchief from his pocket. He picked up the .22, inspected the pistol to make sure a round was chambered and then he put his hand behind his back with a grin. He nodded to Alfonso.

"Have him come in. I might be able to fix this mess you made. If you get really lucky, he brought his meddling mother with him, too."

"I don't understand. Oscar is nothing. He is just the family conscience. He left his father's legacy to rot two decades ago. He means nothing, he is nothing," Alfonso said.

Alvarez shook his head.

"You are wrong there, Alfonso. Oscar is crucial now. You have alerted the prey to a danger. They can sniff it in the air." He made a sniffing motion, the gun hand still behind his back. "They can smell the blood, the cordite, and the lies you are trying to pile up. If you want to pin something on Carlos, and from there also include Manny, you must make it personal."

"But, Henry was a friend of the family. He was—"

"He was NOTHING TO THEM!" Alvarez screamed, spittle flying across the table. "He was MY KEY TO SABOTAGING THEIR OVERSEAS OPERATIONS YOU TWIT!"

Alfonso cringed. He began to doubt his safety. Alvarez's face was red and a large purple vein stood out on his prominent forehead. His free hand began to swing in a rhythmic motion

"I had no idea," Alfonso managed.

"EXACTLY! You have no idea."

Alvarez composed himself.

Quietly, slowly, he said, "You do not see the big picture here, Alfonso. You only see your own greed, your own quest for petty power. You have no idea what it is like to have the pressure of three nations riding on your neck. Don't presume to think anymore. Just do. One more mistake like this and I will consider our agreement null. You will then indeed be on your own."

"I don't take kindly—"Alfonso tried desperately to gain control. It was his own HOUSE!

"That was no threat, Al. You need to step back and see where you are perched."

At that, Vic entered with Oscar. Vic was armed, but his machine pistol was holstered. He had a smirk on his face as if he could see how this would all transpire. He seemed amused by it. Alfonso had difficulty seeing any humor whatsoever.

Oscar walked with false confidence. Alfonso understood, of course. Oscar had always been a peaceful sort. This confrontation was completely out of character for him. Maybe that explained why Alfonso could feel the hairs on the back of his neck rise. Alfonso could see fear and determination in Oscar's eyes. *Careful a cornered cat*, he remembered.

"Oscar. Welcome to my home."

"I have been here before. I remember you being so proud about your art collection and your women." Alfonso also remembered that day. Oscar had not changed much. Some gray peppered his mustache and his sideburns, he had put on a little weight at his neck and waist, but he still had the piercing brown eyes and quick wit of a Villarreal.

"Yes. I was younger and dumber then, right?" Alfonso laughed. He really wanted to grab Oscar by the lapel of his wrinkled button up camp shirt and shake him. Slap him around a little. Really embarrass him, remind him how much of a coward he was. Alfonso had an idea that actions like that would widen the gulf that was developing between him and Alvarez.

He noticed Oscar glancing to the side at Alvarez. The agent was staring at him, his face still red with anger. Alfonso suddenly felt sorry for Oscar. He should never have come. He did not need to be a part of this, no matter what Alvarez said.

"Who is your friend? I don't believe I have ever met him. My name is Oscar Villarreal."

Alvarez was slow to speak. He smiled slowly.

"We know who you are, Oscar. How is Manny lately?"

Oscar raised his eyebrows, surprised. He shrugged, noncommittally.

"He is off on some adventure, taking photos. I haven't seen him in a couple of days. To whom am I speaking that knows of my family? I am afraid you have me at a disadvantage."

"You have no idea. Sort of like our friend Alfonso here."

Oscar smiled.

"Why have you come, Oscar?" Alfonso wanted to change the subject. He was losing control.

Oscar looked at him, all humor aside.

"I want you to reconsider your course, Alfonso."

Alfonso tried a disarming smile, and a turn to Alvarez with a shrug.

"I don't know what you mean, Oscar. I haven't seen you in years and now you show up with a cryptic warning? Why would you presume to know what my course is?"

Oscar looked uncomfortable. He seemed to gather some intestinal fortitude, some vaunted Villarreal boldness.

"I know you intend to have Domingo killed."

Alvarez coughed, possibly a laugh.

"See? It is obvious, just like I said. In America, we would say that you telegraphed your pass and it was intercepted." Alvarez laughed again.

Alfonso was not impressed. He did not appreciate being laughed at. He wanted to choke Alvarez.

Even more, he imagined that he could put the cold barrel of the .22 against Oscar's temple and watch him as tears ran down his cheeks and he begged for his life.

He gathered himself and smiled at Oscar. This was all a big joke, all a misunderstanding. He needed to convince Oscar of that lie if he were going to save face with Alvarez.

"Oscar. *Mi hombre.* What can I say? Why would I want to kill Domingo?"

He could see Oscar grit his teeth, see his jaw work. Alfonso trusted that Vic had already checked Oscar for weapons.

"Why would you want to kill Henry?"

He raised his eyebrows in mock surprise.

"Indeed. Why would I do that? Who said I did? I will kill the son of a—"

"Don't lie to me, Alfonso!"

Alfonso shook his head. Oscar had stepped closer to him, his hands clenched at his side.

Alfonso intended to continue to deny he would kill either Domingo or Henry. He did not have a chance.

Behind him, he heard the report of the .22.

A bead of red appeared on Oscar's forehead, just over his right eye. Oscar's head jerked back like someone had grabbed his hair. Blood and bone splattered the wall behind him.

Another shot popped, and Alfonso had enough presence of mind to flinch. He watched as Oscar's eye disappeared. Oscar fell to the floor, his body limp. He was dead before his head hit the multicolored Persian rug. Alfonso supposed it would be better to burn it now and just get a new one.

Alfonso shrugged and turned around to face Alvarez. He was smiling. Alvarez stared down at the body on the floor and shot him again through the back.

"There. Personal. Tag that on Carlos and now you have a vendetta. Now you have attention drawn away from you. This is the last help you get from me, *mi hombre*," Alvarez mocked.

Alfonso was shaking. He was partly scared, partly angry. He glanced at Vic. He had his hand on his machine pistol, but it was still in the holster. He looked grim. Alfonso could count on him.

He tried a smile.

"Thanks, I guess? I think we could have talked it out, though. I can be pretty convincing when I need to be. Besides, something you may have not considered is Mrs. Villarreal."

"Don't worry about Lucia. She is already in the fold."

Alfonso looked confused.

"How do you think Oscar got here in the first place?"

"But, I don't understand—"

"I know that, Alfonso." he looked very smug as he wiped the gun with a white cloth from the inside of his jacket. "Lucia doesn't know that she works for us. She has for years."

"The US government controls the Villarreal organization, doesn't it?" Alfonso was beginning to see the bigger picture. He was not sure he liked what he was seeing.

Alvarez shrugged.

"I suppose you can say that elements of the US government have always had an interest in the agricultural success of our global allies. Consider that this interest allows certain individuals to continue to have a purpose, continue to profit from broader relationships throughout the world by profiting on distribution, delivery, and the paean of the free world as we protect them—theoretically, of course—from the evils of terrorists, the vile cartels, and the awful enemies of capitalism. We don't really want to eliminate them: where would that truly lead us? But, if everyone has a collective impression that they are safer, then we can continue this ruse."

He put a hand on Alfonso's shoulder. Like good buddies.

"That is where you come in, Alfonso. If you don't screw it up, you can profit from our imaginary crackdown on cocaine."

"It sounds so simple."

Alvarez smirked.

"It is actually quite complicated. There are so many balls being juggled, I am not sure anyone can be assured that they won't all hit the floor at once. The good thing is that with so many balls going around, no one can focus on more than one ball at a time. It is difficult to follow them all, even for the jugglers."

"What if I want to be the one doing the juggling?" Alfonso was not sure it was wise to play his cards like this. He could not stand feeling out of control.

Alvarez lost the smile. The change was immediate and frightening. Alfonso could easily imagine this man, so sophisticated and strange, as a serial murderer or a sadistic maniac. For all he knew, maybe he was.

"Is that a threat? Should I be worried, *mi hombre*?" His tone was sarcastic, but Alfonso could feel the tension practically radiating from him.

"All I am saying is that maybe it would be best if I took the brunt of the action from here on in. I would be glad to be the arm that delivers the blow to the Villarreal family." Alvarez relaxed.

"That blow has already been delivered, Alfonso. Allow Carlos to come home and put this on him, lay it in his lap. I have to return to the States soon. This can all take place while I am away. I don't need protection, I am virtually untouchable."

Alfonso listened, convinced even more that Americans were a cocky sort. He was positive it would be the downfall of Alvarez—his overconfidence and feeling of invulnerability. Alfonso knew he could somehow use these qualities to his benefit. He was not sure yet how. For now, he just nodded and smiled as if he agreed and understood.

Alvarez took his leave and Alfonso instructed some men to clean up the mess in his den. He would have to shut this room off for a few months. He was afraid that the ghosts of Henry and Oscar would speak too loudly. He did not want Carlos to suspect what was in store for him until it was too late.

Alfonso strolled to the kitchen. Suddenly, he was famished.

Nothing like fresh death to make a man hungry, he thought.

He reached into the massive refrigerator and ate right there, taking olives from the jar with his fingers and pulling huge chunks of cooked pork shoulder from beneath some tin foil. He wrapped up some tortillas and filled them with crumbled queso fresco and chunks of pork.

He stood there eating, wishing his staff had baked some cheese *arepas* or *pandebono*. It dawned on him that he needed to get used not always getting what he wanted. It was not a feeling to which he would ever grow accustomed, he thought.

CHAPTER THIRTY

She was sure that she heard a voice say something in English. For an hour now, she had been awake listening to the incessant yelling and broken conversation in languages that she did not understand. She could make out a word or two, but in the end, she could not put anything together.

Partly, she knew, this was due to the pounding headache and the numbing fear that threatened to overtake her. Her hands were tied and her eyes were blindfolded. She could feel the ground beneath her, rough and dry with pebbles the size of marbles. She tried to keep shifting, hoping to push a clear spot. It made her backside sore. She was outside. She could feel the sun on her skin and the breeze blow her hair from time to time.

It was daytime and she had no idea how long she had been away or how she had gotten here. She had been kidnapped, but she could not tell by whom or where they had taken her. The only thing she knew was that she was among people she could not understand and that they smelled foul.

The English speaker was talking again and this time she could make out what he was saying. It sounded like he was on a speakerphone. His voice was strained and yet had an air of authority.

"I don't care what Alfonso said. Keep the woman out of Barranca and take her to the mountain. Alfonso is no longer in charge of this."

The men answered him, but in Spanish. They did not sound convinced.

"Who is paying you? Where do you get your M16s? Your ammo? Your night vision goggles? Huh? You better remember who is in charge here and do what I say."

Someone grumbled. Someone else said, "*Si.*" She knew what that meant.

There was some heated discussion between some people nearby. She could make out three different voices. One of them sounded like a woman. She was angry.

Was she going to be taken to a mountain or to the city? What would be the difference?

Where was she now? And who was this American speaker who had so much authority? And who were these people that were supplied guns and military equipment?

She had read some in preparation for this journey, but her kidnappers could be any one of a dozen different groups. For all she knew, she could be in another country altogether. She wished there was a way to get some answers.

She heard men discussing her. One of them said, "chica."

She tried hard to translate, but they spoke so quickly, she could not understand. She heard boots and a movement of cloth. She figured they were in a tent and had come outside.

Someone gave an order in a shrill voice. Rough hands were on her. She could smell the tart scent of sweat mixed with jungle. She could smell gun oil and cordite, coffee breath and alcohol.

"Please. Let me go," she pleaded. Her voice was a croak. She needed something to drink.

Someone laughed and mocked her. It was a female voice. She translated what she said into Spanish.

"Please. Drink. I am thirsty."

The female voice translated again. They all had a laugh at that and then she heard a sound like a cork. She was splashed with wine. It coated her blindfold and ran down her hair onto her bare shoulders and pooled at her feet. She licked some from her upper lip and cringed as they laughed louder.

Someone grabbed her chin and pulled her mouth down. Warm wine flowed, choking her. She gagged and fell to her knees. Several hands grabbed at her, picking her up by her forearms, around her waist and one grabbed at her breast.

The laughing continued until someone yelled, "*Arrete!*"

Claire felt humiliated. She had read about people getting kidnapped, but had never imagined herself in this situation. She struggled to understand why anyone would want to kidnap her. She had no money, her family had no money. No one would call trying to claim her except her father.

Why me, she wondered.

The tart wine was mixed with the bile from her gagging. It did nothing to quench her thirst. She was ready to panic. She was confused by her treatment.

She felt strong hands grab her again and she was moved forcefully to a tall metal bench.

It was a truck bed, she realized. They lifted her and she crawled away from them. Her shoulder bumped a padded bench. She guessed it was a troop transport vehicle. She could smell diesel and the dankness of old sweat.

Someone was barking orders. She cringed, feeling someone close by. Hands grabbed her blindfold and it was yanked from her face. Sunlight almost blinded her. Through slitted eyes, she saw a veritable army strung out behind her watching with amusement and boredom. Everyone had guns.

A woman approached her, her dark curly hair framing her face. She was pretty, but Claire could see the danger in her eyes. She reached into the back of the truck and grabbed Claire by the front of her blouse. She stepped up onto the bumper and looked Claire in the face. Claire could smell her rank breath and her body odor.

Claire sucked in her breath. She felt her eyes go wide with fright. Her heart thumped against her ribs. The woman appeared to be satisfied with Claire's obvious horror.

"You stay. They take you from here now. Understand?"

"Stay in the truck. Yes," Claire answered, grateful that someone understood.

The woman shook her and let go. She turned and gave some more orders.

The truck started with a rumble. Claire watched the crowd of camo-clad soldiers milling about, some with guns, as the truck pulled away. Fear clung to her like a new skin, raw and itching. She did not know where she was or where she was going. Her body ached, her throat was raw, and she was disoriented, confused, and scared.

She wanted to check her head. There was a pain there on the crown of her skull and a burning like someone had scraped her scalp. She was afraid someone may have struck her at some point. Maybe she had a concussion.

Soon they turned a corner and the dusty road gave way to a rough, paved road. They were traveling quickly. She could feel the men in the truck staring at her, their eyes tickling across the exposed skin of her legs and arms.

She concentrated on the road behind them, the cloudy sky, and the canopy of trees. She focused on understanding how she had gotten here, and how she could escape.

She tried closing her eyes, but the smells of diesel, gun oil, and sweat mixed with the movement of the old truck made her sick to her stomach. Besides, she knew she had to be alert. She glanced at the five men in the back of truck and knew instantly that she could not trust any of them.

Each carried a rifle: ugly, military rifles with stained grips and ammo magazines seemingly held together with red electrician's tape. They passed what she believed to be reefer between them, silently. They each took a drag, held their breath and passed the little brown cigarette to the next soldier, nodding or coughing.

Claire tried to see the cab of the truck through the dirty glass in front, but all she could make out were two dark shapes at either side. They were going downhill, so she figured they were going back to Barrancabermeja. She gathered her hope that their rebellious attitudes were in her favor. They were disobeying the orders of the American speaker. Maybe that was a good omen. Barrancabermeja was just upriver from Yondo. Maybe Manny would look for her there first.

She chastised herself. Why would Manny look for her? What was she to him? They had kissed, sure. But, he barely knew her. Certainly, he would not want to get mixed up with kidnappers. Her better chance of getting out of this mess was the American Consular in Bogotá.

Paul would know the procedures, she was sure he and his wife had dealt with matters such as this before. Experience mattered. Time mattered. She realized that clinging to the hope that a man she barely knew would come to her rescue was absurd and juvenile.

Claire continued this self-abuse for a few more miles, ignoring the leering of the men guarding her, and fighting against the exhaustion that threatened to overwhelm her. She felt drugged. The persistent tug of sleep assailed her, made her eyes droop, her thoughts muddle, and her body relax. Her last thoughts before drifting off were of Manny.

CHAPTER THIRTY-ONE

As the helicopter rose beyond the smoke coming from the oil refinery, Manny settled into his seat, staring at his phone. He simply could not believe Henry was dead.

He sat there stunned, the rotors a loud whir, the pilot focused on his job. The co-pilot was flipping switches and talking loudly into a headset. Manny could barely hear him.

Manny struggled to decide whether to call Lucia, Paul, or Domingo. He did not want his mother to worry. Paul had enough on his mind right now. Manny was pretty sure the news of Henry's demise absolved Domingo of blame.

With a start, he realized that he might be going in the wrong direction. He should be heading straight west for Alfonso.

According to Stefano Durand, the mercenary who had answered Henry's office phone, the rumor was that Henry was murdered by Alfonso. Speculation as to why was all over the map, but most of the guesswork centered on Alfonso's ambition to have his own cartel.

Manny had known about Alfonso's ambitions, his lack of loyalty, and his freelancing. He had allowed it to continue, knowing that Alfonso was just a small player and would never be able to amount to a threat. Besides, he was family. Domingo had never insisted that anyone serve him unconditionally. Even Manny had been able to leave with relatively little repercussions.

Was it a coincidence that Henry was murdered and Claire taken by Carlos? Was Carlos working for Alfonso? Or was this a case of two unrelated events: Domingo kidnapping an American woman in his company, and Alfonso (or someone else) murdering Henry?

The helicopter banked hard to the south. He considered putting on his headset and telling the pilot to head to Bogotá. Instead, he stared at the cell phone in his hand. It seemed foreign to him. It contained no numbers other than the one he just dialed. It was not registered to him. He had been able to buy a black market phone with cash and a phony name. Old habits die hard.

He glanced at the bag under the seat in front of him. Would he have to use the Kel-Tec again? He had used it for good and for evil. With it he had killed men who had threatened the lives of his family and he had killed young men who were in the wrong place at the wrong time. Timing was everything. Those lives, all of them, both the warranted and the innocent were upon his hands. They were upon his soul.

He glanced below them as they coursed through the valley cut out of the jungle by the Rio De Magdalena. He had been washed in that river. Water that could not cleanse Pilot from the death of Christ had for Manny been his burial and rebirth.

Despite that, Manny struggled to put his past behind him and paint his future with peace. He prayed that Domingo was innocent, prayed that he was safe. If Alfonso was responsible for this, the murder and the kidnapping, he would have to answer for his crimes. Manny was sure that he could get the authorities to intervene and allow justice to reign. That would be preferable to getting his hands filthy with the blood of another on his conscience.

Finally, he decided to call Lucia. She had connections in the right places. It had amazed him, as he had led Domingo's covert operations and personal security, how often his mother's presence occurred. It was especially notable that any time he dealt with a government official, especially corrupt ones, his mother's name would crop up. Often it was just in casual conversation. After ten years of working inside and around the Colombian government, Manny had begun to suspect his mother was more than he had imagined.

Her connections could prove helpful. Also, she would be quick to absolve Domingo of wrongdoing. Manny decided not to mention Carlos or Claire. He was not entirely sure where his mother's clearances lay, but he was pretty sure it was not working with assassins and mercs for hire.

What son would be guilty of suspecting their mother of such a thing? He smiled as he sat back and called the familiar number. No one answered. He checked the number, but was certain he had dialed correctly. He tried her cell number. She picked up after three rings.

"Hello?" She sounded upset. She had been crying.

"Mom?"

"Manny?" Her voice cracked.

"Yes."

"I can barely hear you over that noise in the background!" She was shouting, but Manny could hear panic in her voice.

"Yeah, Mom, it's me! I'm coming home!"

"I hope you just said you are coming home!" She shouted.

"Yes! I am! I will be there in an hour!"

"Good! Because Oscar is dead!"

He was not sure he heard her right. The sun was still climbing in the sky, the rays of heat and light magnified by the glass in the front of the helicopter. He stared at the refracting light, blinking and squinting.

"WHAT?! Did you just say that OSCAR is DEAD?"

All he could hear on the other end was a sob.

"Just COME HOME! We can talk about it when you get here! What airport?"

Frustrated, Manny yelled at his mother.

"Mom, did you say that Oscar is DEAD?"

"Yes. Dead. Get home so we can talk. What airport, Manuel?"

"I was actually heading to see Domingo, Mom. I didn't want to say."

"You don't have to apologize," he had not apologized, he thought. "I will meet you there, Manny."

"It will be dangerous, Mom. Stay at the apartment."

"No. What we need right now is a Villarreal reunion."

"I said it will be too dangerous!"

"Don't you know by now, Manny, that *I* am dangerous?"

"I've known all along, Mom. Stay home."

"I will meet you there in an hour." She hung up.

Oscar. Gone; the damage done.

Manny was numb and wired at the same time. His spirit was wild within him. He was angry, sad, vengeful, and disbelieving.

How could Oscar be dead? What could his mother not discuss over the phone? Why was the Villarreal estate an acceptable meeting place to discuss his oldest brother's death. Did this mean that Domingo was involved?

Was his mother's words cold and calculated? Even though he could easily attribute her yelling and emotional distance to the distance, the noise of the helicopter, and her normal manner, he suspected it was something deeper.

Manny knew perhaps better than anyone in his family how manipulative and effective his mother could be. Lucia always had an agenda. Maybe yelling at him, telling him of Oscar's demise was a way for her to motivate him to do a deed he would not normally consider.

He struggled to control his emotions. Oscar dead. He played those words over in his mind and it defied logic, flew in the face of reason. Why would anyone ever kill Oscar, of all people?

Manny faced a test of faith. Oscar was a God-fearing man. He was devoted to keeping peace. Oscar would bleed for a cause, he would remain steadfast. Oscar was hard-working and dependable. He was a rock.

Where did that get him? A pawn in a dangerous game. A game designed and played to deadly precision by his father. Manny and Domingo had given their lives over to continuing that game, of perfecting it and growing their domination. Now Oscar—poor, underappreciated and tortured, Oscar--had paid the price.

Manny faced another test: one of trust. Could he depend upon his mother? Was she secretly using this tragedy to further the family's power somehow? Could he trust Domingo? Carlos had certainly taken Claire. But, Carlos could be working for just about anyone. He had assumed it was Domingo, and so he was not as concerned as he would be if he had suspected an unknown player. Now, he worried he had been rash in deciding to send Paul to find her.

Could he trust himself? Could he make the right decisions? Claire's life was in the balance. Maybe Paul's. With Oscar dead, it was probable that Domingo and Lucia were in danger. What had he thought would happen, anyway? When he had left, he understood that no one would ever be as diligent as he was at protecting the family.

The reality was that the Villarreals owned a cartel. They were drug traffickers. They dealt in small arms, covert operations against competitors, illegal overseas trade, fraud, embezzlement, murder, and government corruption.

They ruined lives of millions by supplying narcotics, killing hundreds, corrupting the poor, taking advantage of farmers, and suppressing the underprivileged.

How could they ever expect to remain untouched with that kind of record? God would have his vengeance. A reckoning was coming.

The despair that Manny felt then was almost unbearable. He remembered this feeling. After his father died, he came home and sat under a yopo tree, peeling the long pods apart with his nails and wishing he was back in America. He had stayed because it was his family. He could not run from his responsibilities.

He had never felt close to his father. His father had been a business man. He had been unyielding, cruel, and greedy. Yet, as Manny sat there making a pile of yopo beans and wondering if he should dry them and make them into a snuff, he found a purpose for his life.

A decade later, he regretted that decision. Not the decision to save Domingo from the jungles of Venezuela. Not the decision to get the family plantation running smoothly again. Manny regretted all that he had done to enable Domingo to succeed. He regretted honoring his father's legacy. He regretted the blood on his hands.

Now, he was faced with a similar situation. Should he turn the helicopter around and go back to search for Claire? Should he go meet his mother and discover her version of the truth of what had happened to Oscar? Should he face off with Domingo and threaten him to dismantle the family legacy, to destroy all that they had created and nurtured?

He had already begun to clear obstacles in his mind. The easy choice would be to go to Claire. It was what he really yearned to do. He was afraid to face his family right now. The disaster that had befallen them felt too much like retribution. It would represent a test his faith may not be able to overcome.

Besides, it was easy to see that he was falling for Claire. He realized he already had. Perhaps that was why he had run. He did not want his strong emotions for Claire to affect his search for her. He was afraid what he might do if he found her hurt.

The co-pilot, Beltran, turned and flashed a smile. It faded away.

"Are you alright?" he asked.

Manny nodded. He was clenching the cell phone so tightly the case left indentions on his hand. He smiled.

"How much longer?"

Beltran was a small, dark-skinned man who had a perpetual smile on his face. Manny had met him before. Beltran played defender for Deportes Tolima. Manny had cut him twice in one match. After the match, he invited Beltran to join him for a few beers at a local cantina. After that, Beltran had helped Manny in small ways from time-to-time. He always joked about Manny's shins being made of iron.

Beltran looked down at his instruments and shrugged.

"Maybe thirty, forty minutes. You in a hurry to see Domingo? He is a tough one, your brother."

"I am in a hurry to see my mother."

Beltran smiled broadened. He put a finger in the air and gave his partner a friendly punch in the arm.

"Well then! Onward! We must get this man to his mama." He turned in seat, chuckling.

Manny did not correct him. The helicopter surged forward and dipped closer to the looming trees. All he saw was a blur of green for the rest of the ride, as the sounds of the rotors washed over him.

CHAPTER THIRTY-TWO

The cell phone lay buzzing on the table. Domingo did not answer. Maria stood in the doorway staring at him with her hands on her hips with an imperious look on her face.

"Why don't you answer it?"

"It's Blanca. I don't want to talk to her right now."

"I thought you didn't care that she was sleeping with the Moroccan prince?"

"You didn't say he was a prince."

"You didn't ask."

"What else aren't you telling me, Maria?"

"Whatever do you mean, sir?"

"You stand there, your eyes cold as those ice cubes in my drink, and you calmly tell me my wife is cheating on me. In the same way you tell me a colleague and friend of mine was murdered by my cousin. You seem unfazed by all this. Have you no soul?"

"I have a soul, Domingo. That is why I tell you these things. You need me to be calm. You need me to be professional.'

"Do you like working here, Maria?"

"Of course."

"Did you grow up dreaming of becoming an assistant for a drug cartel? Is this your calling?"

"Now you are mocking me."

"I am merely pointing out that I sense something about you does not smell right."

"Are you going to continue to be coy, sir, or are you going to make an outright accusation?"

"I don't know."

He stared absently at the phone, the red light blinking madly. He raised his eyebrows and finished the gin. She never moved. He figured he had made her mad. He could see tears in the corners of her eyes. He did not want to feel triumphant, but he did feel like he was finally getting somewhere. He had struck a nerve with her.

"By the way," she said, her voice choked with emotion just enough to ruin the thin sheen of invulnerability and cool she wore like a second skin. "I came in here to tell you Oscar died."

Domingo dropped the tumbler on the table, knocking the cell phone to the carpet beside his foot. He sat up, his eyes bulging.

"You!" He cursed her, the words feeling like fire coming from his mouth.

"Don't call me that," she said firmly. "I should not have told you at all. You are in danger, more than ever."

She was calm. Too calm. She still did not fear him.

"Oscar!" Domingo could feel a heat radiating across his face. He could not tell if it was shame, fear, or grief.

"Yes. My sources say he—"

"Your sources!" Domingo stood and crossed the room toward her, his anger radiating from him.

He thought for a moment he would lose his mind and strike her. Somehow, he held back. It was her eyes. They looked hurt, vulnerable. At the same time, they were wild and judging him. Had he hurt her? Oscar was dead. Why would he care if he hurt her?

"Why do you tell me now, Maria?" He asked.

He held her elbow tightly. She flinched, but did not back down.

"I knew about it for over an hour. I wanted to be sure; I wanted to have more information."

"You are not playing me right, Maria. I am NOT stupid. Tell me who you really are. Now, before I have my men string you up in the courtyard."

She hesitated. She did not believe his empty threat. Despite this, he could tell that something in her wanted to tell him.

"I can't say," she stammered.

"You CAN say! And you will, or I will—"

"You will what? Domingo, you do not know how to threaten me! You do not truly know me, so you do not know what I fear."

"I can teach you fear," he seethed.

She spoke to him as though she were scolding a child.

"You are soft. Because we want you to be soft. We—"

"We? Who is this "we," Maria? Who do you work for?"

She stepped back, her eyes wide, her lips trembling. She had her hand behind her back. He knew she never carried a gun, but he was suspicious.

"Who do you work for, Maria?" He tried raising his voice.

"YOU! I work for YOU! Manny wanted me to weaken your organization, wanted me to sabotage the business, your business, to make it hard for you to keep it."

He laughed.

"You expect me to believe Manny put you up to this? You want me to believe that Manny wanted the family business to fail?"

"It should belong to him." Her eyes were red, her hand shaking. The metal bracelets on her thin wrist clanged musically.

It began to dawn on him. Alarms went off in his head. He was angry at himself for not seeing it before. Why were guys like him so oblivious to stuff like this? He had not seen the Moroccan prince thing coming and now this. Perhaps this was more devastating.

"You are in love with Manny, aren't you?"

She looked as though he had shot her.

She turned away and he could see the tears forming in her eyes. He did not want to hurt her. He had always known she was attracted to Manny. He also knew that Manny had refused her. Or, at least, he assumed that he had. Before Manny had left, he had grown cold toward her.

"You aren't denying it, so I guess I am right."

She did not respond. He had never seen her upset, never seen her ruffled. Even when Manny had begun to ignore her, snap at her, and brush her hand away when she put it on his shoulder, she had responded neutrally. Now, she was obviously upset.

He tried to look past the obvious. What was he not seeing?

"You are not wrong," she whispered. Maria had been hiding a thin leather book behind her back. She brought the book out in front of her.

"What is that?" He was curious. He had never seen this book before. He thought briefly that it was a thin Bible.

"It is my journal. I was writing in it," she said. Her voice had a dead quality. She sounded defeated, vulnerable. He wanted to hate himself for making her feel this way. He could not stop himself, any more than he could keep himself from fulfilling his destiny as the *Capo* for the Villarreal cartel.

"I cannot believe Manny would sabotage my organization."

Maria did not answer. She stared at the cover of the book and picked at the cloth bookmark that hung from it like a silk tail.

Standing there in that light cotton dress, fragile, and distressed, he found it difficult to see how Manny had resisted falling in love with her. She was magnificent. And she obviously cared for him. Her obsession with Manny had led her to betray Domingo's organization.

But how? And why? And was she ultimately responsible for Oscar's death or merely the messenger of his demise?

"Maria, I don't understand. Help me to understand what you have done."

"Everything," she said. She did not look up at him.

"Did you kill Oscar?"

Her hands trembled.

"No." Her answer was firm, but he was on the right track.

"Did you have Henry killed?"

"Of course not." A tear fell from her eye, staining the dress at her bosom.

"How are you guilty of betraying me, then, Maria?"

"I have lied to you."

"How? Why?"

She sobbed, one hand going to her mouth, the bracelets jangling as her body heaved and shook.

"Maria. You have been one of my most trustworthy associates. I have depended upon you since Manny left to keep things together. You have been tremendous. Is that all a lie?"

"Yes."

He wanted to grab her and shake her. He wanted to hit her. His rage had built up within him and it was all he could do to control himself. His conflicting desires aggravated him even more. He could not hit her, couldn't hurt her, but he needed to. He needed to lash out.

He felt in danger for the first time in a decade. He had a hard time believing that the one who had gotten him out of that scrape was now responsible for this one. She knew, or at least thought she knew.

He had to be patient. He could tell he was close. He had never seen her this emotional.

"Can I see the book?" He tried to keep his voice low, demanding.

She trembled and shook her head. She looked up at him, her eyes tinged with red, her mascara running down her cheeks. He could see the fear in her eyes. He stepped forward.

"Give me the book, Maria. Now."

Reluctantly, she held it out to him. He snatched it from her.

"I will get the answers in here, won't I? What you don't want to tell me, this awful secret, it's in here?"

"More than you want to know, *señor.*"

He cautiously opened the book to the middle, just before the place she had marked, and quickly scanned the writing there. Maria had a beautiful flowing script, feminine and bold. He could see her beauty, her intelligence, and her grief right there without reading.

He did not trust her, though. It would not be wise to read it, engrossed in it while she stood by.

"Maria, please have a seat over here on the sofa." He led her gently by the elbow to the sofa. She complied, sniffling and moving with her head bowed low. As she sat, he handed her a handkerchief from his pocket. It had his initials embroidered in red.

"I am sorry." She said between sobs.

"No worries." He hated himself for saying that. *No worries.* His oldest brother was dead. Henry was dead. And his life—or Manny's—was in danger.

He wanted her to feel safe. She was. He had no intention of hurting her now, no matter what her involvement. He, nevertheless, needed her to feel safe. If she felt that he posed no threat, maybe he could expect the same courtesy.

"You can read it. It will tell you what I cannot. I cannot say. I cannot repeat the treachery of my life."

He stared at her, disbelieving. Was she serious?

"I will read it at another time, Maria. Tell me now what I need to know. Am I or is Manny in danger?"

"No more than usual, I suppose." She shrugged.

In the distance, he could hear the beating of propellers. It did not register at first. He was used to the sound of aircraft around this base, so far up and remote in the mountains south of Bogotá. It dawned on him that perhaps this sound was his impending doom.

"We have visitors. Who are we expecting?"

Maria looked confused. She looked past him to the mountains to the south and east, shaking her head.

"I know of none," she sounded somewhere between confused and scared. It made him even more nervous.

The sound got closer and then a civilian helicopter flew overhead, shooting north recklessly as it descended to a promontory just uphill from the main house. He could see the familiar form of Manny exit the opposite side. He ducked and came walking briskly downhill. Manny carried a large duffle bag. He looked mad and determined, his face set in a grimace as he searched ahead.

He saw them sitting on the veranda and he waved. Still no smile.

"It is Manny," he said. Maria was silent.

He glanced at her and saw the truth. She loved him, but she was scared of him.

Suddenly, she lunged for the journal still in his hand. She caught him by surprise, both by the suddenness of her action and the ferocity of her determination to pry it away from him. Her nails raked his hand, and she pulled with the other.

He resisted, pulling back his hand. She lunged with her head, her mouth open in a scream and she bit his forearm. He jerked away, the journal flying against the wall.

"He can't see it!" Maria cried.

With his other hand, he slapped her hard across the jaw. She collapsed between the sofa and the glass coffee table. She laid there, her hand to her cheek. His handprint left a pink mark on her cheek and a sliver of blood ran down the side of her mouth, spilling onto her chin.

Manny was at the door.

"What's going on here?"

Domingo had not seen Manny in weeks. He looked haggard and angry. He must know about Oscar, Domingo thought.

"She betrayed me."

Manny squinted.

"You too, huh?"

Domingo knew he was missing something. Perhaps Manny could enlighten him.

"Manny, Oscar is dead."

Manny nodded.

"I know. Mom will be here soon." His voice sounded dead. There was a smoldering fire in his eyes that warned Domingo of Manny's anger.

Domingo did not know how to respond to that.

"Is this a good idea? Isn't this a security issue, all of us here in one place?" Manny ignored him. His eyes were hard.

"Domingo. Before Mom gets here I need you to answer one thing for me."

Maria sobbed on the floor, covering her face and turned on her side. Domingo was distracted, but there was something in Manny's voice. He had heard this tone once before from him.

"What it is it, brother?"

"Did you kill Henry?"

Domingo was relieved. This was the same question he had asked Maria. He knew the answer to this one.

"No!" Maria screamed.

She got up from the floor, scrambling. Manny stepped aside as she stumbled over the coffee table and lunged for the journal. She was quick. Domingo watched as she picked it up and ran from the veranda back into the house. Domingo started for her, but Manny grabbed his arm.

"Don't you want to get her?"

"I don't want to have anything to do with her right now." Manny's tone was grave. "Answer me, Domingo. This is important to me."

"No, of course not. Manny, I don't know what is going on. Maria won't tell me, but she has confessed to betraying me. She says she is not responsible for Henry or Oscar's deaths but that she has tried to bring my organization down."

Manny nodded.

"It is true, I suppose."

"That is funny." It was Domingo's turn to throw out accusations. "She said it was your idea."

Manny smiled. There was little mirth there.

"You didn't read the journal, did you?"

"No. She tried to take it away from me."

"Don't bother. I can tell you most of what is in there."

"Do tell, Brother."

Manny sighed.

"She aborted my child." Manny's face was drawn.

"Oh. That explains much."

"I can never forgive her."

With so much between them, Domingo felt odd talking about this. He was torn. Should he dig in and ask more or should he broach one of a dozen other conversations that they should have right now?

"I understand." He bit his lip. "Does that explain why she has acted so strangely today?"

"She is bereaved for her mistake. She is obsessed over her loss."

"The child or you?"

"Both, I suppose."

Domingo took that for the end of the conversation. He was anxious to move on, anyway.

"I am sorry. I understand better now why you had to leave."

Surprisingly, Manny said nothing. He just stared hard at Domingo, darkness like flint in his eyes. Manny was ever the protector, ever the avenger. Domingo thought he had put that all behind him when he took up with the missionary and started attending church services every week. Maybe some habits die hard. Maybe you would always be who you are at the core. That depressed him more than the accusing look Manny had fixed on him.

"Did you have a hand in Oscar's murder?" Manny asked through clenched teeth. Domingo noted his fists. They were tight against his hips, his nails digging into his palms.

He saw Manny's muscles in his forearms flexing. He knew Manny was barely containing his rage. Domingo wanted desperately to suggest that they pray. Maybe God could help him contain this savage beast. Domingo had seen what Manny was capable of doing. He wanted no part of Manny's anger or revenge.

It was a good thing he had nothing to do with Oscar's death. He would not have to lie.

"No."

Manny's gaze bored into him, seeking the truth. Domingo allowed him to search his eyes. He had nothing to hide from his brother. Manny knew his many sins intimately, had taken part in them and more.

"Be at peace brother. I believe you. You cannot lie to me. You never could."

That was true. Even as children, Domingo feared Manny more than their father.

"We need to find out who did this. Does Mom know?"

Manny shrugged.

"Mom says Alfonso did it. Is he not working for you anymore?" Domingo didn't miss the accusation in his voice.

"He is rogue at best. He is attempting a coup at the worst."

"That is pretty obvious. What are you doing to prevent an assassination, brother?"

He hooked a thumb over his back.

"I have Maria on it."

Manny smiled at that.

"Well, you're in good hands, then."

"Where's Oscar's body? Are we sure he's dead?"

"I don't have access to that information. I assume the government is investigating. Two murders in his house in the span of two days doesn't bode well for Alfonso. He can't keep this under wraps for long."

"It seems odd to me. Our cousin is ambitious, for sure, but I don't see him murdering Henry or Oscar. How does that fit whatever plans he has hatched in that sick mind of his? How in the world could either of them be in his way or threaten him?"

"I am wondering the same thing. Oscar wouldn't hurt anyone. The only thing I could come up with was that maybe Alfonso was intending to draw me out."

Now Domingo had to decide how much to tell Manny. He could tell him all that he knew, or withhold information. He quickly decided that the more he put on the table now, the less suspicious Manny would be of him in the long run. Domingo was extremely determined to live.

"Um. About that. Manny, Alfonso had you tailed. He sent Carlos to kill you."

Manny did not look surprised.

"Nice of you to warn me, Brother."

Domingo shrugged.

"I figured you could handle yourself. Carlos always had more love for you than our cousin."

"Carlos cares only for the money, Domingo. Besides, all Carlos did was kidnap a friend of mine."

Another surprise.

"What?! Who?"

Domingo heard footsteps coming. Lucia stepped onto the veranda, her silver hair flowing around her shoulders, her eyes heavy with grief and barely contained anger. She was as dangerous as Manny when she was mad. Domingo cringed.

"The young American lady that hired you, isn't that right Manny?" She answered for Manny.

"Yes."

"Alfonso has to answer for all of these crimes," Lucia said. Her voice was harsh, like she had been crying. She was composed, though.

"The government will do nothing but slap him on the hand. They will certainly sweep these under the rug as well."

"We have to remember the living as well," Manny chimed in.

"What do you mean, Manny. You don't want revenge? You don't think that this debt should be paid in blood?"

Lucia's eyes were cold as she questioned her youngest son. Domingo could see Manny steel himself at her onslaught.

"I want Domingo and you to live. I want Claire to be returned. I want Paul to be safe. These things are more important. Killing Alfonso will not bring Oscar back. He is in God's hands now."

Lucia stepped forward, spittle coming from her mouth as she yelled.

"GOD? What God? How could there be a God that lets an innocent man die? How can there be a God that takes my husband from this earth and allows my family to be torn apart by a madman?"

"We are not immune, Mom. God's love protects us, but not in ways we comprehend." Manny's voice was calm, soothing.

"Don't patronize me, son! I expected more from you."

The venom in her voice cut through his soul. He had never heard his mother talk to anyone that way. Domingo had always thought that Manny was her favorite.

"You can expect that I will do what I can to keep you and Domingo safe. You cannot expect me to repeat the sins of my youth."

Lucia spit.

"That is what I say to your God."

223

Her eyes were rings of red. Tears of defiance rolled down her cheeks.

"That is what I say to your misplaced sense of honor and righteousness. You are weak, I see that now."

"You can spit all you want, Mom. I will not do it. Alfonso will pay the price, if he is indeed the culprit."

Domingo felt helpless. Why was no one asking him to do something? He suspected they only considered him to be someone who needed protection. He had spent the last decade getting soft, surrounded by hired guns, levels of security, remotely located, and with the ever-dependable Manuel Villarreal as a brother and body guard.

"I raised cowards!"

Manny looked thoughtful for a moment.

"Is that what you told Oscar before he went to see Alfonso?"

Domingo watched his mother crumble.

It was mostly in her eyes.

She looked defeated, guilty, distressed, and wounded at the same time. He had grown to think his mother was impenetrable. She was the rock that held the family together. She was fearless, determined, and crafty. Now, she looked on the verge of tears.

Lucia bit her upper lip and turned from them. She stalked out of the outdoor room and back into the complex. Domingo started to follow her.

"Mom—"

Manny grabbed his bicep, drawing him back with hands that felt like iron.

"Don't. Let her go. She needs to deal with her guilt herself. She is deflecting it on us—me."

Domingo looked up at his younger brother. Had he always looked up to him?

"But, it's Mom."

"And it is time for her to learn how to grieve. It is time for her to learn to lean on someone besides her own intelligence and manipulations." Domingo last saw Manny look so set when he had pulled Domingo from the burning wreckage the night he was rescued from the Venezuelan mercenaries. He saw that same look in his eyes.

"What do we do now?"

"Make sure you are safe. Get Claire back. Then, we can figure out what to do about Alfonso. That would be a good start."

Domingo nodded. He knew Manny was right. They had to get their priorities straight.

"So what do we do first, little brother?"

"Call Carlos."

CHAPTER THIRTY-THREE

The truck had slowed. It wound through streets, down close alleys with dark, empty buildings on each side. She watched the progress from the floor of the military transport as they passed entire families begging on street corners, vendors crying out their wares from ramshackle structures, and men carrying weapons everywhere. They passed a tank surrounded by military. During this encounter, the men became quiet and sober, fingering their rifles.

The look of death was everywhere. Claire was worried that she might be hallucinating. Perhaps the injury on her head was more serious than she had thought.

Defiance and distress vied for attention with vice and entertainment.

Artists on one street painted portraits for the soldiers. On another street, a woman banged a cymbal while a grizzled old man with one eye played a guitar with only three strings. The woman sang in a high, ululating voice in Spanish. She sounded like she was singing of a dead child or an innocence lost. Men in green fatigues with machetes and rifles laughed and threw change at them.

Children ran naked. Prostitutes patrolled the richer parts. She watched this all as though drugged. She soaked up this world that was so foreign and familiar. It could be any place in America where too many people gathered in too small confines in hopes of security in numbers. It could be any destitute third world country. The difference here was the proximity of death, of violence. It was a malevolent presence.

The feeling was pervasive perhaps because of the men in the transport. They leered and sharpened their knives, stared and cleaned their weapons. She found it hard to avoid staring at them at intervals.

Which one would be the first to violate her?

She could make no sense of anything they said. It was a bigger handicap than she would have ever imagined. She had traveled all over the globe, never bothering to learn another language. She had always made due with an interpreter.

She could tell when they neared their destination. Her guards, previously uninterested and lethargic, became more animated and paid more attention. They stood her up at a stop and made her sit on the narrow bench. Two soldiers dropped the gate and sat on the back. They waved at people as they passed, yelling and shouting greetings.

People cheered them as they passed through a neighborhood that was made up entirely of homes constructed of pieces of discarded metal, old canvas tents, and pieces of molded and warped plywood. Dogs ran after them, their fur matted and their tongues hungry. Their barks joined the hoots and shouts of the children.

Then they slowed and pulled in a wide circle in a large square, surrounded by two-story structures that looked like they were straight out of downtown New Orleans. The men jumped from the back of the truck and turned. She was shuffled between them and she hopped down clumsily. Her bag was shoved into her hands. She struggled to take it all in. There was so much commotion. She was hungry and thirsty, scared and paralyzed by the thought of being captive among all these people who she could not understand.

She allowed herself to be pushed forward. She had no sense of destination or direction. The sun was a powerful agent, glaring down on her head, making her squint to see through all the dust. She could still smell the river. Its moist scent was mingled with the smell of people huddled close together for a long time: sweat, dung, sex, fire, and blood. Over it all was the river. Somehow, it gave her hope.

She clung to the bag, cradling it in her arms. She was moved along toward a tall building with sandbags stacked near the door and around the dilapidated porch. A gun emplacement was positioned pointing out toward the road they had entered, a man in dark clothing and a red bandana about his head stood beside it, chewing on a cigar. He stared at her as she walked by, escorted by her captors.

No one spoke to her. It was as if she was an animal or a decoration, a piece of furniture to be moved into this new home for a while. Claire continued to walk, her mind numb and her mouth parched. She really needed water. What was the word? Aqua? Agua? She wished she could remember.

"I need water," she said, her voice plaintive and hopeful that someone understood. Of course, they knew English better than she knew their language.

The man in the bandana by the large gun with a chain of bullets spilling out of it reached behind him and brought her a canteen of water. It was tepid. She did not mind. The wetness was a welcome feeling on her dry lips and down her parched throat. She wanted more, but the man removed it.

"Not too much now. You will get sick. Go inside and we will take care of you. Get a bath. You smell almost as bad as Hector here." He punched the man to her left, jovially. A crooked grin covered his face. He nodded to the men, a gesture to move them along into the house.

The others just stared at him and at her. The water spilled down her blouse and pooled between her chest and the leather satchel in her arms. She heard chuckles.

She found this did not bother her at all. She was just glad someone spoke English.

She was careful not to get her hopes up. She still did not know what they wanted.

The shade of the porch and the interior of the house was a welcome coolness after the heat of the sun outside. She waited for her eyes to adjust to the dark. The room was plain with sparse furniture. Desks, chairs, some bedding in a corner.

Claire was escorted to a room near the back of the house. Her restraints were removed and she was warned not to leave. The men dropped a towel and a bar of soap on the bed and closed the door.

She could see the river from her window. In the distance she could see a metal structure in the waters rising above the river. It was Christ on the cross.

She continued to stare out the window, her hands on the pane. She knew that not far from that statue of Christ, just downriver, she had delivered a eulogy yesterday. She had been free. She was so close. Now, no one knew where she was. She stood there for a few minutes, wondering about her chances of escape. She was worried that with so many armed men, she might get away initially, but they would catch her and she could not guarantee that it go well for her. It just was not worth the risk.

A knock came at the door. Bewildered, she turned and opened it.

"Hi," an older woman said. She had gray hair piled high on her head in pins. Sweat ran down her neck. She seemed familiar.

"Hi," Claire tried to think of something cordial to say. "I am Claire Eppington."

The woman smiled.

"An American. You are a welcome sight, Claire. I was told to make sure you are comfortable."

"Sure. I was about to take a bath."

"I see you have a towel and some soap. I will wait here while you get ready. I will make sure no one will come while you are vulnerable."

Claire laughed, sort of a cough.

"I didn't think I could be more vulnerable."

The woman smiled sadly.

"I want you to feel as safe as possible. It is just a little comfort." She had stepped inside and carefully closed the door, peering out into the hall as she did. "We are alone for now. The men are more interested in drinking and telling tales right now. That may not last. You best get that bath."

Claire could not help letting her guard down around this woman. It seemed she had known her all her life. She seemed like everyone's favorite grandmother or aunt.

"I'm sorry, I didn't get your name."

She seemed taken aback by this comment.

"Oh. I suppose you are right, Claire." She laughed—a kind and gentle laugh. Claire decided people who could laugh at themselves were perhaps the best kind of people.

"My name is Nina, so glad to meet you, Claire."

Claire's hand that she was about to offer in the universal sign of greeting suddenly went to her mouth. She could feel eyes bulging and her mouth forming an "O."

"Nina Rodriguez?"

Nina looked at her quizzically.

"Yes," she said with a nod and a smile.

"I know your husband, Paul," she said, breathless.

"Where did you see Paul?" Her eyes sunk and she bit her lip.

"Just yesterday in Yondo."

Nina grew grim. She looked out the window. She brushed carefully by Claire as if in a trance. She traced a finger along the window as she looked out upon the river.

"So close," she whispered. She was barely audible.

"He was with Manny."

Nina turned, her smile returning.

"Good. He is in God's hands." She looked at Claire, her head slightly tilted. "You believe in God, don't you, Claire?"

She considered this more than she ever had before. The question had been posed so innocently. Claire could tell it was important to her, though. The possibility that God did *not* exist was strange to her. That was perhaps her biggest reason for admitting that she did believe in God in some remote way.

Besides, how could people as good and wholesome as Paul, Manny, Jhoana, and Nina believe in a God that did not exist? They were as smart as she was and more convicted. Conviction was what she was missing, maybe. Could she believe in someone else's version of God? Could their faith somehow save her?

"Sure," was all she said. She did not feel comfortable expounding on the answer.

"Good, because I am going to pray now." Nina got on her knees by the bed, her hands tied before her. "Come. Join me. I will pray for us both and then you can bathe."

Claire knelt beside her and placed her bag on the bed by the towel.

Nina prayed fervently for almost five minutes. Claire watched her out of the corner of her eye. Nina squinted, her skin lined like leather around her eyes.

She prayed for them both, tears leaking out of her eyes as she poured herself into the prayer. Claire had never heard someone pray as though they were talking directly to God. It was like a respectful but conversational discussion more than a formal prayer.

Finished, Nina grasped Claire's hand and squeezed it gently as she looked directly at her.

"How did you get here?"

"I was taken from Jhoana's home last night during the night, I guess. I woke up in a camp blindfolded. How did *you* get here?"

"I was sent here for demonstrating against government corruption in a small village north of here. It isn't the first time. I know Hector and Saoul, personally."

"You know them?"

Nina frowned.

"It's a long story. Basically, I have helped them in the past. Claire, we may be here for a while. I am here to make sure you are comfortable until someone comes for us."

Claire felt like crying.

"Like Manny or Paul?"

Nina looked sad.

"Maybe. Let's hope not. I was thinking that we could get you out when my aid group gets released in two days."

"Released?"

"The American government pays for the safe return of aid workers. They try to keep it hush-hush, but this will be my third time being kidnapped in a decade. I am sort of used to it now."

"So, what about Paul and Manny? You said you hoped they didn't try to find us."

Nina looked out the window again, her face long with sorrow.

"It is too dangerous. Besides, Paul needs to stay away from Barranca."

Claire could see Nina's eyes filling with tears. Despite this, Claire had to admit Nina was one of the most heroic, determined women she had ever met.

"I don't want Paul to get hurt."

Nina smiled.

"That is kind of you. I don't either. Sometimes with men, the less they know the better. I suppose he probably knows you're missing. Hopefully, Jhoana can talk some sense into him."

"Has he never come for you before?"

"Darlin', he has only once known that I was gone. We spend as much time apart as together nowadays. We have so much work to do. I work in the villages with many of the foreign aid workers. I train farmers how to change their farmlands over to legal crops. I speak out against racism, help protect orphans, and deliver food, clothing, and medicine to some of the more remote villages. Paul, he likes his masses." Her smile was beaming. It was obvious that she was proud of her husband. "His ministry is in the city and the larger villages with people who can read, have jobs, and can contribute to the needs of those less fortunate."

"Sounds like you two are quite a team."

"I like to think God has an intricate plan where our work will someday produce some peace here. Right now I am happy when just one child grows to an adult, finds Christ and becomes a functioning citizen."

Claire felt a sad smile grace her face. She admired this woman with a quiet strength of character and a heart as big as anyone she had ever known.

"You are so dedicated to helping people. Help me understand a couple of things. How are you going to get me out of here without Paul's help?"

"I can't promise anything, Claire. There are three of us set for release. Maurice has been shot in the leg. We don't think he'll make it. It is just awful for me to say this, but desperate times call for desperate measures. It is possible if he doesn't make it, we can—"

"No. I can't do that."

Nina smiled a crooked smile.

"Let's hope we don't have to, Claire. You said you needed a couple of things answered."

"Yes. Why have they kidnapped me? Who am I to them?"

Nina pursed her lips and tapped her chin.

"See, that concerns me. I overheard Hector arguing with someone on the phone. It seems you weren't supposed to be here. You were supposed to go with the FARC main army up deeper into the mountains. This group here is a small recruitment outfit. If the AUC find them, there will be gunfire. Bringing you here was dangerous. To them and to you."

"I heard an American man telling them that at the camp. They drove me the opposite way, from what I can tell, but I don't know why."

"It sounds like a power struggle, but I can't tell you who or why. An American, you say?"

"Well, he spoke English." She shrugged. "And the way he threatened them with money and guns, I assumed he was American."

Nina nodded.

"I'll tell you what, Claire." She handed her the towel from the bed. "You go get that bath and when you are done, I will go get some 'intel' as they say in all those spy books."

"You'd do that for me?"

Nina scoffed.

"Honey, any woman would do that. We gotta stick together. We ain't got no one else but God on our side. He should be enough, but when we put our heads together...Woo! Watch out!"

Her energy and enthusiasm was contagious. Claire found herself chuckling despite the situation.

"I'll be back soon, then," she said, grabbing the bar of cracked soap as she made for the little room separated by a curtain from her modest room. She felt stronger already.

"Honey?"

Claire turned.

"You don't happen to have some lip balm in your purse, do you?"

"Well, not balm, but there is some moisturizer. You are welcome to it."

"I am so grateful. God bless you," Nina said, her eyes as warm and welcoming as Paul's had been.

Despite her circumstances, she felt some hope. Her every fiber was screaming from the danger, from the exhaustion, from the absolute travesty of her condition. But, this remarkable woman had somehow been a balm to her worried spirit.

"You, too," she said, as she shut the door.

CHAPTER THIRTY-FOUR

"We can't jump to conclusions, Paul," Jhoana had never spoken to him so bluntly before. Her cheeks were red, her hair still a tangle sticking out from beneath her hastily tied head band. He was worried for her health.

"Claire gone and Nina missing at the same time is not a coincidence," He tried to keep the frustration and fear from his voice.

"Manny can get them both back without much trouble at all, I am sure. Let him do what he does best. You are not the type of person who can get these sort of things done, Paul. You might get hurt."

"I don't think I agree. We are talking about Nina."

"What are you going to do, Paul? You going to pray with them? Give them a Bible lesson in exchange for a prisoner? Give them God's protection from the government?"

"I don't think violence is necessary if that is what you are implying."

Jhoana shook her head. She had her hands on her hips and she exhaled sharply.

"You are a great man, Paul. You are naïve, though, if you think you can reason with criminals. That is what they are. They feel they are right, they think their ends justify their means. Their sense of entitlement overshadows the evil things they do in the name of political and social ideals. You cannot use logic or a sense of what is right with them."

Paul put his hands on the kitchen counter. Somehow, the cold steel was comforting. He leaned forward. He wanted to yell, to get angry, and to demonstrate his ability to force his will. He knew that would be strained. He also knew he would be projecting his anger on Jhoana. She did not deserve that. His conviction, though, remained the same. He needed to do something.

"Jhoana, surely you understand I cannot stay here and do nothing. I have to do something."

She removed her hands from her hips and approached him. Her face softened and her frown disappeared. She put a hand on his shoulder. He could feel the warmth through his shirt.

"You can do something. Call the police. Call Manny."

"That's just it, Jhoana," he kept his voice low, controlled, "Manny knows. He is the one who tasked me with finding Claire."

Jhoana nodded. She seemed resigned.

"Then do that. Find Claire."

He looked at her eyes, so full of sorrow. Maybe she was right.

He knew that he and Jhoana shared a grief. He also understood that as far as his fear of losing Nina, Jhoana wanted him to accept that he was limited to God's will. It was harder for him to accept that now than ever.

He had always known the danger. He had recognized Nina's recklessness after the death of their daughter as she threw everything into her ministry to hide her pain and occupy her restless spirit. Nina was a tireless worker and the people loved her for it.

Paul wished there was an outlet for him. He and Nina shared a passion to deliver the Gospel to a persecuted people. They had sought different paths of ministry. He felt helpless. Maybe Jhoana was right. By helping Manny find Claire perhaps that would be the activity he needed to occupy his mind.

"God help me, Jhoana. I cannot lose Nina." Tears were forming in his eyes. He had never cried so much in one week since his daughter was murdered.

He was slightly shocked as Jhoana wrapped her arms around him without a word. Her body was warm against him. She held him as he stifled a sob.

"What makes you think you are losing her?"

"I haven't heard from her for over a week. I tried reaching her before I woke you." He paused, concerned that he would let the emotions well up again. He tried his best to trust in God. "I don't think that it is a coincidence."

"I know this isn't the first time she has been missing, Paul."

"It's different."

"How? Because of Katherine? Because of Claire? Because of Emily?"

He closed his eyes. The last thing he wanted was to lash out at Jhoana. He knew she was not trying to be cruel.

"I can just feel it in my heart that she is in trouble."

He felt her nodding next to him. Her voice was sad and convicted.

"I understand the power of love. You are probably right. Maybe it is just coincidence. Maybe when we search for one, we will discover news of the other."

"Where do I start?"

He choked back the desperation and the whiny voice that wanted to come out. Composure seemed the biggest struggle of his life. He never had to pretend for Jhoana. For his own sake, he needed to sound confident and competent.

"I know someone we can check with in Barrancabermeja. She knows many of the organizations there. She supplies them with fresh vegetables and temporary workers. Maybe she has heard of something."

"It's a start."

"We can take my car."

"We can't call?"

She shook her head.

"We can, but she will not tell me anything over the phone. We will have to meet with her in person if we can."

Paul nodded.

Soon, they were traveling across the bridge connecting Yondo to Barrancabermeja. Jhoana's old Nissan Patrol rattled and spit black exhaust into the air as they passed checkpoints. This section of the city was less picturesque than the north end near *Cienaga De San Silvestre*. The lake was famous for its fishing and its beauty.

The oil refinery, Eco Petrol, dominated the waterfront for almost a mile to the south of the bridge. They wound through streets alive with celebrations and vendors, children and militia. The things that Paul remembered most about Barrancabermeja were the graffiti, the art, and the murder of his only child. The energy and happiness of the new Barrancabermeja was marred by his memories and his realization that like most of Colombia, the outward pride and joy shown on the streets hid the inner pain and violence that lay under all the smiles, laughter, and proud stares.

"I will book us a room at the Hotel San Carlos. Alejandra lives not too far away, close to *Iglesia Del Inmaculada.*"

"I didn't want to stay that long."

He avoided looking at her. He continued to stare out the window, his spirits low. He saw only the blood on the street, his daughter's body lying crumpled and broken as members of his congregation ran screaming and crying into nearby houses. He struggled to see the world as it was.

Paul closed his eyes. The sound of Jhoana's Patrol drowned out the world around him. He could not hear the *vallenato* music, the shouts of vendors, or the laughter of children dancing. He could not hear the beat of his heart or the voice of God. His teeth ground together. He was suffused in self-pity and self-loathing. The anger, loss, and deep, unfathomable hurt welled inside him. He felt it pool in his stomach, a heavy pit. He felt like his body was lead, his mind a sharp sword cutting his insides.

"You are beating yourself up again, Paul. I know that look."

He tried to smile. It came out as a grimace.

"Stop it right now or I will pull this truck over and tickle you."

Paul could hear the playfulness in her voice. Without looking, he knew she was smiling. He wanted to resent the audacity to joke when he was in so much pain. He remembered the way he had brought Jhoana out of depression when her daughter had been diagnosed with the disease that had taken her life. He had poked fun at one of her paintings, teasing her until she got mad and finally she had broken down laughing and crying.

"It won't work, Jhoana. Nina has never found my ticklish spot. Trust me, she has looked." He looked at her, craning his neck and doing his best imitation of a smile.

Her eyes were on the road.

"You sure could use a good laugh, my old friend. When I volunteered to bring you here to look for Claire and Nina, I thought you were being reckless. I had no idea I was signing up for suicide watch." Her voice was hoarse.

He had not realized how selfish he was being. Of course Jhoana could understand, could empathize with his loss. He never imagined that she would also recognize when he was getting close to despair.

"I can't lose Nina. She is all that is holding me together. She is the glue that binds me."

"Really? I thought it was God?" She said, mocking him.

"It is hard to find God in all this."

"Really, preacher? You say this to me now? Don't be pathetic. You can cling to God as easily as you can cling to your anger. Paul, you know as well as I do that the easiest way to shut out God in your life is to seek out self." She was fiery.

"Now who is the preacher," he said with a chuckle.

"I'm just sayin'."

He felt helpless in the face of her will. She was right. He was completely engrossed in himself. He had lost sight of his mission. He steeled himself for the mental chastisement in which he knew he could indulge. Instead, he glanced at Jhoana, and tried to control his emotions.

"I'm glad you did. Thanks. I need slapping around from time-to-time."

"Every man does. I'm glad I could fill in for Nina so well," she nodded proudly, her eyes scanning the street ahead. "We're here."

He did not realize they had been traveling so long. He sat up, finally bringing his attention to bear.

The warehouse was a two-story brick building several dock doors along its north side. Men and women sat on the dock, eating and laughing. They had arrived during the lunch break.

Jhoana parked and they entered through a decorative side entry. Inside, they walked down a hall and were promptly greeted. Jhoana spoke to the receptionist and they were directed to an office suite upstairs. They sat in plush seats while they waited for Jhoana's friend, Alejandra De La Cruz.

She came out and greeted Jhoana with a warm hug. Alejandra was younger than he had expected. Her eyes flashed with an inner fire. She looked smart and capable.

"I want you to meet my good friend, Paul Rodriguez. Don't be fooled, he is an American."

Alejandra extended her hand, her smile mirrored in her eyes.

"Good to meet you, my esteemed friend. I have heard much about you and your wife. Your work here in Barranca did not go unnoticed."

Paul suppressed the shiver that came unbidden. He wanted to be diplomatic. He knew it was best to keep things light. No need to burden this woman with his memories. He let go of her hand. It was warm.

"Good to finally meet you. Jhoana has spoken about you several times. She has never told me how you two met."

Alejandra chuckled.

"We met at the hospital in Bogotá while each of our daughters was fighting cancer. My Lia was younger, of course. Jhoana and I became friends through our trials. Saw the same doctors, went through the same tests and treatments. Drove through the same ELN checkpoints. Situations like that bring people close, sharing misery and fear."

Paul nodded. He understood how important it was to have a shoulder to lean on, especially someone who could truly understand your pain. It was easy to see that the well-meaning folks who had no real tragedies in their lives could not begin to comprehend your situation. That was the main reason why Paul clung so tightly to Christ. It was good to have a reminder every now and then.

"Well, we are faced with possibly another situation, Alejandra. Paul is concerned that Nina has been taken."

Her only reaction was a sudden frown. Paul could see the determination in her eyes, a subtle hint of the fighter within.

"Well, it is possible I have some information on that."

"Good. We can use all the help we can get."

"We are also looking for a young American lady named Claire. She brought Katherine's ashes to Yondo for the ceremony yesterday," Paul said.

"I regret not being able to attend," she said to Jhoana. "When was she abducted?"

"Claire was taken from my home last night."

"It is good that you have come to me so soon. How long has Nina been missing?"

Paul shrugged.

"I haven't heard from her in over a week. I cannot contact her. And she wasn't in Yondo yesterday. At first, I wasn't worried, but then when Claire was missing…"

"It is likely. There was an American aid group that was kidnapped three days ago. I can make a few inquiries."

"Don't the authorities know?"

"Of course. But, the local police do nothing. They allow the AUC to walk the streets with guns out and strutting their stuff through Simon Bolivar barrio. Things seem more peaceful than they are."

"You aren't giving much hope," Paul opined.

Alejandra shrugged.

"These situations often resolve themselves. Especially where the Americans are concerned. Often times, the government pays the ransom or deals with the group in some other way. There are never any guarantees, though."

"But, how does this help us find Claire?"

Alejandra looked down at a stack of papers in front of her.

"I get female abduction reports almost every week. Most of them aren't abductions at all. Some women are forcefully displaced, which means they are given a home somewhere else. This usually has some ties to forms of racism or activism.

Conversely, the FARC control only a few areas of Barranca. They are covert units. They specialize in captive transport and protection. They are the ones who usually collect and deal with the government representatives. My hope is that this group has collected Claire. It is also possible that if Nina was with the American aid workers in San Luis last week, then she may be here as well."

Paul knew that she was trying to put him at ease. He could not help the panic that threatened to keep him from breathing. His chest felt tight. His throat was dry. It hurt, but he knew he must ask.

"How can you be sure they are here?"

"I can't, Mr. Rodriguez. I am only speculating. But, I can find out quickly. There are three activist groups that operate here in Barranca." She turned back to a desk and flipped through an old Rolodex. She pulled a card out. "I will call my contacts at CREDHOS and PBI. My best hope is that OFP has heard something. They are a women's group that operates a training center and helps women with jobs, food, and housing. They are likely attuned to the activities in Barranca more than I am. We will see."

That made Paul feel better.

"Have a seat in the lobby. I will be right with you."

"Thank you so much," Paul said. He was fighting back tears.

"Don't thank me yet," Alejandra responded, her eyes sad and her face grave.

Paul nodded. Jhoana winked at Alejandra and took Paul's arm and led him to the lobby.

He took a seat, and put his head in his hands. He knew from experience waiting was always the worst part. Despair hung like a shroud from his shoulders. Jhoana rubbed the middle of his back, trying to reassure him. He did not hear a word she said.

CHAPTER THIRTY-FIVE

Alfonso hated Americans. He had grown up revering them. They had all the trappings of freedom and riches. They were cocky and brash. They could say what they wanted. They could live out their fantasies without reproach. Even criminals were often placed on pedestals. He recalled Bugsy Siegel, Al Capone, Dillinger, Jesse James, Billy the Kid, and John Wesley Hardin. They all were famous outlaws—movies, books, and media coverage popularized their deeds.

He had always wanted to be a gunslinger. A Tommy-Gun anti-hero. He had watched *Scarface, The Godfather, Butch Cassidy and the Sundance Kid,* and dozens of westerns and mafia movies. He had purchased replicas of great American Old West pistols and knives. They were stored in his trophy room.

Now his image of Americans was tarnished. Agent Alvarez had destroyed all that Alfonso had hoped to create. He had put Alfonso in more personal danger than he had ever experienced.

He realized that his own ambitions had brought Alvarez into contact with his dreams. He had hoped to use Alvarez's contacts, influence, and their mutual interests to fulfill his goal of becoming the Capo of the Villarreal organization.

His only solace was that he was facing an opportunity to place some of the blame on Carlos. He was anxious.

This had to work. If he could deflect some of the blame, perhaps, he could lay low for a few months and gather his strength to pull off the take-over on his own.

His organization grew larger by the day. He had some of his most trusted associates out recruiting from the poorest parts of the *Valle de Cauca.* Ex-Cali mercenaries and political activists were looking for opportunities. Alfonso considered himself anti-political. He could care less about the political bent of his followers. All he cared about was Colombian pesos and American dollars.

That was one thing about America he continued to like. The money.

He had to make a decision. Once he had the deaths of Henry and Oscar pinned to Carlos, he would have to decide whether his relationship with Alvarez was still beneficial to his vision. Right now, he wanted to strangle him. He wanted to curse him. Alfonso choked down his anger and resolved to consider their partnership further once he had cleared himself.

The most awful part was that Henry's death was the only blood on his hands. It was no matter, though. No need to feel sorry for himself. Alfonso expected Carlos to enter his home any moment. He rubbed his hands in anticipation.

Of course, he could not kill Carlos here. That would be too suspicious. He had considered meeting him in public. He decided that was too risky.

When Carlos had contacted him saying the American woman was at the camp, he had told him to come to the house to collect his payment.

Carlos had insisted that the payment be mailed or shipped through channels. Alfonso had assured him that was not possible. He told him he had earned a bonus for his extra work. That had made Carlos suspicious. He was concerned that since he did not eliminate Manny that his mission was a failure.

Alfonso assured him that his expectations had been met. The idea was not to kill Manny (although, now in retrospect, Alfonso had to admit that would have been more convenient), but to ensure that Manny was out of the picture, and of course, to ultimately link Henry's and Oscar's deaths to Carlos.

A furtive knock sounded at his door.

"Come in."

He was expecting his assistant. It was Carlos. He had a scowl on his face. He slipped into the room, closing the door carefully.

"Carlos."

"Alfonso."

"I was expecting my assistant to announce your visit."

Carlos shook his head and shrugged. He seemed to be favoring one leg. He kept his weight off of it, only the toe touching the thick carpet. A dirty white bandage was on his right index finger. Alfonso did not think he had ever seen Carlos look so…positively vulnerable.

"I was told to come right in. I knocked out of courtesy."

Alfonso wiped a bead of nervous sweat from his upper lip. He wanted to rise from his seat, to shake his hand, to look him in the eye. He was not sure it was safe yet. He fingered the trigger to the shotgun taped to the bottom of his massive oak desk.

"I am afraid maybe that you have eliminated my entire security staff just to get to me."

Carlos chuckled humorlessly.

"You overestimate me, I think." He shrugged. It was a subtle gesture that belied his cat-like grace and strength. Carlos appeared tired, drained.

"Perhaps. I am cautious."

"That's not what I heard."

Alfonso frowned. He did not like the attitude that Carlos was taking. He was supposed to be cowering, afraid for his sister, ready to quit the mercenary business at any minute, and totally malleable. He seemed to be exhausted, irritable, cocky, and hiding some secret. He could not allow him to have the upper hand.

"You have been misinformed, then. I thought you had the best intelligence in Colombia. I guess I was mistaken."

Carlos tilted his head.

"So, then Oscar Villarreal still lives?"

Alfonso's jaw clenched. *The nerve of this insolent...*

"Of course not. He is as dead as Henry Fronçeau."

"Then it is true. You murdered Domingo's closest friend and his oldest brother. What? Was Lucia Villarreal too hard to kill? And why not just kill Manny or Domingo?"

Alfonso could feel the anger radiating from him. He tried to harness it, to use it to concentrate. The hairs on his neck were raised, pinpricks of sensation bristled against his skin. He knew this was a dangerous situation. He was out of control. He plunged right in, reckless as ever.

"It is just a matter of time, Carlos. I thought you came here to get your bonus, not taunt me."

Carlos nodded, his eyes boring holes through Alfonso. He tried not to squirm.

"You did mention a bonus. I don't know what you had in mind, but I had some ideas of my own."

"Oh, you did, did you?"

"Yeah."

"We can discuss that later. You said on the phone that the American woman was safe. Was she taken to the mountains?"

Carlos shuffled his feet and glanced at the empty chair. Alfonso nodded. Carlos sat, his eyes averted.

"I left as soon as I dropped her there. I got some rest and then checked my contacts this morning. No one knows where she is."

"What!?" Alfonso screamed. He bolted forward, his palms flat on the desk.

Carlos nodded, his eyes still on a point at the corner of the desk. He sighed.

"Evidently, your friends in the FARC have taken her somewhere else. I was told that someone in the American government had tried to force them to disobey your commands." He smirked and shrugged, his eyes coming up to stare Alfonso down. "I guess they figured that it was best that neither of you had access to her."

"But why? To what end? Who was in charge?"

Carlos scoffed.

"Who *ever* is in charge? No one can tell. Just when you think you are, someone else is thinking that they are. It gets awfully confusing, really."

"Now you are mocking me." Alfonso was livid. The woman was an important cog in his plan to keep Manny occupied. The only good thing was that he did not know where she was either.

"I guess it doesn't matter, though, right?"

Alfonso put his hands together, the fingers touching. It was one way he found that he could calm himself.

"As long as she is somewhere that Manny can't find her."

"That was your plan? Pretty good, actually."

"I am glad you approve. Now, if you don't have any other 'intelligence' to share with me, then I guess we are finished."

"Finished?" Carlos rubbed his finger and thumb together in the international sign for money.

Alfonso smiled. Maybe Carlos had not changed that much after all.

"Oh yes. Of course. Your payment."

He reached behind him, swiveling in the chair. The small bag of American hundred dollar bills was on the credenza.

"The bonus I had in mind, by the way, was that I wanted to give you back your pistol," he said as he turned back around.

He was stunned for one second by the barrel of the .45 held in Carlos' steady hand.

Carlos was not smiling. Anger and exhaustion were etched on every inch of him. The dark circles under his eyes seemed to swallow his face; the brown of his irises swam in a sea of red. He looked like he was about to cry. Despite this, his hand never shook once.

Alfonso tried to smile. It came out as a nervous tick, his face twitching.

"You mentioned a gun. It wouldn't happen to be the .22 you used to kill Henry and Oscar, would it?"

Carlos spoke through clenched teeth. Alfonso tried to concentrate on looking at his eyes past the barrel of the gun. It was hard to do. Alfonso wanted to shout, *I didn't kill Oscar!* He swallowed instead.

"It is the pistol I took off you at your apartment three days ago," Alfonso said slowly.

"I was told not to kill you. It will be hard for me to not do that. It *is* what I do. I can't let you get away with trying to frame me for killing those men." Carlos' voice was lower, his face dark with hate.

"I can assure you that I only want to pay you for your services. If you don't want your pistol back, I will keep it as a reminder of our partnership."

"Bah."

"You don't trust me."

"Only in the grave."

"What is stopping you, *mi hermano?*"

"I made a promise."

"It is good that you keep your promises. So, what do you want?"

"Leave Domingo alone. Leave the Villarreals alone. One more death will mean my promise is void."

"Why should I fear Carlos?"

Carlos smiled, his teeth bright white against his dark skin.

"Don't fear me, *hermano*. Fear Manny Villarreal."

Alfonso felt trapped. Of course Manny had told Carlos.

"It's too late, Carlos. You might as well kill me now."

Carlos tilted his head.

"Don't tempt me. The only thing between a bullet in your brain and your life is a promise."

Alfonso shrugged.

"An assassin has already been hired. The deed will be done. I cannot stop it now."

Carlos cocked the hammer. Its click was loud in the quiet of the room.

"An assassin. Who, if not me?"

Alfonso weighed his options. He could live to fight another day. His dream was to have a cartel of his own. The quickest way to that goal was to remove a weak link. He could not do that if he were dead.

"I hired the 'Ndrangheta."

"The mafia? Why?"

Alfonso hesitated.

"Giovanni Tegano has a grudge. I just figured he would have an additional inspiration to carry out what I needed done."

Carlos took in a sharp breath, as if he realized something. His eyes were wide.

"*That* is the death you wanted to frame me for." It was not a question.

Alfonso was impressed. Carlos was smarter than he had anticipated, really. He shook his head.

"Giovanni isn't known for his subtle measures. He is quite messy. I think it will be easy to link him to the crime but harder to catch him. He and his uncle have been high profile criminals in Italy for years. There is no danger of you getting framed. I am giving you back your .22, so how could I be manipulating you?"

"I still don't trust you. I should just kill you anyway."

"And go against your promise to Manny? Not a good idea even for someone as talented as you." Alfonso was nervous. He had pressed his security button three times already during the conversation with his foot. No one was answering. Where were his men?

"Manny doesn't want innocent blood on his hands. You aren't innocent, Alfonso. All you have said, all you have done has indicted you."

"When did you become the dispenser of justice, Carlos? The last I knew, you were just an expensive mercenary for hire. An assassin with a conscience," Alfonso taunted.

"I am no longer for hire. I have retired. Maybe law enforcement is my new gig?"

Alfonso scoffed.

"I see. Lieutenant Carlos, now is it? You can't even protect your own sister. Where is the whore, now, Carlos? I told you I would come back for her. Now you are Marshall Carlos? The new law in town? Where's your badge?"

"Right here."

The impact of the bullet at such a close range spun Alfonso around in his chair, blood splattering the credenza behind him. Carlos stood, wiped the bloody barrel of the .45 on Alfonso's shirt and laid it on the desk. He grabbed the bag of money. He unzipped the bag, careful to avoid the blood. He extracted several stacks of bills and stuffed them into his satchel. He checked the pocket of his shirt to make sure his airline ticket was still there and turned and walked from the room, leaving his old life and Alfonso's corpse behind.

CHAPTER THIRTY-SIX

Claire wished she had been able to enjoy the bath. The water was tepid, but the soap and the rinsing of the grime of the road from her body refreshed her. In the back of her mind, she could not escape the fact that she was being held captive. Even after meeting Nina, who had given her a slim hope of rescue, she still despaired for their lives. Every time she thought of Manny, she would remember all those guns, all those people with death in their eyes.

The thought of Manny risking his life for her made her sick. For the first time in her life, Claire found herself concerned for someone else. She felt cleaner on the outside but she had found her spirit growing more desolate.

She stepped out of the bath and toweled off. There was no mirror, but she could plainly see the bruises on her arms and legs and across her stomach. She was still sore there, but she was determined not to let them win. They could beat her if they wanted; she was not going to let them have the pleasure of seeing her cower. She resolved to keep her dignity, regardless of how much she was abused.

She stepped carefully into a clean pair of underwear. She slipped on some Bermuda shorts and a button-up cotton blouse. The bathroom was humid and stuffy.

She wanted to get out.

She was anxious to talk to Nina some more and to formulate an idea of how they were going to escape and get back to Yondo before Paul got into trouble trying to find them.

Although it was not the most ideal circumstances, Claire was glad she had met Nina. She hoped that she would get an opportunity to spend more time with the couple.

She wrapped the towel around her head and opened the bathroom door.

Nina was sitting on the bed, Claire's journal from her mother on her lap. It was open to a collection of black-and-white photos, their edges curled and yellowed. Nina looked up, tears streaming from her eyes.

"What—" Claire began, surprised. She struggled with competing emotions of anger and compassion.

"I'm sorry, honey. I just came across it and opened it out of curiosity." She stammered, her voice choking with emotion. She put her hand to her chest, her fingers squeezing a tissue. Her hand shook as she grappled with more. "It is one of the most touching things I have ever read…"

Tears fell onto the sheets of her bed.

Claire did not know what to say. She was stunned. She had shared the journal with Manny, expecting what? Approval? Sympathy? She never finished reading it herself. Now, someone she barely knew was pawing through it, blabbering on. She wanted to be offended at the invasion of her privacy. Somehow, she could not manage it. She pitied her. It was such a trite thing, pity. She felt the frown sitting heavy on her face.

"Look at me. Crying like a little baby," Nina said. She wiped her nose with the tissue and closed the book. She looked imploringly at Claire.

"I thought when I saw you that you reminded me of Emily. Now, I wish that I had been a better mother to her. God help me. I should never have brought her here. The cost was too great. Paul will never forgive me." She sobbed—great, heaving sighs, her bosom rising and falling. Her face drew down and Claire could see the age and the great loss etched there.

Abruptly, she placed the journal in the middle of the bed and turned her back to Claire. She swung her legs off the opposite side of the bed and hunched over. She continued to sob, her back jerking.

Claire wanted to console her, wanted to say something. She stood there in the doorway to the bath, her shampoo held loosely against her chest with one arm and the other at her mouth. She felt paralyzed.

"I'm not Emily, Nina," she whispered. She was surprised at the emotion in her voice.

"I know," Nina said between sobs.

Claire crossed the room and climbed onto the bed, her knees sinking into the lumpy mattress. She put her arm around Nina's shoulders from behind. She scooted forward, her feet dangling off the side of the bed and scooped up the journal in her right hand.

They sat like that for several moments. Claire stared at the journal, the porcelain shards of her mother's favorite china glinting in the sun coming from the window. The sun felt warm on her back. She wanted to remove the towel, but she knew Nina needed her there.

Nina sat with her face buried in her hands. The sobbing subsided. She sniffled from time-to-time.

"I have only had this a few years. I never opened it until this week."

Nina looked at her then. Her eyes were red from crying, her nose had a sheen of tears. Claire could see that her lips did indeed need some balm.

"Why?"

Claire shrugged. She pulled the towel off and let it fall to the bed behind her.

"I suppose I have always been afraid of dying. Afraid of death, you know, the Great Unknown."

Nina nodded. Her sad smile was comforting. Claire could see her strength, could see how she had managed to survive and to serve so long regardless of heartache and loss. It took a toll, but she was stronger for it.

"It is not an unknown, Claire," she said quietly. "I weep not for Emily. I know where she is. I weep for my loss. It is so selfish, so vain. Regardless, grief and compassion are what make us human. It is what brings us closer to God. When we understand our place in all this, that is when we realize God's will."

"Is it?" She did not want to sound bitter. It just happened. She expected the other woman to judge her harshly. Instead, she smiled.

"This wonderful gift," Nina said, indicating her mother's journal "is a legacy of love to you, Claire. It is a tender heart dedicated to God that put these pages together."

"My father made the cover. He's devoutly atheist."

She just shook her head.

"He loved your mother. What is the story behind the cover, for instance?"

Claire looked up at the ceiling and blinked quickly to clear the tears from her eyes.

"I broke my mother's favorite china when I was nine. This was shortly after my mom died. My dad scolded me, but I realized that he was just grieving my mother. He picked up the pieces and then almost a decade later, he gave me this journal covered with the broken pieces of my mother's plate."

As she finished, she looked directly at Nina. Her eyes were shining with pooling tears again, but she was nodding.

"See? This gift is as much a legacy of your mother's love for you and her desire for you to become a woman of God as it is your father's legacy of love to your mother. He probably resents God for taking your mother from him."

Claire had to agree.

"Yes. He does. I have always known that and I forgive him for his anger and resentment. But, it is unfair to be raised thinking there is no God, there is no Heaven. I have always worried. Worried that...that—"

Claire could not finish. She was choking on the words.

"We don't fear death, Claire. We embrace the gift of life. We honor the gift by living our lives dedicated to the ones we love, dedicated to our God who has given life to us. This is what your mother speaks about in her journal. Have you discovered the passages yet?"

"Some. Mostly, I have read her accounts of her illness and her family's history. She talks about the long line of her family all being Christians."

"Yes. I saw that. I also saw that she wanted the same thing for you. She wanted also for your father to come to love Christ as well. But, she knew that he was bitter. Her illness took a lot out of him, didn't it?"

"I don't remember much. I don't remember being truly happy. I knew he loved me, but sometimes, when we were sitting at the dinner table staring at each other not saying anything, I felt like he wished he could, you know, trade me for Mom." She had never said that to anyone before. She had never even admitted that to herself. She had hid it away, like the feelings of loneliness and the fear of dying like her mother.

"He didn't feel that way," Nina said with conviction. Claire almost believed her. She wanted to believe her.

"I think you are right. When I was young, it felt as though it was all my fault."

"But it wasn't. Look at us now. We are both just feeling sorry for ourselves. We need to find out why you are here and how to get you back. Trust me; the best way is not to get loud and bossy." She chuckled at that. "I already tried that. All it got me was a bruised ego, a bruised noggin, and an extra day here."

"You're right," Claire said, putting both hands on the journal. She looked intently at Nina. "Thank you. I wanted to be upset that you saw it. I couldn't. It was more that this is like a wound. I keep picking at it, making it worse."

Nina put her arm around Claire.

"Sorry I tore off the scab and let it bleed, hon. Sometimes, that is for the best. We'll just bandage you up and send you back out again. You'll just get stronger and soon enough it will heal. You'll see."

"I feel better already. I never looked at it that way. I never thought that her journal was a legacy of love. I always thought it was some sort of way to hurt me from the grave—to remind me of her death, to remind me of my father so unhappy, so confused, and so angry."

Nina nodded.

"We all deal with pain differently. It is best most time to just feel it. Let it wash over you and remind you that you are *alive*. While we are alive, darling, we have stuff to do. It is the dead that are at rest. Come on," she said, standing up and grabbing Claire by the arm. "Let's go meet Saoul."

"Do you think Maurice will be--

Before she could finish, several loud explosions and gunfire sounded outside. Nina grabbed her and they ducked beside the bed. Claire banged her knee on the wooden floor. She could feel blood drip down her shin as she crouched, Nina's body covering her.

Claire listened, feeling Nina's shallow, quick breathing above her. She could hear men shouting, more gunfire, and vehicles moving. Somewhere nearby, a woman yelled.

The door burst open. Nina crawled off her and she looked up to see Saoul standing in the doorway, his face stern and blood running down his thigh from a gash in his hip.

"Saoul! Let me help you. You are hurt."

"Don't worry about me, woman. You two have to get out. We are under attack."

"By who?" Claire asked, her voice cracking.

Saoul looked at her like she was crazy.

"Does it matter? Quick, go to the river. There is a boat at the dock behind this complex. Take it downriver and to the other bank. It should be safe there."

He handed Nina a pistol, slick with blood. Nina shook her head.

"I won't need it."

Saoul only tucked it in his pants with a nod.

"I suppose it won't help you any more than it did Hector."

"What do you mean," Nina asked.

"He's dead. They killed him before he could even get the fifty-cal started up. I told him he made a great target. He wouldn't listen. Anyway, we'll all be gone soon if you don't get to the river. Now, go."

Nina turned and took Claire's hand. She practically dragged her past Saoul. Claire could smell blood, sweat, and smoke. She tried to look Saoul in the eye as she passed, but he just bowed his head and shut the door.

Nina took them outside. The gunfire was louder, but she could tell that the sound was getting farther away. A truck was smoking in the middle of the square, several bodies lying immobile in the dust.

She watched as several soldiers came forward in a group. They wore green berets and dark uniforms. The FARC rebels that had kidnapped her outnumbered them, but the enemy showed no fear. Their weapons were in better shape, their gear newer.

They were more professional, more sure of their abilities. She could tell by the calm looks on their faces as they fired their weapons.

She saw one woman with an old rifle and a bandana go down, her arm flailing and her weapon dropping to the ground with a thud.

"Stop staring! Move!" Nina commanded. She pulled her around the corner of the complex and then Claire's back was to the tumult. She could hear the whine of bullets around her, feel the tug in the air, the danger of death so near. It hummed in the air all around. It mingled with the moisture of the river and the dankness of the moist soil of the riverbank. The fetid air of death overwhelmed it all.

Saoul had been correct about the dock, such as it was. An old wooden boat with a pull-start engine sat tied to a wooden dock that was little more than a few two-by-fours jutting out into the water, suspended on two rotten posts protruding from the water.

Together, she and Nina stumbled down the bank. Behind her, Claire could hear Saoul yelling orders. She could not make out what he said. He was speaking Spanish. Just before they reached the dock, she heard more explosions behind her and felt the ground rumble. Grenades, she thought.

Nina was in the boat now and holding out her hand to Claire. She had never gotten into a boat this small and for reasons she could not explain, she feared she would capsize it just by stepping in too briskly. She hesitated. Nina yelled. It was caught up in another explosion, but Claire could read her lips.

"For God's sake, Claire, get in!"

"I can't!"

"You can! Get in, now!" She reached out again, one foot stepping back onto the dock to steady the boat.

Claire stepped down into the boat, taking Nina's hand. Immediately, she sat down on the middle seat, clutching her mother's journal. She had not realized that she still had it. She held it against her heaving chest. She was breathing so hard, it was incredible.

Nina stepped around her to the back of the boat. Claire was startled as the boat engine roared to life. Nina revved the engine and fiddled with the choke as it began to sputter. Smoke from the engine oil plumed all around them. The boat began to pull away from the dock and the engine was chugging away, disapproving of the sudden expectation to work properly.

As they pulled through the smoke hanging over the river, a shadow interrupted the light from sun ahead of them. A large boat loomed, bristling with guns and rockets. She could hear voices echoing on the water.

The patrol boat slowed and turned slightly against the current. Claire felt a pull in the air and then an explosion behind them as mud churned on the bank. Another volley of gunfire exploded across their bow, the water splattering as bullets ripped a path just past them. Nina panicked and the engine shut off with an angry click.

They drifted for a few feet and then their boat turned. Nina was trying to get them to the opposite bank, but without the engine, they would never make it.

The patrol boat came closer, the muddy waters of the Magdalena churning along its bow.

"Nina! It's going to hit us!"

"That will be better than it shooting us!"

Then the world went black. Claire felt as if someone had suddenly compressed her lungs and stopped her ears with cotton. Her mouth had been open to say something to Nina, but it was now full of water. She felt her body floating, could feel her mother's journal against her chest, one arm flung out, her eyes shut against an irresistible pressure.

She could feel herself falling, being pulled by a strong current. She reached up, dropping the journal, feeling it floating nearby. She tried to open her eyes. She fought against the urge to breathe through her nose.

Her life seemed to coalesce into one enormous fight. She just kept feeling like she was sinking, the waters of the Rio de Magdalena a brown, and liquid grave around her. From somewhere above her, she could hear her name called. Desperately, she fought the current, her hands brushing her mother's journal, the sharp edges of the porcelain decoupage reminding her of her mother's legacy, of her father's pain, of God's plan and Christ's love.

An explosion above her lit the stained waters of the Magdalena with an orange glow. Claire closed her eyes. She felt so heavy. The pressure around her eyes, the lack of oxygen, and the warm waters of the river made her sleepy. She kept slipping, unable to fight anymore.

CHAPTER THIRTY-SEVEN

Manny towered over Maria. He wanted to avoid a repeat of the last conversation they had before he left his brother's employment. She had gotten in the last bitter word.

He hated himself for what he was doing. He needed to do it for his own sanity. He needed to make at least this part of his life right. It would haunt him forever.

"Get up, Maria. I don't need you kneeling at my feet. I want to talk to you face-to-face." He grabbed her hand. It was shaking. She had a tissue in the other. Her face was drawn and she could not look him in the eyes.

He never enjoyed making women cry. He just seemed really good at it. It dawned on him, though, that sometimes it was the most effective emotional tool a woman had at her disposal against the opposite sex. As a means to an end, crying was much more honorable than most men's compulsion in an argument: physical violence. It was odd; most times crying got better results.

"I won't tell you to stop crying. I understand you are upset. But, I need you to talk to me. I need to know, Maria."

"What? What more do you need from me?"

His gaze was sad: bitter disappointment mixed with pity.

"I have never required anything from you but the truth, Maria. It seems I have never gotten the truth, though, have I?"

She still could not meet his gaze. She kept turning the ring on her right hand. She kept biting her lip. She could be so beautiful. Manny remembered her body, remembered touching her cheek as they had lain together. He remembered her eyes, so full of life and merriment.

That was before she had betrayed him. That was before she had deceived him and then extinguished the life they had created. The life he had never known might be possible until she had already had the fetus removed in the first trimester.

Now, he could barely look at her. He had seen her eyes, so full of hurt and anger when he had found her in this study. It was deep in the center of the complex, no windows anywhere. The room was dark. The only light was a halogen lamp on the desk by the far wall. Books lined the room, statues and maps of Colombia.

"No," she said. Her voice was a tortured whisper.

He tried to keep the heat from his voice. He tried to keep from hurting her. He just needed to finish this.

"You owe me the truth now, Maria. I know you still care for me. Give me what I need. Who are you?" Manny resisted the urge to grab her shoulder. He fought to control the lump that was forming in his throat. He had never been an emotional person, but he found himself struggling. "I know you were forced to take our child's life. Whoever it was, you feared them more than you feared losing me."

She looked at him. Manny could see there all the anxiety and pain he had mistaken before for anger. He could tell she wanted to tell him the truth. But, it was killing her.

"I never wanted you to find out," she croaked, desperate. "I never wanted to hurt you." She sobbed, her fist going to her mouth, her brow furrowed, her hair falling across her face.

"Then, why, Maria? Why did you do it?" He could not say it again. It was too much pain to say it aloud. He could barely think about it without teetering between rage and a deep sadness.

"I had to! He wouldn't let me carry a baby! He said he would take me away from you. I was never supposed to fall in love with you…"

She gasped. It looked like all the energy drained from her eyes. She turned the ring on her finger again.

He knew this was a delicate part, but she had finally admitted that there was someone else. He could not let this opportunity slide by without probing. He felt as though time was being pulled through a tight hole.

"Who wouldn't let you, Maria? Who made you abort our child? Who would do something like that?"

"The Americans."

"Who?"

"Agent Alvarez was my handler. I work for the American government. I was placed here to spy on your organization." She looked at her shoes when she said this. She just stared ahead, turning the ring.

"I don't understand, Maria. Why would they want you to seduce me?"

"You have better intel than they do. You have more connections in organized crime. With me in place here, they had the same information, the same connections." Her voice sounded robotic. It was as if she had practiced this speech before.

"Then, why did you stay when I left?"

She looked up, tears in her eyes.

"They wouldn't let me leave. And, I — I believed you would come back," she said, defeat in her voice.

"Alvarez made you take our child?" He asked this, bitterness and resentment in the edge of his voice.

"I didn't have a choice, Manny. I wanted you. I thought that someday we could make a family." She paused, her voice cracking. "I made a big mistake. I suspect Alvarez is rogue. I think he is working for the Mexican cartels."

Manny clenched his fists. *So, this is what my life comes down to?*

Cocaine had ruled his life since he was a kid. It took his father, it took his friends, it had his brother in its grips, and now he learned it had taken his unborn child.

When he had left his family's cartel, the guilt he experienced regarding the nature of his family's business was secondary to the blood on his hands from protecting it. The loss and emptiness he had felt at the news that the woman he loved had betrayed him had led him down a path of discovery and guilt that led him to seek out his friend Paul and eventually Christ. Now, he saw that all along, the culprit was cocaine. The blame for all the pain and loss in his life could be traced to Colombia's most prolific and famous agricultural crop.

He could lie to himself no longer.

"Where is this Alvarez?"

"He works at the American embassy in Bogotá. He is a member of the Plan Colombia Task Force. I work for DEA, and he is my superior. I have other contacts in the agency, but I am supposed to be dark, completely undercover." It all came out in a rush. She must have been feeling a sense of relief to be able to finally just get it all out.

"How connected is---"

Before he could finish, he heard shouts in the hall outside. He heard the clarion blare of the security sirens.

A male voice announced over an intercom in the hall, "We have a perimeter breach. Alert. We have a perimeter breach. All personnel to arm immediately. Repeat. Arm immediately. Security protocol Red One."

Red One was Maria's invention. She had introduced the security protocol shortly after the Villarreals had crossed the 'Ndrangheta. Before he could wrap his mind around why the Teganos had chosen this day in particular to attack a well-defended complex, Maria had grabbed both his hands. Her eyes were wide with fear.

"It's Alfonso! Come with me!"

He did not correct her. She had no idea that he had warned Carlos before going to see Alfonso. Although Manny had instructed him not to kill his cousin, he knew that Carlos would have difficulty going against his nature. That was something Manny understood intimately. Besides, what would Alfonso have to do with the 'Ndrangheta?

What was his cousin thinking?

CHAPTER THIRTY-EIGHT

Paul wanted to drive. Not because he thought he could get them there any faster. He just would be more comfortable. Jhoana's friend, Alejandra, drove like a mad person. The little Patrol darted down the street, Alejandra laying on the pathetic little horn as she jerked back and forth through traffic.

Where's a policeman when you need them, Paul thought.

His knuckles were white as he pressed them against the dashboard to keep himself from sliding into the door. Jhoana was shouting directions from the back seat.

They had heard on the radio just moments before they left that a paramilitary unit of the group AUC had been dispatched to Barrio de Arenales in *Comuna 1*. That neighborhood was where the local FARC group supposedly held Claire and possibly even Nina.

Paul was scared. Most immediately, he was scared of dying before they got there. Alejandra De La Cruz was doing her best imitation of an American movie stunt scene, knocking over a sign for a local cell service provider, hitting a sidewalk once, and barreling through intersections. He did not know how to interpret the smile on her face as she drove.

Paul always feared the unknown. God he knew. The Bible he knew. The outcome of moments like these, were not so sure. He tried to remain calm, tried to pray despite the jolting vehicle and Jhoana's shouts from the back seat. He tried to push the images from his mind of Nina being pushed to the ground, her hands tied and some brute cracking her skull with the butt of a rifle.

He resisted the images: an AUC officer shooting Claire through the chest as a policeman looked on, the girls running, chased by a tank. He knew his imagination was getting carried away. He concentrated on his white-knuckle ride and his prayers.

"When we get there, I propose that I skirt around any violence and get to the river."

"The river? Why?"

"It is their escape route. The FARC group there has specific escape routes that they use to elude the AUC forces. We need to get there before they do."

Alejandra glanced over at him again. He wished she would keep her eyes on the road.

"You looked scared, Paul."

"I am!" He shouted.

"I want to warn you: there will be gunfire there. We won't be safe."

He looked over at her. She jerked the wheel to the right and they narrowly missed a fruit truck, its diesel pluming in the air as it changed gears. The Patrol zipped by.

"I'm not safe now. I think I would rather dodge bullets than trucks."

She smiled.

"Not me. I think I can drive better than they can shoot, but they have lots of bullets."

Paul just shook his head.

He felt a hand on his shoulder. He looked in the back seat. Jhoana leaned forward.

"It will be fine, Paul. We will make sure Nina is safe."

He smiled, trying to feel reassured. The drawn look on Jhoana's face did not hide the fact that she did not feel as confident as she sounded.

He could smell the river before he saw it.

"The compound is just up ahead."

"How can the FARC hide from the AUC in a compound?"

"It's just a small square on the peninsula. Some old warehouses and run-down apartments. Some families live there, their sons and uncles are workers at the oil refinery." She motioned upriver with her eyes. The peninsula swerved south, a finger jutting out into the brown waters of the Magdalena.

Looking upriver, Paul could see where Barrancabermeja had gotten its name: "reddish-colored ravine." The riverbank was a thick red-brown line wending its way past the Barranca-Yondo Bridge toward the Atlantic Ocean.

Paul could hear explosions and the sharp report of gunfire up ahead of him. It reminded him of a fireworks display, the pops and whistles echoing across the water. He gripped the dash harder. Ahead of them, two personnel carriers were parked, several black-clad soldiers taking cover behind them.

"We can't get through!" Jhoana shouted.

Alejandra smirked.

"I know a shortcut," she quipped.

She jerked the wheel to the right, toward the river. Paul had a sinking feeling.

They went through a small alley between two houses at break-neck speed. Doors and windows, toys and trash scattered around them. The alley was empty of people. Paul sent a quick prayer of thanksgiving.

"There! Up ahead! There's a courtyard full of soldiers!" Jhoana pointed ahead.

"I thought we didn't want to go there!" Paul was panicked.

He wanted to see Nina there. Everyone was clad in blue-green camo or dark black military fatigues. Everyone was shooting weapons or running for cover. Paul struggled to see Nina's red hair or Claire. He saw some women, but they were neighbors running, pushing children to safety or crying over bloody bodies in the dirt.

Alejandra slowed and downshifted quickly, the engine whining in complaint. She steered sharply left through a gate and they were on the road, the personnel vehicles on their left. They crossed the main street, Calle 1, and then drove through the narrow space between two houses.

Alejandra slammed on the brakes and whipped to the right, just past the back of the house.

A dog ran out in front of them, dust billowed, and he felt the tires leave the ground as the Patrol rocketed ahead. The vehicle jumped a small ditch and they all grunted as the wheels touched down hard on the other side.

They were on the eastern side of the square in an opening. The AUC forces were pinned down by gunfire from the houses near the river.

Paul craned his neck as Alejandra shoved the stick into third. The Patrol screamed, its big tires grabbing the loose red dirt of the square and bolting ahead. He still did not see Nina.

"I don't see her!"

"She's probably down there in those buildings!" Jhoana shouted.

"Hold on. We'll get there. I want to come in by the river," Alejandra said. Her voice was controlled.

"I'm glad you drove," Jhoana said, patting Alejandra's arm.

"I know you are," Alejandra said, a proud smile on her face.

Paul could hear more gunfire behind them. He looked around, frightened that their flight had attracted the gunfire from either of the forces across the square. He did not see anyone even paying them any attention at all.

"I'm going to park over there behind that building away from the gunfire, but I need to cut behind this house first."

"Thanks for the update. Do it," Paul said. His hands were sweaty. He noticed the palm marks on the dash. He was almost embarrassed.

Alejandra slowed the Patrol and then they came to an abrupt stop. Paul grabbed the white napkin they had the presence of mind to bring. He saw a swarthy man approach with a rifle in hand.

He smiled when he saw Alejandra.

"Aren't you a sight to see in a war? Who are your friends? Why are you here?"

"Slow down, Saoul. We came looking for Nina, Paul's wife. And an American woman named Claire."

Saoul frowned. He half turned, pointing with his rifle.

"I just sent them to the boat. A patrol was there and sunk their boat. I came back here to get a rocket."

"What! Nina's in the river?"

He nodded.

"Then let's go!" Jhoana shouted, grabbing Paul's arm.

They were running down the bank toward the river. Paul could see the forty foot plumes of flame from Ecopetrol's refinery just north of them.

He could smell the rancid, moist odor of the river. Sounds and smells all melded together and time seemed to drag. He felt the jolt of each step as he careened down the gently sloping bank, the wet grass slippery beneath his feet.

He was amazed at how unfocused his mind was despite how attuned he was to one image: Nina clinging to wooden plank, floating in a brown river of flotsam and debris.

He saw the looming hulk of a thirty foot patrol boat bristling with big guns and eight men looking overboard at their handiwork. He clenched his jaw. Hate and fear, love and pain mingled in a mesh of emotions so strong he thought he would explode.

Instead, he picked up his pace and dropped Jhoana's hand. All thought went to Nina. He could not lose her now. *Not like this.*

He ignored the men in the boat. He understood that his hatred would paralyze him. He had to focus on the love he felt, on the fear of losing Nina.

"Where's Claire?" Jhoana asked.

Paul tried to ignore her.

Didn't she see his Nina floating in the water, vulnerable and scared?

"Señor! Wait! Get down!"

"Drop to the ground, Paul!"

He shut out the cries from behind him. He did not understand.

"Danger close! Get down!"

Paul heard a WHOOSH! It came from behind him. Heated air blew past his hair and he felt himself falling forward, pitching face-first into the wet grass.

He caught himself with his hands, trying to keep his head up. His nose buried in the soil, and he tasted the musty grass and dirt. His lip burst, pain and blood filling his senses.

He felt himself skid across the grass. As a kid, he would have gotten up laughing at the fun of it all. He would probably climb the hill and dive again just for the sensation of being out of control sliding down an embankment. Now, he struggled to get his head up and look for Nina. He had to find her.

Just as he looked up, he was blinded by an explosion. The patrol boat, just thirty yards from Nina, went up in flames. He watched Nina struggle and lose her grip on her board. She slipped beneath the water.

"No! What did you do? She's going to drown!"

He watched in horror as the burning boat began to sink. He jumped up to his feet and sprinted down the hill. He saw a rickety dock at the water's edge.

He made for it, feeling the boards sway and bow under his weight as he ran across it. He reached the end and jumped into the water, his hands out in front of him.

He was amazed as his body hit the water at how warm it was. It was thick with debris. He could not see much of anything. His heart hammered in his chest. God forgive him if he failed her.

He could hear voices echoing off the water. Some were calling his name; some were screams he thought for sure were coming from the burning boat. He tried his best not to gloat at their demise. He concentrated on Nina, not vengeance.

Ahead, he saw hair floating in the water. Below the hair, he saw a slim body drifting downward, a hand held up and one against its body. It was Claire.

Panicked, he searched for Nina. His lungs ached. He needed oxygen. He started to see spots. Fat droplets of darkness spotted his vision. He felt a prickling sensation in his fingers.

He stopped swimming forward and then powered his way to the surface. He shook his head, his hair spraying brown droplets across the river as he came out of the water. A dark black stain marked the sky where the boat had plunged into the water. Ahead of him and downriver, he saw Nina clinging to another piece of wood. She looked at him, desperate and excited at the same time.

Their eyes met and Paul's heart almost stopped. He could see Emily's eyes there, could see her face framed with curls. He had failed her. He had held her while her killers had scurried away. No justice.

"Paul! Snap out of it! Claire is down there! She is drowning! You need to save her! I am too weak to get her up. I gave her some air, but I don't think she'll make it." Her voice echoed across the water like she was right next to him.

He nodded, his vision blurring. His eyes stung, his lip burned, and his lungs complained. He took a deep breath, feeling his ribs constrict and then dove beneath the water.

His heart sank at first. He could not locate her.

Then he saw her hand below him. The waters were deep here and dark.

Paul shoved off with his feet and pulled water past him with the powerful strokes of a man half his age. He felt the water pull around him.

He grabbed her hand. He saw her eyes were closed. He felt a deep sadness. Losing Nina would have been devastating, but seeing someone with a spirit so bright would be a wicked blow to his spirit. He knew he had hoped Claire would meet Nina someday. He never would have wished this on her though. Why was God so cruel sometimes?

Paul began to steel himself and changed his position in the water with his free hand and let his legs drop below him. He dropped lower on Claire's body and wrapped his arms around her from behind. He was startled when he felt something sharp at her belly. He ignored it, focusing on moving. He knew time was crucial. She was limp in his arms. She was not breathing.

Paul struggled to the surface, his body screaming in protest. He strained beyond his capabilities, fighting the urge to breathe out, fighting the urge to just give up.

The air was hot and stifling around him as he reached the surface. Flames danced upon a rainbow-colored slick just a few yards away. He frantically looked around for Nina. He had become disoriented under the water.

He took in huge gulps of air and brought Claire's body close to him. Her head tilted back and her mouth came open. He reached up with one hand while treading water with his legs and slapped her gently on the cheek.

"Claire! Please Claire. Please God. Please Claire."

"Paul! Come this way! Bring Claire here! We've got Nina!" Jhoana was standing at the edge of the river, cupping her hands. He tried to wave. He tried to answer. He failed.

Paul felt his energy wane. It was like he was a toy running on batteries that were giving out. He could feel the tug. He just wanted to sleep. He wanted to hold Nina again. It had been so long this time. He realized how much he had missed her.

If only he could sleep. He could wake up happy if he knew Nina was there. He would do anything. He promised God to devote himself even more to His work if He would just let him sleep.

"Paul!"

He heard a splash and a dark face was coming toward him in the water. A hand grabbed him by the forearm. His eyelids drooped and he saw Alejandra on the bank ahead of him pulling Nina from the muddy waters. He smiled and closed his eyes.

Thank you, God, he thought. *Thank you.*

CHAPTER THIRTY-NINE

Manny followed Maria as she opened the door into the hall. It was dark except for a red strobing light. She slipped into the hall and headed for the north wing at a run. It was where Domingo had his offices and living suite. He followed a step behind, his instincts kicking in, his mind racing.

Most of the gunfire seemed concentrated on the perimeter. Manny glanced over the rail into the courtyard and saw several of Domingo's security forces setting up defenses. A tall, swarthy man pointed to places of cover and directing the men to position for defense.

Manny could tell from the scene below that this was no small threat. He wondered at the force that the 'Ndrangheta could unleash. Would they ally themselves with rival cartels? Hire mercenaries from ELN forces or disbanded ex-Cali cartel thugs?

It did not matter. They were here. He was not so far removed from his job that he did not immediately assess the situation and begin devising his own plans for survival and counter attack. Cut the head from the snake.

He had thought Alfonso dead. So, the snake had more than one head. He did not have time to puzzle it all out. Maria had knocked on the door to Domingo's suite.

A large man in a designer suit holding two submachine pistols opened the door, one pistol trained on the hall behind them, his eyes scanning back and forth.

"Come in," he said, curtly.

Manny did not know this man. He was tall, thick through the chest and had dark skin. One of Henry's specialists? A seven-inch long, black SOG SEAL Team knife was strapped to his hip and a Ka-Bar Kukri machete was mounted on his back.

The man meant business, that was for sure. The two COBRAY M11s were on a custom sling that allowed him to drop either one to his side at a moment's notice. He also noted a no-nonsense .45 caliber M1911 in a holster under his left arm.

Manny approved. This man would make a great bodyguard. He knew how to outfit himself for personal protection. It was odd to see so many weapons on a man in such an expensive suit. It was a contrast that spoke of necessity and professionalism.

They would need both.

"Any heavy artillery? Gunships, or tanks?"

"Not yet. Just small arms fire and a couple of soldiers with rocket and grenade launchers. The gatehouse got blown into bits."

Manny nodded.

"Where's Domingo?" Maria asked. Her mascara had run and her hair was matted to her head.

"In the safe room. I have two men guarding the entry from in there, two in each of the adjoining rooms for crossfire and two in the room with him."

He looked at Manny with cool eyes.

"But, they will have to get by me first. That will not be easy." He did not seem brash. He was speaking as a matter of fact. Manny was not going to argue with him.

"Henry train you?"

He nodded.

Manny offered his hand.

"Manny Villarreal."

"Domingo's brother. You should be in the safe room with—"

"Manny!" Domingo came into the room, his face a mask of concern.

Manny was stunned for a second. The bodyguard turned, alarm on his features. He held up a hand and pleaded.

"Sir! I told you I cannot keep you safe if you insist on exposing yourself. They are here for you. I cannot allow them to kill you as well."

Domingo flashed his most charming smile.

"Nigel, your father would be proud of your commitment. I will be fine. Manny and Maria here will watch over me. You go and help out my security folks. They sound like they have their hands full."

"But, sir—"

Manny grabbed his bicep to get his attention. He flexed and Manny felt the ripple of steel there.

"You are Henry's son?"

He turned to Manny with eyes sad and determined.

"Yes. I was not there when he died. He was a friend to your family. I must protect you now in his honor. I can't if—"

Manny nodded.

"My brother can be obstinate and dangerous. Trust me, I know. I protected his backside for almost a decade and got his precious fat out of the fire on several occasions personally. You just have to do the best you can. "

He looked miserable.

"Stay in position for now. I will talk some sense into my brother, Nigel."

Domingo had already struck up a conversation with Maria. His two body guards stood nearby looking pale and nervous.

"Are you saying this is the Mafia? Why?"

"It doesn't matter now. You have to listen to your security personnel. They know what is best for you."

"I am tired of being protected all the time. Maybe it's time for me to protect myself for once." He stuck out his chest and extracted a pistol from inside his jacket.

"Give the gun to Maria, you fool," Manny demanded. He was ruthless. His experience had always been with Domingo that you had to be rude to him to get him to listen. Being nice and diplomatic would just get you trod upon.

Domingo turned, his eyes ablaze with hurt and anger.

"Who's in charge here, anyway, little brother?"

"Whoever's alive after this attack, I suppose. If you think you can defend yourself, I guess the odds are in favor of Nigel over there." Manny indicated Henry's son standing by the door, his machine pistols in hand and a determined scowl on his face.

"Oh, he just volunteered his services this morning. I think it's a coincidence that he showed up the day we get attacked. What do you think?"

"I think he is here to save your skin in honor of his murdered father. You don't even know who to trust anymore, do you?"

Domingo looked surprised. He glanced at Maria for a second.

"No."

"Give Maria the gun, Dom." He turned, trusting that his verbal abuse of his brother would do the trick.

"I see you aren't packing a gun. How are you going to survive this?" Domingo asked smugly.

Manny turned slightly, a smile on his face.

"I'm going to pray and trust in God for a change, Dom," he said as he walked into the bedroom.

The safe room was a concrete and metal closet in the corner. A bank of televisions lined one wall. That was new since he had left. Security cameras showed Domingo's forces holding the line at the perimeter against over twenty armed men. The grainy, black-and-white cameras did not show much, but he could see gun flashes and men moving around.

On one screen he noted a group of men walking down the hall leading to the suite. They all wore suits. One man, tall and gaunt, had a limp. Giovanni Tegano. The perimeter skirmishes had been a diversion. Manny quickly counted ten armed men and Giovanni.

Even on the low resolution, Manny could make out the facial scar and the permanent scowl on Giovanni's face. He could see determination and murder in that stare. Tegano pointed at the camera and one of the men shot it, the screen going fuzzy a moment later.

"They're coming!" He yelled.

Manny bolted back into the living room, just as the door was ripped to shreds by a spray of bullets. He saw Domingo duck and Maria crawl behind a sofa. Nigel stood his ground, just to the right of the door, crouching beside a huge exotic lamp.

The two body guards leaped in front of Domingo and knelt on the carpet, their AK-74's trained on the door.

A boot came through the door. Then the door was flying onto the floor. Manny saw all this in slow motion; saw the black canister float through the air the instant the door was breached. Manny recognized it immediately. He wanted to shout, but knew it would be too late. As soon as the canister hit the floor, they would all be blinded and deafened. He braced for it, turning his head toward the opposite wall and diving for the floor.

A loud THUMP sounded as he skidded on the carpet burning his forearms and cheek.

His ears rang painfully and he was disoriented. The good news was, he avoided the worst of the blinding flash. He got up on his knees and scanned the entry. Two men stood there, their rifles spilling spent cartridges onto the carpet. Manny could not hear, so it looked like watching a gangster movie with the sound down.

He saw Nigel cut one man's hand off with the machete and then slash the other man across the neck with the back cut, all while spraying the M11 at a man charging Domingo's position. Flashes from gun barrels lit the room.

He could not see Maria or Domingo.

He charged across the room toward where they had been, dodging a table that had been toppled for cover and saw a body sprawled there. It was one of Henry's security team. His ears still rang and his legs were aching from the effort it took to run in a crouching position, his head held low and up.

He saw the two men guarding Domingo. One was down and the other was bleeding badly from his leg and face. He continued to fire ahead, his eyes squinting in pain.

He was probably still blinded. They were outnumbered and outgunned. Manny knew it was desperate.

He chanced a glance at the doorway and saw the figure of Tegano enter, pushing aside his two soldiers. He held an M-16 at waist level and shot the ceiling in a long burst. The sound of the gunfire was Manny's reminder that he had retained his hearing. Spent cartridges rattled on the teak floor.

"Put your guns down or you all will die!" Giovanni yelled. His smile was mirthless, just barely an upgrade from a frown.

Nigel stood behind him and brought the machete around in a long side swipe, meant to decapitate him.

Remarkably, Giovanni ducked and then brought the butt of the rifle backward in a quick motion, hitting Nigel in the crotch. Giovanni turned and his rifle flared. Nigel's face disappeared in fountain of gore and blood. It happened so fast that Manny did not have time to look away.

The man beside him grunted and then screamed. His rifle jumped and Manny was startled as bullets ripped the air beside him. The man to

Giovanni's right, closest to the wall, went down holding his knee, his rifle skittering to the floor.

Manny did not move. He seemed rooted to the spot. That was when he saw Maria. She had Domingo's pistol in her hand and she leapt in front of Manny, screaming.

He watched as Giovanni turned, a smile creeping onto his face.

"Alvarez's little prostitute. What a surprise. I didn't expect you to stick around for the festivities." Giovanni leveled his gun at Manny. Maria fired once and Giovanni flinched like someone had punched him.

Manny reached for Maria, to pull her down to the floor. Two more soldiers in black t-shirts and camo pants stood outside the door. Both were aiming down their sights. Manny lunged. As he did, he saw Domingo out of his peripheral vision on the floor face-first, behind cover, his hands over his head.

He managed to push Maria forward, her head snapping back as he pushed her between her shoulder blades. He used his momentum to leap over her, pinning her beneath him, pressing her into the carpet as bullets came flying overhead from the doorway. Manny felt his shoulder rip as a bullet hit him high on the tip of his deltoid. It hit a bone. Pain shot up his neck and he pitched to the side, the force of the projectile moving his entire body to the right. His right arm went numb and he landed hard on the carpet, unable to get his hand under him.

More bullets passed overhead. He prayed none hit Maria. He almost lost hope. He could hear more men coming and Giovanni had turned back to them, pain and anger written on his features. He held one hand to his chest, blood soaking through his grey shirt. His other hand held the M16, its muzzle trained on the floor at the moment.

Manny knew what he needed to do. His arm was not cooperating. He struggled back to his knees, his left arm on the floor. He put his feet under him, meaning to take the three point stance of a defensive lineman and tackle Giovanni and pin him to the floor. Manny was not sure if he had the strength to pull it off. The pain in his shoulder radiated to his neck and back. His whole body was tight as a wire.

He managed to get his head up and get his aim directed just as Giovanni began to lift the rifle. Then, he was shoved aside. He fell over to his right as a small form darted past him. He saw Maria just as his shoulder crashed into the carpet again, waves of agony crashed over him.

She ran, her body low to the ground, her head down. She crashed into Giovanni, the same move he had planned on executing. The only difference was that Maria may have weighed a hundred and ten pounds. Manny cringed from the pain and the realization that Maria would never be able to bring Giovanni down with a tackle. And she would be up close to him with the rifle aimed forward point blank. Giovanni was big. Manny grimaced, expecting the worst.

It was only a second, but it seemed the moment hung in the air. Just as Maria approached Tegano, she ducked to the side, one hand grabbing Giovanni's gun hand, the other reaching high up on his shoulder, just above where she had shot him. She circled around him, quick as a cat. She forced his wrist of his gun-hand inward with a twist and dug her fingers into his wound at the same time. Giovanni reacted instantly, his face contorted in pain. He tried to reach back with his other hand.

Maria merely ducked down, pulling his shoulder back, and put her knee into the back of his leg. Giovanni toppled over backward, a howl coming from his lips as he realized what was happening. Her quick movements used his momentum against him and he crashed to the floor. Manny could feel him hit.

He could hear shots behind him as the men in the cross-fire room filled the living room and quickly dispatched the incoming mercenaries. He watched as bodies fell and blood splattered in the hall just outside the door. Men's cries filled the room.

He managed to get back up. Standing was such an effort. Maria stood over Giovanni, the pistol back in her hand. She had a grimace on her face, and blood ran down her leg.

"Hold still, you bastard! I will put a bullet in your eye if you move." She was crying, he saw.

"Maria. It's alright. It's over."

Then, he heard Domingo moan. He turned and saw Domingo sitting up against the table, the two bodyguards at his feet, dead.

He saw no injuries on him, but Domingo looked around the room with haunted eyes. Manny remembered that look. He turned his attention back to Maria and Tegano.

Manny stumbled over, holding his shoulder. He looked down at Giovanni on the floor on his back, staring up at him. He ignored Maria, who stood there breathing hard, the pistol held shaking in a two-hand grip.

"My brothers will avenge my death. They will come for you. They will destroy the Villarreal family!" Giovanni spat.

Manny shook his head.

"They can't avenge your death if you still live. You are going home empty handed, I'm afraid. Forget about Colombia. Forget about the Villarreals. You will live longer, be more profitable, and your family will hold you in high regard that you have chosen the path of wisdom rather than the path of vengeance and pain. That is all you will find here."

He could sense Maria staring at him, incredulous.

"You're not going to let him live! He has to pay for all these deaths."

"Vengeance is mine, says the Lord," Manny said, still staring at Giovanni.

Giovanni smiled.

"Now he is a man of God! Manny the charitable. Manny the gracious," Giovanni said, distaste and mockery lining his voice. Manny placed his foot over Giovanni's wound and tamped down. Giovanni squirmed, his face twisted in pain.

"I am a man of God, but don't expect much more mercy, Señor Tegano. You will be escorted back to Italy and handed to the authorities that have been trying so hard for so long to find you."

Maria huffed beside him. He still could not meet her eyes.

"I am sorry, Manny," he heard her whisper.

"I forgive you," he said, still not looking at her. He blinked rapidly, holding back the tears that would not come.

CHAPTER FORTY

Her first thought was that Paul and Nina looked perfect together. A monitor beeped. Claire saw Nina brush Paul's hair back and lay her hand across his lap. He looked at her sheepishly. It looked like they were dating, not married for thirty-five years. It was so cute, she had to smile.

They were so wrapped up in each other they had not noticed she had woken up. She did not want to ruin the moment, so she just raised her eyebrows and watched them. She was truly grateful to both of them. They deserved to have this moment.

She had been in the hospital for two than days. She had been unconscious for a full three minutes underwater, but her brain was still functioning well. She had needed to rest. She had never felt so exhausted. Manny had sat with her last night and told her the whole story of what had happened. He had seemed more distant, but happy to see her again.

Claire knew that with the death of Manny's oldest brother, he would be in mourning and contemplation.

So much death. So much violence.

She did not feel she could live in a country so fraught with danger and such a disregard for human life. Based on her past five days, she would have to consider carefully whether she was ready to commit to another assignment here.

Of course, her employer, Cremation International, had already contacted her. The president had called, giving his sympathies and condolences. He had a beautiful bouquet of roses delivered and had her return arrangements scheduled on an open ticket so she could take her time to recover before returning home. Her travel supervisor had called. Sally had mentioned that she would get hazard pay and that there was already a note in her file to schedule her assignments closer to home in the future.

Claire had assured Sally that she was open to continue to travel. She did truly enjoy it. She met such interesting people. No one quite as unique as in Colombia, though. And that was why considering her stay and her possible return was bitter sweet.

Paul glanced up, perhaps feeling Claire's stare.

"She's awake."

"Oh."

"How long have you been awake?"

Claire smiled.

"Long enough to know you two are made for each other."

Nina blushed.

"We have been apart for so long, we just—" Paul began.

"I'm teasing you. You don't need to defend yourself or be ashamed. Seriously, I am glad you are here. I want to thank you for saving my life."

It was Paul's turn to blush. He recovered nicely.

"It was nothing. In fact, I was thinking that after all our talks together, I had never mentioned baptism to you and yet there you were buried in the water."

Despite herself, she chuckled.

"Well, I am glad you were able to get the ceremony in with all the bullets and bombs."

"Don't encourage him. His sense of humor is getting worse with age," Nina chided.

They had a good laugh.

Claire's room was bright with the afternoon sun when their visit began. They talked for several hours, the room darkening. Claire enjoyed laughing with the Rodriguez's, praying with them, and catching up on the local news.

Finally, Claire had to ask.

"So. Where's Manny? I haven't seen him since last night."

Nina and Paul shared a furtive glance.

"Manny and his family are attending to the funeral arrangements for Oscar. Viewing is tomorrow. He has asked us to invite you to the ceremony. Domingo has asked Manny to preside. He is home writing some thoughts."

"Of course I will go."

Claire could not help feeling a little disappointed that Manny had not asked personally. She supposed she was being silly.

"He did mention that he would stop by tonight before visitation is over," Nina added.

Claire glanced at the clock on the wall out of habit. Visitation was over in less than an hour. Was Manny going to come before visitation was over? Was she resigned to not seeing him again until the funeral? She decided not to say anything. She felt anxious and selfish.

Paul took her hand.

"Claire, we have been so blessed to have met you and gotten to know you. Nina and I have discussed this. We are going back to the States this winter."

"Really? But your work here—"

"Will be continued by someone younger and fresher," Nina finished for her.

"We are thinking about moving to the Chicago area. There are some mission opportunities in the inner city that we are interested in assisting. We would like to visit you once we move. Would that be alright?"

"Of course! You can meet my dad. He will be a little huffy with you being a Christian and all, but since you saved my life, I think he will be fine," she said with a smile.

"We look forward to meeting him. We want to take the opportunity to congratulate him on raising such a fine daughter."

Claire was taken aback by their praise. She had never felt so welcome and loved. She felt herself getting emotional.

"Oh, dear. Don't cry. We will see you again by the grace of God," Nina said. She came over and gave Claire a big hug. She squeezed her tightly.

"I love you," Claire said. Her voice was muffled by the choking sensation of emotion in her throat. Nina patted her back and Claire could feel her smile against her shoulder.

"We love you, too, Claire." She pulled back and looked Claire full in the face.

"We will see you again tomorrow at the funeral, then. Do you know when you are shipping out?"

Claire wiped the tears from her cheek and sniffled.

"I get out early tomorrow, so I thought Monday would be best. I wanted to meet your congregation in Bogotá again. They were such wonderful people. And, I thought I could spend some time with—" She was almost ashamed to say Manny's name.

She knew her affection for him was obvious. She was past all the juvenile games of clandestine romance. But, something made her hesitate.

Maybe it was the fear that the timing of her romantic interest was in bad taste and inconsiderate since Manny had just experienced the loss of his brother.

Nina came to her aid. She was nodding with a sad smile. She tilted her head, her hair framed in the waning light from the window.

"Manny, right?"

"Yeah. Pretty obvious, huh?"

"Well," she said, smiling. "I haven't witnessed the two of you together, but Jhoana tells me you two were getting pretty acquainted the other day."

"Speaking of Manny, he should be here any minute. We should give you two some privacy. Besides, I need to get some grub."

"Yeah. You two go on. Get something to eat. Call it a date."

Paul chuckled.

"A date, huh?" He looked at Nina with a glow on his face. "We haven't had a date in years. That sounds good to me."

"Me, too," Nina said, a hitch in her voice. She looked at Claire with sad eyes and traced a line down Claire's crisp cotton sheets with a finger.

"Claire, promise me that you won't break Manny's heart."

Claire was surprised at this request. She frowned.

"Of course not. What makes you think that I will."

"It's not that I think you will. He just can't bear another setback. Oscar isn't his only loss, you see."

"Oh. I'm not sure I follow, but I trust you."

Paul gently grabbed Nina's arm, his eyes serious and pleading.

"Nina. This is something that Manny can discuss with her, darling. Something he needs to decide to share with Claire if he feels it is necessary."

Nina nodded.

"You're right. Goodbye dear. Take care. We will pick you up in the morning and get you ready for the service."

"Thank you again for everything. God bless you."

"And you, young lady," Paul said with a wink.

Claire could see a weariness that she had not seen in the days they had spent together. She figured their adventures had taken a toll on him.

Claire sighed as they left.

She had much to consider. Their visit had stirred strong emotions in her. She had finally begun to feel complete. She realized the thing in her life that she had missed was someone she could admire, someone to look up to.

At the same time, she struggled with the bitter realization that it was her mother that she should miss most. She glanced over at her meager belongings sitting on a bureau by the little bathroom in her hospital suite. Her mother's journal was there, the pages bloated from exposure to water.

Nina had picked the grass and weeds from it earlier. The lights from the street lamp outside gleamed off of the porcelain and bead cover.

Several pieces had fallen off in the river, leaving the black board exposed that her father had used to glue the pieces of the plate. Looking at the journal made her sad. Not because she would never be able to read her mother's words contained within.

It made her sad that she could not remember her mother's voice, her mother's face. She was a foreigner, a stranger. She was a legend. Claire did not have memories of her mother. She just had that journal.

It was ruined now, but she felt it did not matter. She would never be able to put a false memory of her mother into her heart based upon some pictures and words in a journal.

It just did not resonate with her. Maybe it was because she had always felt cheated. Maybe it was because it was hard to feel a loss of someone you had never known.

Of course, it was different for her father. That was another factor, to be sure. The effect on her father, the effect on their relationship was a palpable entity. She held a grudge against her mother for dying, for succumbing to her illness before she had a chance to be a mother. She hated her mother for giving in to the disease and leaving her father a husk of his former self.

And perhaps she had resisted the idea of a God for so long for the very same reasons. She had denied His existence because she had blamed him. It was not so much her father's stance that had influenced her as it was her own experience. It was just convenient to blame her father. Claire had found that it was convenient to ignore how selfish and unforgiving, irrational and petty she had been.

Claire was beginning to yield to self-pity and self-loathing when she heard a light rap at her door.

"Come in."

"Hi," Manny said sheepishly as he entered. He held a plush teddy bear and a card. A clean bandage covered his right shoulder.

"Hi there," Claire returned. He looked so sad. His face was drained of energy and his eyes were hollow. She was glad he was here.

She wondered what Nina had been meaning to tell her. What other loss had Manny experienced? Manny had told her about his father while on their way to Yondo. Perhaps that is what she had meant.

"I brought you some gifts."

"That is thoughtful. Thank you. I am sorry I wasn't more talkative last night. I was just so tired."

Manny sat next to her and leaned forward, grimacing.

"Claire, it's fine. I understood. I was in my own funk, as well. I was glad to see that you survived, but I regretted that I was forced not to be there."

"Paul filled in admirably. Besides, I think he needed to play the part of hero."

Manny looked impressed.

"It's funny you say that. I think you are right. Saving you from drowning was certainly an act of heroism."

An awkward moment passed as Manny stared at her, playing with the plush toy. She could tell he wanted to say something more.

"How's your shoulder?"

Manny shrugged and closed his eyes.

"It still hurts, but only a little. They didn't admit me. I had some arrangements to oversee."

"Paul said you invited me to come tomorrow."

He did not take his eyes off the bear.

"I need you to be there. It's a small ceremony."

"How's your mother doing?"

Manny hesitated.

"I think she blames herself. That is my fault,. I sort of called her out." Manny's mouth was a hard line, his eyes maintained a sadness.

"Now who is blaming themselves? From what I have heard, there was nothing either of you could have done."

Manny grunted.

"Oscar was always the peaceful one. He was the normal one."

Claire tried to tap into her new-found fledgling faith. The words of Jhoana and Paul came unbidden into her mind.

"Well, at least we know he is truly home now."

A tear streaked down Manny's face. Claire leaned forward, her exhaustion gone. She touched his cheek, her thumb tracing the tear.

"Manny. It's alright."

Manny leaned forward, resting his face on her thigh. She could feel the wetness from his tears through the thin sheets.

She stroked the back of his hair. She loved how it felt between her fingers.

She cherished this moment, selfishly enjoying the opportunity to provide Manny some comfort.

He looked up, sitting back in the chair, wiping his mouth. His eyes looked haunted. Manny locked her eyes in his.

"We can't do this, Claire. I am a broken man. You have so much ahead of you."

"Don't," she said. She could feel a lump in her throat. She wanted to say more, to protest more, but the lump prevented it. She could feel the tears coming fast. She could not have stopped them if she wanted.

"I have to. I want to see you again. I need to see you again. But, we have to go our own ways."

"Manny. Give us a chance," she pleaded.

"How? Domingo wants to shut down the business. I have to help him pick up the pieces, to transfer the holdings, sell the land, find protection…"

"Then come and see me when all that is done. You are free, Manny. I can't tell you that it will be perfect. I just feel we need a chance. I can't explain how I feel for you."

Manny bit his lip. He looked down and then back to her, his eyes penetrating, haunting. The pain etched there broke her heart.

"I truly feel the same way. The only problem is, Claire, you don't really know me."

"I know enough."

He shook his head.

"No. You don't," he said firmly.

She sucked on her bottom lip. She swallowed, knowing that what she was about to ask him might cause him more pain. She had to know.

"Nina mentioned…another loss. That losing Oscar wasn't your first loss. I thought he meant your father. Does this have anything to do with that?" She struggled to maintain her voice. It cracked, a great sob wrenching her body as she finished.

Manny considered this. He put the bear down on the desk by his chair and scooted the card underneath.

"Not my father," he said, looking aside as he said it.

"Then who?"

He turned to look at her again, his face drooping, his eyes tortured.

"I should have been a father, Claire. The baby was taken, aborted." He swallowed, grimacing. "I have never been the same since. In some ways that changed me for the better. In other ways I am battered, wounded, torn up inside."

Claire's breath caught in her chest.

A father? But—who was the mother?

"I'm sorry," she muttered.

Manny's eyes glittered for a moment.

"The mother—well, my lover, anyway—isn't in the picture anymore. That's not what I am trying to say. It's what came before that that matters."

"What do you mean?" Claire clutched her covers. She wanted to rip them, wanted to tear them.

Manny swallowed and found a spot on the ceiling behind her. Claire found herself tempted to turn to see what had caught his attention. She understood that he could not look at her and say what was on his mind.

"Claire. I have killed people. Tortured some. I have murdered, stolen, and covered up crimes so heinous that I can't even speak about them. Even to Paul."

Claire stared. She was completely shocked.

She could hear her heart break. Not because she could not love a criminal, but because a criminal with a conscience could not stand to be loved.

"Don't torture yourself this way, Manny. I don't care about your past. I care about our future. Don't torture me this way. It's not fair."

He looked at his hands, considering what she said.

"I look at these hands, Claire. I look at them and think: *how can I make these hands clean again*? I couldn't forgive her for so long. How can I be absolved if I can't forgive?"

Claire sobbed, a low body-wracking cry.

"I thought Paul had taught you better than that," she whispered. Disappointment and dread marked her voice.

Manny nodded.

"Yeah. He tells me all the time that I am forgiven. It's just that my past continues to haunt me."

Claire smirked. She grabbed his hands, kneading his fingers and seeking out his eyes. She pressed his fingers to her lips and then touched them to the tears on her cheeks.

"I know what you mean. I just came to the realization recently that I have to put the past behind me. I have to learn from my mistakes, let them help me grow. I can't hinder my future by tripping over the past."

"I know you are right," Manny said, looking at her eyes. He swallowed. "I know why you are so dear to me, Claire. Maybe when I am through with cleaning up Domingo's house here in Colombia I can come see you in the States."

She squeezed his hands. Her heart leaped. She was careful not to show too much emotion. She knew he was still fragile. She did not need him changing his mind again.

"I would like that very much," she managed.

"There's just one thing, though."

Claire cocked her head and raised an eyebrow. Her heart had taken a three hundred and sixty degree turn in the last moment. She held her breath.

"Can you cook?"

Her surprised laughter could be heard down the hall.

EPILOGUE

Lucia opened the office door without knocking. The plush carpet seemed new. The dark paneling and brass features were old, probably here from a different era.

It hurt Lucia's heart to think of her Colombia. It had been at war with itself for over forty years now.

She regretted that Oscar could not see the beginning of the new Colombia. A peaceful Colombia that attracted world renown. A Colombia that finally capitalized on its rich bounties of natural resources and passionate, capable people.

She focused on why she was here. She was here for her country. She was here for Oscar. She was here for her brave sons. She was here for her deceased husband. She was here for her own pride and peace of mind. She was here to make up for all the mistakes she had made over the years. She was here for revenge.

The office was larger than she had expected. A man sat at a desk opposite the door under a bank of windows. Good. She could see the Colombia she was protecting. The city stretched out behind, the mountains in the distance with the glitter of Bogotá reaching out for miles. Millions of people would be avenged today. Millions of Colombians.

Alvarez looked up.

His eyes were ice. His eyes were predator eyes. She had looked into eyes like that all her life. She had never felt fear. She felt no fear now. She had purpose. She had a plan.

"Excuse me. I'm not taking visitors right now—" He stopped, his mouth closed, his eyes getting bigger as recognition hit him. He swallowed.

"Mom?"

"Hernando."

He stood up, coming around his desk. He seemed nervous. He glanced at the papers on his desk furtively. He looked confused for a second and then smiled. Her son rarely smiled.

"Mother, why are you here? I thought we agreed not to meet during the day. You have never—"

"Why did you kill my son?"

For one second she saw it in his eyes. A sense of pride. The monster she was afraid he had become. She had been able to shape the lives of Oscar, Domingo, and Manny in some small ways. Hernando had been denied that influence.

No one could ever know. The secret she had kept for over three decades had been one of pride at first. It was necessary to save her marriage.

At the time, it had become a pleasure for her to know that she had an alternative life, a life she could pretend had been hers all along. Along with the death of her husband and the demise of her lover had come the realization that she had been foolish in her youth.

Hernando put his hands behind his back and raised his eyebrows. His rumpled suit sat awkwardly on his body.

"I thought my efforts were successful in saving Manny's life, actually." His smirk was perfect.

"You know I mean Oscar."

He turned, staring at the carpet.

"Oh yes. Oscar. Poor Oscar. I suppose I can't pin that one Al, can I?"

"I know better. Investigators have cleared Alfonso. Carlos paid off all of Al's henchmen. One even agreed to testify in exchange for the release of his cousin. He implicated you."

Lucia let this lie sink in. It seemed plausible enough. She wanted the gambit to work. It had to work.

Alvarez shrugged.

"Why are you here then, Lucia? Where are the police? Where is the Director? Where are my superiors? If this testimony is out there, then where is the justice, Mom?"

She remained cool. She expected him to doubt.

"The wheels are in motion. A mother works more quickly than our government."

He nodded. He paced the carpet, his head down, his hands behind his back, his lips a narrow line on his long face.

"I see," he said. Lucia walked towards him carefully. She had to stay close. "So, you are here to warn me? Is that it?"

It was her turn to shrug. She kept the movement subtle.

"A mother has to know the truth. I can't protect you if you don't tell me the truth," she said in a soothing voice.

He looked at her, his eyes narrowing.

"You sound like a lawyer, Mom. You want my confession? Dad raised me as a Protestant. I don't need a rosary or a priest. My conscience is clean."

"Good. So you didn't murder Oscar."

She watched as his jaw clenched.

"Let me ask you something."

She almost had him. She needed to play the game. She had been playing the game for longer than Hernando had been alive. She had to be patient and not rush him.

"Anything, darling."

He frowned and put his hands in his pockets. She tried not to notice the bulge in the right one. The one with the gun.

Why did an agent carry a weapon in such a strange and obvious place?

She knew her son had been unstable for some time now. She did not realize that it had affected his common sense.

He began to pace again, his hands in his dark, wrinkled jacket.

"Why did you come to me when I arrived in Bogotá? Why did you feel compelled to tell me the truth after all those years of secrecy? You broke your promise to my father and your agreement with your husband."

"Your father was a true American. I was excited that he had raised you to be patriotic. I was glad you felt compelled to serve here in Colombia, your true home. I had hoped that after all those years your father would understand. A mother never forgets."

"But, I had a mother. The truth didn't set me free. It shackled me. It made me feel guilty, dirty. It made me hate Sheila. It made me hate my father. You stole my entire youth from me. You denied me my true home and my true nature."

She saw now how much she had hurt him. She had no idea. Their relationship over the past decade had been a close one. She had consoled him when Everett Alvarez—his father and her lover—had died. She had been there as Hernando had been promoted and had successfully eliminated over a dozen ELN cells and eradicated hundreds of thousands of hectares of coca.

Despite her pride in and her suspicions of Hernando, she had never revealed their relationship to her other sons. She wanted her relationship with Hernando and Everett to remain her little secret. She saw now how damaging it had been to him. She had selfish reasons, but she had also been concerned over the hurt and judgment that Domingo, Oscar, and especially Manny would feel.

"I never meant to hurt you. Is that why you murdered Oscar?" She tried to ask in as neutral a tone as she could manage. Her anger and disappointment was welling up in her chest, constricting her throat. She had blamed herself for tempting Oscar as she had. Now, she began to realize she was more complicit than she had ever thought was possible in killing her oldest son.

Hernando stopped pacing and half turned towards her. He raised his eyebrows.

"Yes…Yes. I—I wanted to…I wanted you to love me like you loved them. I knew of them. I knew of their little outfit in the mountains. I knew how you protected them. You never told them about me, did you?" His voice was choked with emotion. She had not seen him this upset since Everett died.

"No. I told you I wanted it to be—"

"Our little secret. Yeah. I remember." He turned his back on her then, walking around his desk. "Like the secret my father kept from me. He lied to me, saying my birth mother had died. Sheila lied to me, saying that I was truly hers. Secrets are poison, Mom. Secrets make us lie to the ones we love."

"Our secret makes me lie to my family. Not to you, Hernando."

"Don't coddle me. I'm not twenty-six anymore." She had to wrap this up soon. Her time was running out.

"Hernando, I want you to turn yourself in." She knew she was skating on thin ice now. She owed him this much, though. It would go easier for him if he did.

He chuckled.

"You lied better when I was younger," he said, bitterness tainting his voice. "You don't want me to turn myself in. You *are* warning me, though. You are *telling* me to turn myself in before you have me arrested. Isn't that correct?"

"I want you to have a chance."

"A chance." Hernando squinted, hate and resentment radiating from his brow. "You know what this is all about? Do you know why for the last few years I haven't been the same? Because no one truly likes change." He pointed out the window. "This country has been at war with itself for the past forty years because they don't want to change. People in the villages have been poor and malnourished because they are afraid to change. Drug traffickers continue to poison the world with their filth because people don't want to change. They don't want to change, Mom, because they just want to survive."

Lucia let him rant. Her time was almost up and she had very little more to say. As far as she was concerned, this was done.

"Changing the way we act and live is how we survive, Hernando." She looked at him with sadness in her gaze. It was sincere. He was her son, too. She had failed him as surely as she had failed Oscar and Manny. "When did you lose your honor, son?"

Hernando jerked like someone had shot him. He blinked rapidly and pulled the pistol from his pocket.

"Honor? You dare speak of honor? You judge me, yet you pat Domingo on the back. You coddle Manny. You allow Oscar to trot into Alfonso's domain like some American cowboy. They aren't heroes, Mom. They are *criminals* and *cowards*! They hide behind a fence of henchmen and corrupt government officials. Everyone turns their heads the other way. Well, I can play that game, too."

"They can be redeemed, son."

"And I can't?" He pointed the gun at his chin.

Wasn't time supposed to stand still in moments like these?

"Don't, Hernando. You don't want to do that," she begged. She began to walk to him.

"You're right, Mom. I don't want to do that." He pointed the gun at her. The barrel wavered. Lucia swallowed. She knew what would come next.

The office glass shattered. She dove towards a stuffed chair in front of the desk as glass rained through the room. She saw Hernando collapsing, surprise on his face.

She felt a sadness grip her. She had done what she needed to do.

Before she could get up, she heard footsteps behind her and men shouting. Someone grabbed her under the arms and picked her up. She turned to see a young officer with a white mic in his ear and grim set to his jaw.

"You alright, ma'am?"

She dusted herself off, absently. Shards of glass tinkled to the floor. Hernando was behind the desk. Two more officers were turning him over and putting handcuffs on him. She approached them. She had to have the last word.

The young officer tried to stop her.

"Miss Villarreal, I suggest we go downstairs now. We need to make sure you are safe."

She huffed. She had just stared down a gun held by her son. She would never feel safe again.

"I just have one thing to say."

Hernando was struggling against the officers. A man in a suit and aviator glasses stepped across the glass. He addressed the officers with a nod.

"Mr. Alvarez, you are under arrest for the murder of Oscar Villarreal. You will be taken into custody and given a chance to hire a lawyer. However, the United States Government has renounced your citizenship on grounds of your birth. Your position as assistant director of the Bogotá office of DEA is now vacated effective immediately. You will be tried as a citizen of Colombia."

Hernando spat on the ground.

"At least I can't be tried on grounds of treason," he said proudly.

Before the Director could respond, one of the other officers spoke up. He had a stack of the papers from Hernando's desk in his hand, his eyes scanning them quickly, and alarm on his face.

"Sir. You might want to look at these documents on his desk. And, his terminal needs to be checked, evidently."

The Director nodded.

"Make it so. You will have other crimes that we can pin on you, Mr. Alvarez. If I were you, I would keep quiet and allow us to bring you in without a fight."

"I don't want to fight," he said, his eyes locking hers. "I just want to know why you lied to me."

She swallowed. Sometimes, the truth hurt.

"Colombia is ready for a change. I am ready for change. I am willing to embrace it." She stripped back her suit jacket, showing him the wire she wore there. "I owe Oscar at least that much."

ACKNOWLEDGMENTS

I would like to thank the following people who helped me in this endeavor. Massive amounts of time and effort have been put into this work and I am grateful for every contribution.

Tracey Michael, Seth Michael, Nathaniel Michael, Eden Michael, Isaac Michael, Amy Hudkins, Danielle Culbert, Kim Smith, Susan Bentley, Sheri Hine, Gayla Alexander, Holly Parker, Shar Fitzpatrick Grant, the community over at Kindle Boards, Create Space, my Facebook writing friends at Deux Magot Shop, Shades of Brown Coffee Shop in Tulsa, the good folks at The Book Place in Broken Arrow and countless others who have touched my life and encouraged me.

The photo used for the cover was purchased from ©iStockphoto.com/ElenaVizerskaya. The font used for the interior of the print edition of this work is standard Garamond True Type based on the original font designed by Claude Garamond in 1561 and the italics designed by Robert Granjon, Garamond's assistant.

ABOUT THE AUTHOR

Robert Michael is a writer and commercial roofing sales director. His love for books, family, and God fill his time and his spirit. He enjoys reading, writing, sports, fishing, and gaming. He lives in Broken Arrow with his wife and four children.

Connect with the Robert at:

www.facebook.com/infiniteword
www.robertamichael.blogspot.com
www.twitter.com/InfiniteWord

Other books available from Infinite Word Press:
DARK MOUNTAIN by Robert Michael
THE VAGARY TALES by Robert Michael

And, coming soon:
MANIC MONDAY by Robert Michael

Get your copy today at http://www.infinitewordpress.com.
Available on Kindle ereading devices as well as paperback.